Praise for *Boy, 9, Missing*

"*Boy, 9, Missing* has a gripping plot, fast-paced action, and memorable characters that you won't soon forget. This riveting debut had me hooked from page one."

—Heather Gudenkauf, *New York Times* bestselling author of *The Weight of Silence* and *Missing Pieces*

"*Boy, 9, Missing* is a stay-up-all-night suspense tale about a tragedy from which a family and town don't recover. The characters come alive as the story twists and turns, and every one of your guesses about what happens next will be wrong."

—Helen Klein Ross, author of *What Was Mine*

"Nic Joseph gives readers an addictive psychological thriller in her gripping debut novel. Exploring unexpected depths in plot, character, and story structure, *Boy, 9, Missing* is a twisted ride of family and revenge."

—*New York Times* bestselling author Michelle Gable

"In Joseph's debut thriller, no one escapes the wreckage of a decades-old crime, as secrets and lies imperil the survivors. An intriguing premise, breathlessly executed."

—national bestselling author and Edgar nominee Sophie Littlefield

Boy, 9, Missing

Nic Joseph

For my sister, Gui.

Published by Sourcebooks Landmark, an imprint of Sourcebooks, Inc.
P.O. Box 4410, Naperville, Illinois 60567-4410
(630) 961-3900
Fax: (630) 961-2168
www.sourcebooks.com

Library of Congress Cataloging-in-Publication Data

Names: Joseph, Nic, author.
Title: Boy, 9, missing / Nic Joseph.
Description: Naperville, Illinois : Sourcebooks Landmark, [2016]
Identifiers: LCCN 2015046815 | (pbk. : alk. paper)
Subjects: LCSH: Brothers--Fiction. | Family secrets--Fiction. | Suspense fiction.
Classification: LCC PS3610.O66896 B69 2016 | DDC 813/.6--dc23 LC record available at http://lccn.loc.gov/2015046815

Printed and bound in the United States of America.
WOZ 10 9 8 7 6 5 4 3 2 1

Chapter One

My brother drowned in a bathtub that was less than one foot longer than he was tall. It was a typical vintage, roll-rim, claw-foot tub with chipped paint, slippery sides, and an air of undeserved elegance.

Morbidly enough, it was also a key factor in my parents' decision to purchase our home a decade earlier.

"But there's no shower," my father had said as we stood shoulder to shoulder with the real estate agent in the bathroom.

My mother was pregnant with Lucas at the time, and she placed one hand on her bulging stomach while she held on to me with the other.

"I know, Alex, but think about the baths." She made the face she sometimes made when she bit into something sweet, like a piece of chocolate, and I could see my father's shoulders sag. The decision had been made.

That my little brother would drown in that very tub just nine years later seemed, at best, a terrible coincidence and, at worst, an inevitable twist of fate that was sealed the day we all locked eyes on that porcelain, showerless beast.

Lucas was small for his age, and still, the accident was, in almost every respect, impossible. "Freakishly contorted" was the not-quite-clinical-enough phrase I heard Dr. R. Rudolph Smith III, the medical examiner from two suburbs over, use to describe the body when he arrived at our home that night in the brutal winter of 1992.

I remember Rudy's face, round and reddened as he stood in my parents' tiled master bathroom, the tips of his boxy, black shoes disappearing beneath the tub. He was still wearing his thick down coat, which made sense, given the single-digit temps outside, but he glowed from a thin layer of sweat inside the hot, stuffy bathroom.

The room smelled of staleness and death, like an old, damp sneeze, and I struggled to fill my lungs with air while trying to remain as quiet as possible. Rudy held a swab in his gloved hand, and his eyes were glued to my brother's body below him, the very sight that would wholly define my life moving forward.

"My God…" he breathed, mostly to himself, and he seemed at a loss for what to do with the tiny, pristine, white cotton swab. I remember thinking that for a man who made his living attending to dead bodies, Rudy didn't seem to be holding up very well. He stared at my brother's body, and I couldn't tell if he was going to cry or throw up. I'd done both only a few minutes earlier. The surprisingly few adults around at that point in the night kept saying they needed to get me out of there, away from the chaos and the death and the heartbreak that had stolen our night. But no one left. I was thirteen at the time. Deep down, I think both of my parents knew I would come out on the other end of it all much better than they would, so we stayed. We stayed, and they sobbed separately in different rooms of our two-story home in sleepy Lansing, Illinois, while I hid behind the bathroom door, alone, covered in my own vomit, watching the medical examiner as he struggled to do his work.

I stood like that for a long time, peering out at the shiny tears as they wormed their way into Rudy's white, feathery beard. I had no way of knowing it back then, but he'd been a medical examiner for thirty-three years, mostly in the Chicago suburbs, and he'd never once cried on the job. But then, Lucas's death wasn't the type you logged away in any rote fashion, checking boxes on a form, measuring splash, and noting the position of the head. His was a painful and soul-crushing death that took with it the lives of many others that night.

In the twenty-three years since, I've said—with varying degrees of certainty and sobriety—that the claustrophobia and panic attacks started right then, as I crouched behind that bathroom door. It was the first time I ever encountered the painfully helpless sensation of feeling trapped inside my own body. I remember standing there, shaking, chest heaving, as the small, confining space between the door and the wall seemed to shrink and grab on to me the way cling wrap sticks to vegetables. I was suffocating. And yet, I was too terrified to move, afraid I'd see even a hint of Lucas's tie-dye T-shirt as it billowed around him in the tub.

Many years later, while on a date, I said something about that being the moment my panic attacks made a serious splash into my life. It had gone over the way most things do when you try, painfully, to lead with humor.

"Francis, you really shouldn't joke about something like that," my date had said, and I'll be honest about my fogginess surrounding her name. "The fact that you would say something like that tells me there are a lot of unresolved issues there."

There was a detective there the night Lucas died too. He was a large man, and he seemed to swallow up too much of the air in our home as he poked around, touching things, asking questions. Like Rudy, he still wore his knee-length wool coat, and he tugged mercilessly at the red-and-black-checkered scarf around his neck.

I think he and Rudy knew each other, because they didn't say anything for a long time after the detective—tall, broad shouldered, and turtle faced—walked into the bathroom and peered into the tub.

"What do you think?" he finally asked.

"Death almost certainly due to asphyxiation following head trauma."

"So he fell and hit his head, then drowned?" The detective stepped forward and peered into the tub. "It doesn't seem right, a child that size."

"That's what it looks like, but I'll need a little time." Rudy's voice cracked on that last word. "Nothing from the other child?"

"Nothing. Weird kid. Think he's mute or something."

"He might be."

The men weren't talking about me. They were talking about Sam Farr, the boy who had been playing upstairs with Lucas when it all happened. Sam was a year older than Lucas, a quiet, anxious kid, but he did speak—though I could understand why the detective thought he didn't. The son of my parents' church friends, Brian and Elizabeth Farr, Sam didn't talk much on an ordinary basis. But since the moment he'd run downstairs, his face blanched with terror, his clothing completely drenched and clinging to his small frame, he hadn't said a single word.

A fact that had caused my mother to lose every single shred of her dignity.

"Say something, you weird little fuck!" she'd screamed at Sam through the tears and the snot when he wouldn't respond to her the first couple of times. She stood at the edge of Lucas's bedroom door, the front of her burgundy, patterned dress soaked from where she'd reached into the tub moments earlier to lift her youngest son from the water before pumping furiously on his chest. "What happened? What happened to my baby?"

Sam hadn't said a word, pausing momentarily to stare at her before turning around and quietly putting his things away. We watched as he packed up his toys before grabbing his mother's hand and pulling her toward the door. This had only infuriated my mother even more.

"Where's he going? Why won't he say something?" she'd asked, spinning wildly toward Sam's father, who was trembling where he stood, unable to respond or defend his son. "Brian, why won't he say anything?"

"Because he's terrified!" Elizabeth had cut in angrily, blocking her son from my mother's valid but batshit response. "Kate, you have to calm down. I'm so, so sorry, but you have to stop."

"*But he won't tell me what happened!*"

Those words would echo throughout the rest of the night.

And then for days after that.

And then for months, and years.

I think if Sam had said something that night—anything at all—we might have spared ourselves the many years of shit that followed. If he'd said, for example, "Lucas and I were trying to see who could hold their breath longer, and he slipped and hit his head" or "I stepped out for a second and came back and found him that way" or anything else that could give my parents something to grasp on to, something to believe, maybe they would have retreated into grief the way most people do. With booze, some prayers. Maybe a touch of belligerence.

Instead, my parents went to court.

They dressed up, grasped hands, and went to war with a ten-year-old boy.

My father, handsome and tearful in his Lansing Police Department uniform, set out to prove that there was no way Lucas's death could have been an accident.

That Sam Farr had, for any number of well-crafted reasons, killed my little brother.

That childhood is not synonymous with innocence, and that inside the mind of this ten-year-old was something vindictive, troubling, disgusting, and terrifying.

Alex and Kate Scroll hired lawyers, the best our money could afford, and they went horrifically, and desperately, all in.

I think their motivations changed along the way. But one thing remained the same: my parents figured that, at some point, Sam Farr would reach his breaking point and say something—absolutely anything—about what happened to my brother that night.

That's all they wanted.

An admission of guilt, or even a denial. A plea for forgiveness.

Anything.

It never happened.

Sam Farr has never once, in twenty-three years, said a single word to a single soul about what happened that night upstairs in my parents' bathroom.

Not to his lawyers, his family, the judge, or a screaming, angry, relentless press. Not even on the day, almost six years after Lucas drowned, when he walked out of court for the final time at the age of sixteen. Not even then did Sam Farr utter a word about what happened to my brother on that awful, frigid night.

He simply looked at us, turned, and walked away.

Someone behind us, in my parents' sea of supporters, called out, egging on the crowd of friends, neighbors, and Lansing police officers.

"He's smiling! Can you believe it? That monster is smiling!"

I didn't see it.

Chapter Two

For eight long years, I kept my name.

"Francis, you're from Chicago, right?" my freshman-year newswriting professor at Madison asked me one day after class. Professor Cal Oakton was tall, thin, and almost unbearably "tufty"—tufts of thick, wiry, salt-and-pepper hair streamed out of nearly every opening on his face, making prolonged eye contact difficult.

"Yeah," I answered, my hand on the classroom door, my gaze landing everywhere but on the fluttering hairs. "Right outside of it."

I'd been waiting for this very conversation since the first day of class, when Cal pushed his glasses up on his nose and breezed through the list of twenty-three students before stopping abruptly on my name. He'd seemed fascinated as he rolled it over his tongue, but he hadn't said anything, not right away. They never said anything right away.

"Wait, not Lansing, Illinois?" he asked as I stood in the doorway. The nose tufts, in particular, liked to dance when he got excited.

"Yes."

"Wow. You're Francis Scroll of that whole..."

I nodded.

"I'm so sorry."

"Thank you."

"So that was your brother." Flutter. "Such a sad story. I was in Chicago back then, you know."

"Is that right?"

"Yep, at Northwestern. Hey, what ever happened to that other boy? The one—"

"Nothing. My parents lost their case against him."

"Well, I wouldn't call that *nothing*..."

He actually trailed off like that, shoulders raised, eyebrows scattering to different corners of his forehead as he urged me to give him just a little bit more. One more nugget to take home to discuss with his wife over mashed potatoes and under-seasoned beef.

By the time I started seeing therapists, I was Francis Clarke. A handful of signatures on the afternoon after my college graduation, and my paternal grandmother's maiden name erased it all. That was the plan, at least. But the therapy didn't last long. At first, I went mostly to talk about the claustrophobia—in my early twenties, I stopped riding trains because of the sudden, inexplicable urge I'd have to get off in between stops. In my late twenties, I cut out elevators altogether. The dirt phobia started somewhere in the middle of all of that—I'd be walking outside, and suddenly every wet leaf, wad of gum, or stain on the concrete would make me gag. I'd run home and jump in the shower, practically clawing my skin off.

My visits with therapists always inevitably ended up in a conversation about Lucas, since that's where I thought it all started, but then, they were the therapists, and they should have been able to tell *me*. Once we got to Lucas, we stayed there, talking about guilt and responsibility and all of this other shit that had nothing to do with the fact that I walked up seven flights of stairs every morning to get to my office because the sight of an elevator made bile rise in the back of my throat.

On the afternoon before everything started, that's where I was, pulling myself up those 152 steps to get to the offices of the *Lansing News*. I'd gone out for lunch, something I rarely did, given the effort it took to get in and out of the office. As I stepped onto the seventh floor from the stairwell, breathing hard, my editor, Cam, strolled out of her office.

"Got a minute?"

I nodded. I'd been a writer at the paper for the past year and a half, and I had to admit I enjoyed the reactions I got when I told people I still worked at a real, crinkle-back-the-corners-and-sit-on-your-patio newspaper. I was on the local beat, which meant I ended up covering everything from library closings to car accidents. My job was fairly straightforward, and I liked that. Gather the facts, report them accurately. Simple.

I'd learned about the job after I'd bumped into Cam on a subway in New York two years ago. She had been in town for a media conference. I'd been living there at the time and was both married and out of work—two things that go together like having the shits and being at an outdoor festival. I didn't recognize Cam at first. She'd been standing right in front of me for a few stops, holding the bar above my head, and I'd deliberately been staring past her crotch out the window on the other side of the train car.

"Francis? Francis, is that you?"

I'd looked up, and she'd been peering down into my face, her forehead wrinkled. Short brown hair tucked behind her ears, large brown eyes that took up a sizable amount of her face. Pretty. Smart looking, whatever that means. Her face had been familiar, but it had taken me a second to place it.

"Cam Merchant?"

"Wow, how's it going?"

We'd caught up during the fifteen-minute train ride about all of the important stuff that had happened since we'd left Marshall

Middle School. She: married once a long time ago, no kids, now the editor of the paper our parents read when we were growing up. Me: still married, one preteen daughter, currently "between jobs." I'd left out the part about Reba and me tiptoeing around the conversation of divorce. Cam was attractive enough that it might have sounded like a come-on, and to be honest, it might have been one.

"Well, if you and your wife are interested in moving back home, I have an opening at the paper," Cam had said as we'd approached her stop and she'd let go of the bar. "Every last reporter I had—or good reporter, I should say—has jumped ship. Apparently, journalism is the new prelaw."

I had taken her information with no real intent of actually following through.

Six months later, I followed through. I called Cam from the front seat of my car, double-parked on a busy street on the Upper West Side, the divorce papers in my lap.

"Is that job still available?"

"The reporter job? Yes and no. I filled the position I had told you about, but we could still use some more help. What changed your mind?" she asked.

"Circumstances."

"That's…vague, but all right. I'm not asking, but I need to know that—"

"I'm getting a divorce."

After nine years of marriage and eight years of divorce threats on both of our parts, Reba and I had finally pulled the plug. Or, I should say, *she'd* yanked the fuck out of it, and I'd slid down the drain. I probably would have spent the rest of my life ignoring that we were slowly killing each other, saying, "That's just marriage; we're trying to make it work."

Cam didn't say anything for a moment. "I'm sorry to hear that."

"Thanks. My daughter, Amy, is thirteen. She'll be staying with my wife for another year or so, but then Reba's going abroad for a project."

"A project?"

"She's a photographer. Something about documenting the human experience in Italy."

"What's wrong with New York's human experience?"

I leaned forward and rested my forehead against the steering wheel. "I don't know."

"And Amy?"

"She'll stay with me when Reba leaves. At least, until she finishes high school."

"Here?" I could hear the hesitation in Cam's voice. "In Lansing?"

"Yeah," I said. "I need something steady. Nobody's biting out here." Seven interviews in the past month, but I figured she didn't need details.

"Okay…" she said. "And after high school?"

"She's moving to Europe with her mother. She's going to take some time off before college. You know, to see the world. It'll be good for her."

"Yeah, it will. Look, Francis, like I was gonna say before, I just need to know that if you take the job, you'll stick around."

"I will. There's just one more thing." She waited without saying anything. "I've changed my name. It's Francis Clarke now."

Cam had barely missed a beat. "If you can file at least four stories a week, the job is yours. I don't give a damn what your byline says."

As I stepped into her office a year and a half later, Cam held up a piece of paper. "Thanks for this," she said, resting both elbows on her neatly organized desk while toying with the paper in her hands. "It was a rough one." She was holding a printout of the article I'd turned in the previous day—a story about a car accident involving two nineteen-year-old parents and their two-year-old.

I nodded.

Cam leaned forward, putting the paper down. "Tomorrow's the big day."

"Yep."

"What time does Amy get in?"

"Early afternoon, I think."

"Anything I can do to help?"

I shook my head. "Thanks, though."

"Is her room all set up?"

"Uh, I guess so. There's a bed."

"What about food? Did you stock the fridge?"

"There's stuff in there."

"No, new food. Good food. Nothing you have to smell twice before ingesting. Go to the grocery store, Francis."

"Okay."

"Tonight."

"Is that all you needed?" I asked, standing up.

She smirked, sitting back in her chair and crossing her arms in front of her chest. Cam's attractiveness was one of those things I tended to ignore for the most part, given our working relationship. But the smirk always got me.

"Has Reba left New York yet?" she asked.

I paused with one hand on the back of the chair. "She leaves next week."

"Damn. Not wasting any time."

I didn't respond.

"Francis..." Cam stared at me, her lips parted, and I could sense that she was having a hard time figuring out exactly what she wanted to say. It was odd, because Cameron Merchant rarely, if ever, bothered to mince her words. Not in the brash "keeping it real" way, but in the sort of endearing "Grandpa can't help but say whatever comes to his mind" way. I knew I should feel special that she was taking such care. She bit her lip. "You do know that you're going to have to talk to Amy at some point. It's not going to just… go away."

"I know, Cam."

"She's going to run into someone, somewhere, and they're going to tell her about you. About her grandparents. About your brother."

I sighed. Besides being my boss, Cam was the closest thing I had to a friend, and I knew she was right. Reba and I had never gotten to have the conversation with Amy about my past, the trial, or my family. Amy had asked once, when she was very young, about why she had only one set of grandparents. I'd instinctively told her that they'd "gone away."

"You just told her they're dead!" Reba had hissed. "What's wrong with you?"

"I didn't say they were dead," I'd said, and I should have stopped myself before the next words came out. "But if that's what she thinks, maybe it's for the best."

"You're the fucking worst."

"Really? The worst?"

"Yeah."

"Of all the things, of all the people, I am the worst of them?"

"*Yes*," she'd said again, because if there was one very reliable thing about Reba, it was that she never backed down.

In reality, my parents had gone on to live separate lives, to the betterment of absolutely every person involved. Alex, my father, retired from the Lansing Police Department a few years before I moved back to town. This had followed a decade of desk work that he'd done after a very extended leave of absence following Lucas's death. My father was a self-proclaimed "recovering-recovering alcoholic," which is exactly what it sounded like.

"Do you know how messed up recovering alcoholics are?" he had asked one of the last times I had seen him. "Why would I want to be one of those?" I remembered the way he asked this question, the glass of brandy dangling from his fingertips, his eyes bright from his excitement about this seemingly novel rationale. "Recovering alcoholic… I'm recovering from *that* bullshit."

My mother, Kate, was living with a man who I had graduated high school with, and that's pretty much all that needs to be said about that. I tried to visit her once after he started living there, and it had gone about as well as could be expected.

"Are you guys even going to try to talk?" my mother had asked.

"About what?"

"I don't know. Anything. The weather. Squirrels. What we're eating, high school. Or not high school. But anything else, since we're all here, and we're all trying. Right? What's the point of sitting in silence?"

Those were the only words said before I left.

I haven't spoken to either of them in years, and as far as Amy knows, I'm Francis Clarke, her parentless, journalist dad who was, at most, getting by. It was who I'd always been to her, and who, with any luck, I would always be.

All things equal, I was moving on.

I'd left it all behind me, and I was okay.

Better than my parents, just as they knew I'd be when they'd left me alone the night my little brother drowned. Not good by any means, but okay.

Yet, it was generally then—when things are moving on and you think you've been through all the hardest bits and you're trying to just go on and live some sort of simple, menial life that you've manufactured for yourself, making less than thirty grand but, thank God, therapy free—that something comes along to ruin the tiny bit of decency you've tried to build back up.

That something is usually the game changer.

The big twist.

The "you *are* the father."

For me, that something came the next morning while I was in the shower, just hours before Amy was set to arrive, when someone broke into my apartment.

Chapter Three

Saturday, 6:10 a.m.

Hello?"

"Dad. It's me."

"Ames?" I said, sitting up in the bed, my mouth cottony, my feet cold because the comforter had spun a full ninety degrees during the night, leaving the bottom half of my body exposed. "Where are you?"

"At home, waiting for the cab. You told me to call you when I was leaving. I didn't know if you meant leaving home or leaving JFK."

I pushed myself up farther and squinted at the clock, but it was just a haze of fuzzy, glowing red shapes. I pulled my cell phone away from my face and squinted at it, the bright light hurting my eyes.

"No, now is good," I said, clearing my throat. "Thanks. You all set?"

"Yeah."

"What time do you land?"

"Ten thirty. Chicago time."

"Okay." I gripped the phone tighter. "I can't wait to see you."

"Yeah," she said quickly. "Me too."

"All of your boxes arrived. I set most of it up in your room."

"Yeah, Mom told me," she said, and then, maybe as an afterthought, "Thanks."

I pushed back the covers and dropped my feet to the floor, the phone still pressed to my ear. Five years ago, I wouldn't have been able to get a word in edgewise during a phone call with Amy. Now, she spoke only in short, quiet, conversation-ending bursts.

"Well, have a safe trip, and call me when you land, okay?"

"Okay. Thanks."

We hung up, and I pushed myself out of bed, stumbling blindly toward the bathroom. I flipped on the shower before turning to the toilet. As ridiculous as it was, I was nervous. Nervous that Amy would hate the bedspread I'd bought her or think my apartment was too small or that she'd be bored out of her mind or think I was trying too hard. It wasn't a question of whether she'd hate living in Lansing, but how *much* she'd hate it. The town is only a half-hour drive from downtown Chicago, but you'd never know it, based on the number of Olive Gardens and Applebees around every corner.

I flushed the toilet and stepped into the shower.

To be fair, Amy had taken it all surprisingly well. "I could just stay here," she'd said when Reba and I had first sat down to tell her about the divorce and her eventual move back to Illinois with me. "Kaitlyn's parents would probably be cool with me staying with them. It's only a couple of years."

Reba had looked at me, and I'd known she was actually considering it, but she had shaken her head when she'd seen my face. We'd agreed to back each other up on this, if nothing else. "No, honey, it's best if you live with your father," she'd said. "I know it's going to be hard to leave your friends, but it's…it's just our reality right now, okay?"

I'd expected a little more pushback from Amy, a final plea, but she'd nodded once and stood up from our living room couch.

"Okay. Well, thanks for letting me know." She hadn't asked again or shown any emotion about the move since that afternoon nearly two years ago. Whenever I'd asked her about it, she'd just shrugged and echoed her mother.

"It's fine. It's our reality."

I poured a glob of shampoo into my hand and raked it quickly through my hair before it could slither onto the floor of the tub. As I massaged it into my scalp, I thought back to my conversation with Cam. She was right, of course; I'd have to tell Amy about her grandparents at some point. But with everything going on—the move, her saying good-bye to her mother, the new school—I hoped I could put it off for at least a few days.

Or weeks.

A few months, tops.

I was reaching to put the shampoo back when I heard the first noise.

It wasn't that loud, but it was distinct—the sound of glass breaking somewhere close by, very close, *too close.* I froze, droplets of water stinging my eyes. The shampoo bottle slipped from my paralyzed fingers, and the steam from the shower suddenly seemed to increase, blinding me. Trapping me. As I gasped for breath, the water beating down, it occurred to me that I needed to act.

Right away.

I pushed the shower curtain back quietly. The bathroom door was not locked, but it was closed, thanks to an irresponsibly placed smoke detector right outside of it. My contacts were in the vanity, and unlike most people who casually exaggerate, I'm nearly blind without them. I floundered for a moment, wiping the water out of my eyes and wishing I hadn't left my glasses on my nightstand.

As I stepped out of the tub, my wet feet hit the cold tile floor, and water dripped down my face and body. I glanced momentarily at the empty towel bar on the other side of the small bathroom and cursed. Like most mornings, the towel was on the floor at the foot of my bed, where I'd left it the previous day. I'd gotten used to walking naked through the apartment each day to find it. Today it was, just maybe, the worst thing in the world.

Think!

It couldn't be Amy, right? No, that didn't make any sense. She'd barely left for JFK. I took a step toward the door and listened, picturing the rooms outside. There was a small hallway that, on one side, led to my bedroom and the spare room I'd prepared for Amy. On the other end, the hallway led to the living and dining areas and the kitchen, which was stocked with the groceries I'd purchased the night before.

The passageway outside of the bathroom contained exactly three things: a small table from IKEA, a lamp, and an ornately framed mirror I'd gotten with Reba from a secondhand store in Queens. I took another step closer to the bathroom door and pushed my ear against it, listening for any signs of life, imagining the disappointment that an intruder might feel upon realizing what little a washed-up journalist for a washed-up newspaper had to steal. With my hand on the doorknob, I tried to count the number of steps it would take for me to get to my bedroom and to my phone on the nightstand.

I cracked open the door and peeked out. And then it occurred to me that the sound of the water must have gotten louder as the door opened, alerting the intruder that I was coming out.

Shit, shit, shit.

I could see nothing, hear nothing, and I wondered which would be the better option—running ass-naked toward the front door, which posed its own problems, or heading toward the bedroom and barricading myself inside. I blinked, using the backs of my hands to wipe the remaining water out of my eyes. Without my contacts, I could barely see five feet in front of me. Gripping the bathroom doorframe, I forced myself to move slowly out into the hallway.

Maybe it was nothing. Maybe I would find that I was a fool once I saw what had made the noise. I moved forward, the rug tickling my feet, the sound of traffic from three floors below shaking my entire body. I was completely naked, an element I hadn't missed, even in my fear. As I moved through the hallway, I reached out and grabbed the only weapon-like object I could see: the tall lamp. As my fingers curved around the long, black stem and my wet hands brushed against the plug, I imagined myself getting electrocuted.

Maybe that would be a better way to go.

I crept through the hallway, the lamp lifted up at ear level as I listened, but there was nothing. No sound, nobody. I moved slowly, inch by inch, my gaze darting around every corner, the lamp trembling in my hands. As I turned into my small dining room, my heartbeat began an impossible increase, sending even more blood shooting through my veins. For a second, I thought I would pass out, fear taking hold of me, the briny taste on my tongue making my stomach flip over with nausea. I raised the lamp higher, up above my head, and I stepped forward again, wondering what I could have done differently to avoid this.

One: always keep glasses and cell phone in the bathroom while showering, no matter what.

Two—

I heard a thump—this noise softer, but somehow more *real* than the one I'd been able to hear from the shower—and I stopped in my tracks. My pulse quickened even more, as all doubt about whether there was someone in my apartment disappeared.

"Who's there?" I called out in a voice that sounded much more confident than I felt. The words flew out of me, and I trudged on, hoping a robber would be reasonable enough to respond, identify him- or herself, and apologize for bothering me on a cold Saturday morning.

"Who the fuck is there?" I called out again. Still no response, and I felt like an idiot, a terrified idiot, calling out to someone who obviously didn't have any plans to respond. I tried to make out the fuzzy shapes in front of me as I inched around my small dining room table toward the living room. I bumped into one of the chairs, and the noise was deafening, but still, nothing. As I turned the corner into the living room, a cold blast of air hit me, and I could see that my patio door was open. I squinted at it, shivering uncontrollably, the heavy lamp shaking in my hand.

I turned toward the arched opening that separated my living room from my front door.

And my heart clenched as I stopped in my tracks.

The lamp dropped from my hand and clattered noisily to the floor.

Standing not three feet in front of me, her back pressed against my front door, was a woman.

Tall, slender, and dressed in all black.

Dark-brown hair floating around her face like a cloud, swirling from the gusts of wind that snaked past us.

She was just far enough away that I couldn't make out the details of her face.

But close enough for me to see what she was holding in her hand.

A small handgun.

Pointed steadily and purposefully at my chest.

Chapter Four

"Who the—" I stepped back, tripping over my own feet, and toppled onto the carpet. Instinctively, my hands flew up to cover my head because maybe—just maybe—layered on top of each other, they would be enough to stop a *bullet* from entering my skull.

The woman stepped forward.

"Cover up." Her voice was deep and confident, her movements controlled rather than forceful. It took a moment for her words to sink in. I hesitated before lifting my head slowly and peeking out from beneath my arms.

"What—"

"Cover yourself, Mr. Scroll. Please."

I was still frozen, my arms lifted high. I glanced at the patio door, which suddenly seemed miles away, and I was 100 percent certain I couldn't reach it before she shot.

Shot.

She had a *gun*.

"Wha…what are you doing?" I managed to choke out.

She didn't say anything, just held the gun steady in one hand and gestured to the couch with the other. I looked back to see my deep-burgundy throw tossed over the arm. I stared at it for a moment, then turned back to her, and she nodded.

I swallowed and dragged myself over to the couch, reaching up to grab the throw and yanking it toward my body. I rolled and tugged awkwardly, wrapping the cover around my waist with shaking hands.

She used the gun again and motioned for me to stand, which I did slowly, my hand still holding the blanket tightly.

"What the hell are you doing?" I asked, my voice cracking on the last word, and she didn't even flinch. "Take whatever you want, please."

She didn't respond. She squared her shoulders and lifted the gun higher, aligning it with my face.

"I'm going to ask you this one time," she said, and my knees buckled again. I slumped back against the couch as she stepped forward, allowing me to make out just a little bit more of her strikingly angular face and tense but deliberate motions. Her eyes commanded mine, and I stared back, panic taking over. "I want you to tell me if you know anything about where my son is right now."

"What?"

"And I swear to you," she continued, coming even closer, "if you lie to me, I will shoot you through the head, and I don't care what happens to me after that. I really don't. So just tell me the truth, for your sake and mine: Where is Matthew?"

I swallowed, and the room swayed around me. *I was going to pass out. I am going to pass out…*

"Where is he?"

"I don't know," I said. "I swear, I don't know what you're talking about. I don't. Really. I promise you."

Her jaw worked, and it occurred to me that this was some sort of lunatic who thought I was an ex-lover, and that lover had stolen her kid, and she, for some reason, thought it was me, and she was going to fucking kill me because of it, and—

"Are you telling me the truth?" It was a whisper, the gun not moving an inch, and she didn't sound like a lunatic at all. "Francis, are you telling me the truth?"

It hit me only then that she'd used my name earlier.

My real name.

This wasn't a random lunatic.

She knew who I was, and she'd come here to find me.

Me.

"I swear to you, I have no idea what you're talking about, or who you are," I said. "But if you tell me, maybe…maybe I can help you find him."

She blinked, and for the first time, she looked away from me, her gaze dropping to the floor. I wondered if I could reach her and kick the gun out of her hand, but it seemed like too much of a risk. Besides, that probably only worked in the movies. I'd never kicked anything out of anyone's hands, let alone a loaded gun.

But I wouldn't need to. After a couple more seconds of staring at the floor, the woman lowered the gun slowly and stepped back. She walked a few steps to my love seat and dropped down onto it, placing the gun in her lap.

I was still frozen in place, the throw wrapped around my lower waist, too scared to move an inch.

"If you don't know, then…" She shook her head, the rest of her body completely motionless. "If you don't know, then what am I supposed to do?"

"I don't—"

"What am I supposed to do, Francis, if you don't know where he is? You were my last hope."

I stepped backward, inching behind the couch so as not to startle her. If I could keep her talking, maybe I could make it back into the bedroom and to my phone.

Or maybe I should just go for the front door.

Shit, or even out the patio door.

"Who are you? Maybe..." I cleared my throat. "Maybe I can help you."

She looked up, blinking as if seeing me for the first time, and she stared, her face almost completely expressionless.

"My name is Miranda Farr," she said simply, and it hung there just long enough for me to choke on the air that had just entered my lungs. "I'm Sam Farr's wife."

Just like that.

She said it so simply.

"*Who?*"

I didn't ask her because I hadn't heard her, or because I didn't know who Sam Farr was, or even because I didn't believe her. I asked her because I needed a moment to let it sink in.

And to catch my breath.

"Sam Farr."

"What are you talking about?" It was nothing more than a hoarse whisper.

"My husband is Sam Farr, and our son, Matthew, is missing." When I didn't respond, she continued, as if she knew how to twist the knife even deeper. "He's nine."

That last sentence was meant to hurt me, to hit home, and it did. I struggled to catch my breath as we stared at each other.

Could she be lying? Why would she lie?

What was she talking about?

Most important: *Why did she have a gun?*

I glanced back and forth between her and the weapon. "How did you..." I swallowed. "How do you know who I am?"

"I looked you up," she said, as if I'd asked the world's stupidest question. "Francis Scroll was an intern at the *Madison Tribune* in the summer of 2002, but he fell off the face of the earth after that. Coincidentally, Francis Clarke's bylines began showing up at the same paper a few months later. When I found your name in the *Lansing News*, I knew you'd come back home. Why'd you come back, Francis?"

It was an accusation, and I blinked rapidly. "It had nothing to do with your son, if that's what you're suggesting. Is that why you're here?"

She stared at me for a moment and finally sighed, her shoulders slumping forward. "I'm here because I need help finding him," she said. "I'm sorry, I…" She raised the gun, then shrugged and put it back in her lap. "I'm sorry I brought this. I just needed you to tell me the truth."

I swallowed. "So it's not loaded?"

"Oh, it's loaded," she said, looking up quickly, and there was something like a dare there, asking me to come closer.

I swallowed again. "If your son is missing," I started, "why didn't you go to the police?"

"I did," she snapped. "They're not doing anything. So I thought maybe you knew something about it, or maybe they suspected you and they just weren't telling me…"

"Suspected me?"

"Yes."

"Why would they do that? Who did you see? Captain Keith Del—"

"Delroy? Yes. I asked him if they would talk to you, and he said he would. Personally. But obviously, that was a lie."

"So you're telling me you think I had something to do with your son's disappearance?"

"No, not you. Your father."

"What?"

"Your father took him."

"You can't be serious."

"Do I look like I'm not serious?" she asked. "I broke into your apartment and pointed a gun at you. I'm as serious as you can get. Alex Scroll has my son. That old, drunk bastard has my child. And nobody in this town wants to do anything about it."

I still felt painfully close to losing consciousness, and I leaned forward against the couch.

"When did…uh…"

"Matthew."

"When did Matthew go missing?"

"Three days ago. He went to the park with Sam, and then…" Her voice broke, and she looked out the patio door. "We were just getting it together, me and Sam," she said, turning back to me. "It's been hard, really hard. You can't imagine what our life has been like—what Sam's life has been like. Matthew was all we had, and now…"

"I'm sorry," I said quietly. "But what makes you think my father was involved in this?"

"Because he was following us."

"What?"

"Your father has been following us for weeks. We've seen him. Confronted him, talked to him about it."

"You confronted him?"

"Yes," she said simply. "I walked up to the bastard and told him to leave me and my family alone. But he didn't listen, and now my baby is just…gone."

I opened my mouth and closed it, and outside of my open patio, a bus blared its horn. We both froze, staring out through the shards of glass as if there were an answer out there for us.

"Did you press charges?" That would at least prove to me that she wasn't making it all up, that she wasn't absolutely insane, even though she seemed to be perfectly in control.

"No, it never got that far. We never wanted it to. We just wanted him to leave us alone." She shook her head and stared down at the gun in her hands. "I can't believe I didn't do anything about it. I never thought he would do something like this. I thought he would eventually go away once he realized he couldn't hurt us anymore."

"When did you last see Captain Delroy?"

"Yesterday," she said. "I know how close he was—is—to your family, so I asked him, point blank, if he would check with you about your father. He said he would. Now he's not returning my phone calls. So I came here myself."

During the year between Lucas's death and my going away to boarding school, I'd spent most of my days with Captain Keith Delroy and his family. My parents had split their time alternately grieving and chasing lawyers to find out how they could best build a case against Sam Farr. Delroy and his wife, Dorene, had welcomed me with open arms.

I'd seen Delroy only twice since coming back to Lansing. Like Cam, he'd been pushing me to reach out to my parents, especially my father.

"He hasn't called *me*," I'd said the last time we'd met, and the words had sounded childish, even to my own ears. "He knows my number."

"You're the one who moved back," he'd said. "You're supposed to make the first move."

"Says who?"

"Says common decency."

The gun was still in Miranda Farr's lap, but it seemed pretty clear that she wasn't going to use it. My heartbeat was settling to a close-to-normal rate, and I knew I needed to take control of the situation quickly. I took a deep breath.

"Miranda, I'm going to go get dressed, okay?"

She looked up at me but didn't say anything. I began to back up slowly, my knees less confident than my voice, and I walked shakily toward the bedroom.

She tensed as I sped up and turned, moving quickly through my apartment in an awkward, clunky run.

"Hey," I heard her call out, but I didn't stop, even as I heard her get up to follow me. "Where are—"

I made it into my bedroom and grabbed the glasses off the nightstand. As I put them on, I spun around. She appeared in the doorway, the gun in her hand but, thankfully, still down at her side. I was shocked by her appearance, now that I could see her clearly. She was in her early thirties, and she was nice-looking, except for the puffy eyes, reddened nose, and mane of tousled, clumpy brown hair that obviously hadn't been washed in days.

"What are you doing?"

"I'm getting dressed and going down to the station."

"I'll come with you."

"No, you won't. Believe me, I'm as pissed about this as you are—"

"Believe *me*, you're not," she said, her eyes narrowing.

I nodded. "Look, I'll have better luck with Delroy if you're not there." I walked over to my dresser and began pulling out clothes. "Do you mind?"

Her eyes widened, and she turned around, stepping away from the door. "Are you going to press charges?" she asked, and it was almost conversational, as if she didn't care how I answered the question.

I stepped into my underwear, watching her back. It seemed like the moment could have been my best opportunity to take the gun from her. She didn't seem like she wanted to use it, but she had brought it back with her. I straightened up and hesitated only a second before inching closer to the door.

"Don't do it, Francis."

I looked up and peered past her into the hallway, and my heart skipped a beat when I saw that she was staring at me in the large hallway mirror, right above the table from where I'd taken the lamp just a few minutes earlier. We locked eyes in the mirror, and I could see that she was tense but still in control and not as vulnerable as I thought she might be.

I turned back to the bed and picked up a pair of jeans.

"Well, are you?" she asked. "Going to press charges?"

"I don't know," I said truthfully as I finished getting dressed and grabbed my keys and wallet.

She turned back to me as I strode toward her, and she walked backward into the living room, the gun still gripped at her side. I walked past her toward the front door and grabbed my jacket from the coatrack.

"You're just going to leave me here?" she asked.

I turned back at the door. "What did my father say?"

"What?"

"When you confronted him about following you. What did he say?"

She stared at me with an expression I couldn't quite read, and her gaze moved to the floor for a second before coming back up to mine.

"'It's not fair,'" she said softly, and I knew immediately she was telling the truth. "He didn't deny it, didn't apologize, didn't seem upset. He just said 'it's not fair.'" Her voice wavered on the last word, and it was the first sign of weakness I'd seen since she arrived.

I slipped on the jacket and zipped it up as I opened the front door.

"Let yourself out."

With that, I turned and bolted across the threshold and down the stairs.

I cut the fifteen-minute drive to the station in half, barely hitting my brakes. As I pulled into the parking lot of the sprawling, brick-and-glass Lansing Police Department, my chest tightened, and I went all death grip on the steering wheel. A major upgrade six or seven years back had turned the structure into something far different than the rundown station I remembered as a kid, and yet it was all too familiar. I got out of my car and walked quickly to the front door.

As I stepped inside, I froze, the warmth and the sounds enveloping me. Even though the aesthetics were different—it was shinier, more modern, and brighter than the last time I'd been there—the station felt the same, *smelled* the same. I was immediately pulled back to the late afternoons I'd spent sitting in another officer's chair, my feet barely touching the floor while my father finished paperwork.

I took a deep breath and walked toward the front desk, my gaze darting through the crowds of tables, toward the captain's office. From the entrance, I could see Delroy's hulking frame behind his desk. There was another cop in the room with him.

I was almost at the front desk when someone called out behind me.

"Francis?"

I turned and tried to hide a groan when I saw Vincent Jeffries, a cop who'd worked with my father for about a decade. There were more than fifty full-time Lansing police officers, and only a handful of them left who might recognize me. But that was my luck. Vince frowned, squinting at me. "Francis? Is that you? Wow, I haven't seen you around here in a while!"

"Hey, Vince," I said quietly. "How's it going? Yeah, long time. Look, I need to talk to Cap. It's urgent."

He looked back at the office where Delroy was currently midconversation. "Well, geesh, I can take you back there, but he's—"

"No problem. It will only take a moment," I said. He nodded and walked me through the scattering of tables but put up a hand as we approached Delroy's door.

"We can wait here," he said. "I'm sure they'll be done soon. So what have you been up to?"

I glanced at the men through the glass wall. "I'm sorry about this, and thanks a lot, Vince," I said before walking up to the door and opening it.

Delroy looked up in confusion, stopping himself midsentence. His eyes widened, and he looked back at the man in front of him.

"Let's continue this in a few minutes," he said.

I still didn't speak.

The man stood and turned, walking past me out of the room.

"Yes, I could have called you, but it wouldn't have done any good, you know," Delroy said, standing up. Keith Delroy was fifty-eight years old, 225 pounds, and six feet tall, with weathered, dark-brown skin, and shoulder-length, peppered-gray dreadlocks. "I know you're pissed, but you know I'm right."

"No, you're not, Cap. You should've told me."

"Francis, we're looking into it," he said. "You know we are. I'm not taking this lightly. We have a few people on it—"

"What did you think I was going to do?" I asked.

"What? I didn't think you—"

"No, you had to. You had to think I was going to do something, like warn him, or what? Did you think I had something to do with it too?"

"Too?"

"Yes. Farr's wife just showed up at my apartment with a fucking gun pointed at my face."

"Shit..."

"Yeah. Shit. And maybe I would have been a little more prepared for that if you'd told me what was going on."

"We'll get somebody on Mrs. Farr right away."

"No, don't worry about it. We resolved it."

He frowned, walking around his desk. "Are you sure? Francis, we—"

"No, it's fine. How could you leave me out of this?"

"I wasn't trying to hide it from you. But you *have* to trust me. We're looking into it, and we're following every lead possible. He's just a person of interest at this moment."

"Just a person of interest?"

"What do you want me to tell you?"

"What the fuck is going on!"

He scowled but didn't say anything, looking quickly over my shoulder to see if anyone else in the station had heard me.

"Look, the woman came to us three days ago and said her son was missing, and we started patrolling," he said. "She also told us who she was and said she didn't want any media attention 'cause they'd had 'more than enough of that to last a lifetime,' you know? Her words."

I nodded for him to go on.

"She said Alex had been following them around for the past few weeks, just watching them."

"How did she know it was him?"

"She got a good look at him, I guess. And there's no one in this town who doesn't know who Alex Scroll is. Especially someone married to Sam Farr."

"She said she talked to him?"

"Yeah, I guess there was a confrontation a week ago, which we're looking into," he said.

"Where?"

"Francis, there's no point in you getting involved in all of this!" He looked over my shoulder again and leaned closer, lowering his voice. "You've got to trust me, okay? We're doing everything we can to find that boy. Everything. But Alex didn't have anything to do with this. That woman has it out for your family. That's why she's doing this. Okay? We got this."

I thought about the expression on "that woman's" face as she stood in my living room, and I knew there was more to it than that. To be honest, Delroy's outright dismissal of her worried me—*he* hadn't seen the determination in her eyes, or the panic that was beneath it. I stepped back from him.

"You don't think it's possible?" I asked. "Not even a small part of you?"

I watched his face carefully. Delroy, and most of the Lansing Police Department, would probably do anything to protect my father, especially if Sam Farr was involved.

"No," he said softly without blinking. "You can't be serious. Do you?"

We stared at each other for a long moment. He was about to say something else when there was a knock on the door and a short, bulky cop walked in.

"Cap, you should see this."

We left his office and followed the cop to a small television in the corner of the room.

"They did it anyway," the cop said, shaking his head.

Delroy and I walked up to the television, and I heard him groan. It took me a moment to recognize the two individuals on the screen.

When I did, I sucked in a deep breath, not sure I could handle what was coming next.

It was Miranda Farr, sitting on a stool next to a thin, lanky man with his hands in his lap.

He wore a light-brown suit jacket over a button-down shirt that cinched his neck. Miranda was staring at the camera, but the man beside her was staring at his hands, moving his lips slightly as he quickly tapped his thumb against each one of his fingers.

Index, middle finger, ring finger, pinkie.

Repeat.

Sam Farr.

I hadn't seen him in years, since the day his trial ended. I'd avoided most of it while away at boarding school, but bad luck had brought me home to pack for college during the very week the trial ended. He looked the same—shaggy, oily hair curling around his ears and neck, bloodshot eyes, and, most noticeably, a twitchy nervousness that radiated from every part of his body. The only sign of age was the obvious rounding of his midsection; other than that, he looked exactly like the boy I'd last seen getting into his parents' car on the day the verdict came in.

"What's going on?" I asked Delroy as I stared at the couple. "What does he mean 'they did it anyway'?"

"She said she wasn't going to the press, that they couldn't handle all of that attention again," Delroy said, his jaw tightening in anger. "That she'd let us do our damned jobs."

I turned back to the screen, shocked that Miranda Farr had managed to go from my living room to being live on Channel 3 News in less than an hour.

The off-camera reporter had just asked her a question, and Miranda nodded, her puffy brown eyes watery but her gaze resolute. "My son, Matthew, has been missing for three days," she said, her voice shaky, "and the Lansing Police Department is not doing anything to find him. That's because one of their own took him!"

Both men beside me cursed.

"Mrs. Farr!" the reporter exclaimed in a singsongy voice, barely able to mask her excitement. She sat across from the couple, one ankle tucked behind the other. She wore oversize, trendy animal-print glasses, and she tapped a pen furiously against her knee, even though she held nothing to write on. "That is a very serious accusation. Just what exactly are you saying?"

The camera flashed back to Miranda Farr, who paused as she chose her next words. "I'm saying that Alex Scroll—the same man who has had it in for my husband for more than two decades—has kidnapped our son." Her voice broke, but she straightened her shoulders, reached over to grasp her husband's twitching hand, and stared directly into the camera. "And if nobody else in this town is going to do anything about it, you'd better believe me when I say *we* will."

Chapter Five

Saturday, 10:42 a.m.

As I walked out of the station, I glanced at my phone and saw that I had two text messages.

Cam: The fuck? Call me.

Amy: Leaving O'Hare.

Amy's text had come through more than half an hour ago, which meant she would be arriving at my apartment any moment now. I cursed, thinking about what she'd see when she got inside. The busted patio door, the glass. The lamp on the floor.

Shit.

I jumped in the car and sped home, dialing her cell phone on the way. It rang four times and went to voice mail. "Don't do it," she said in the message. "Just text me."

Sighing, I hung up and called Cam.

"Hey, I just heard," she said, skipping the pleasantries. "They can't be serious."

I opened my mouth to speak, but absolutely nothing but air came out.

"Hey," she said again, softer, and I could hear the concern. "Say something so I know you're okay."

"I'm okay," I whispered.

"Where are you?"

"I'm driving home from the police station. Amy just got here. She's on her way to my place now."

"Did you go see Delroy?" Cam asked. "Can't he do anything?"

"Yeah, he's looking into it," I said. "Did you know anything about this?"

She paused. "I heard a tip that Sam's son was missing, but it wasn't confirmed yet," she said. "And definitely none of this about Alex. You know I would have told you if I had."

"I know," I said. "I really don't know what to do."

"You need to go see your dad."

"Well, I know that—"

"And you need to talk to Amy."

"I'm going to—"

"No. No more 'going to.' Seriously, Francis. When you get home, you have to tell her."

"I will," I said. "Look, I'm going to need a couple of days off."

"Don't worry about it. Someone will cover for you."

Neither one of us wanted to talk about the fact that we knew she would assign the story to someone else.

I pulled up in front of my building and groaned when I saw Amy sitting on the front steps. "I gotta go," I said into the phone.

There were two suitcases by Amy's feet. I slammed the door and walked over to her.

"Hey," I said.

"Hey." She stood up. I'd seen her four months earlier during my last trip to New York, but she already looked older. A lot older. Her brown hair hung nearly to her waist. She wore a pair of burnt-red glasses and a dark-green peacoat, and she looked so…discerning. We stood there silently, shivering in the cold, trying to read each other. I had the feeling she was doing a better job than I was.

I shouldn't have been too surprised by her appearance. In what I can only imagine was a momentary lapse in teenage judgment, Amy had accepted my Facebook friend request about a year ago, and I'd been able to watch her journey toward adulthood from afar. I'd learned that instead of parties and booze, she spent her time supporting various human rights causes and volunteering to do things like clean beaches and build community gardens. Her passionate, public responses to social injustice both amazed and scared me—there was very little about Amy that was a kid anymore.

After standing there for several seconds, I finally managed to speak. "You okay?" I asked.

"I'm fine," she said. "Where were you?"

"I had to run out. Why didn't you call me to pick you up?"

"Would it have mattered?" she asked, and it wasn't an accusation, just a question. "You weren't here." She grabbed her suitcases and turned to head up the stairs. I stepped forward to reach for them, and she shook her head. "I got it. Thanks."

She moved back when she reached the front door, watching me as I struggled to get the key in the lock. I felt clumsy, awkward. I finally opened it and let her inside, wondering how I would explain what had happened that morning.

"See you up there," Amy said, breezing past me toward the elevator before I could say anything else.

I hesitated. I knew I should go with her, ride with her in the elevator to prepare her for what was upstairs, but in a second, she was gone, disappearing as the sliding doors closed between us. She knew I wouldn't follow her. I turned and made my way to the stairwell, pulling myself up the three flights of stairs.

"Daddy, why won't you ride with us in the elevatuh?" Amy had asked me when she was six, gap-toothed and charming as all hell, her thumb glued to the down arrow in the elevator bank of a Queens parking garage.

"Because the stairs are faster!" I'd said. "I'll race you and your mom to the bottom, okay? Betcha I'll make it first!" I could still hear her squeals of excitement as she raced into the elevator and jammed the buttons. When they'd emerged on the first floor, I was waiting for them, out of breath but ever the hero.

"Tell me, what would you have done if I weren't here?" Reba had whispered in my ear as Amy ran ahead of us. "Let my daughter ride down in an elevator by herself, or carried her through that piss-stained stairwell?"

As I stepped onto the third floor, Amy was waiting for me next to my front door. When she saw me, she moved back, waiting for me to let her inside.

"Ames, something happened this morning that I need to tell you about," I said as I inserted the key into the door and carefully pushed it open. Even though I knew Miranda had left, I scanned the room quickly.

"Okay," she said, walking quickly past me and dragging her suitcases through the living room. "Can we talk later?"

"Shit, Amy, wait," I started, but she walked into the spare room and shut the door. She'd stayed in that room only once before, when she'd come to visit me when I'd first left New York. If she saw the busted glass by the patio door, she didn't say anything about it.

I moved through the apartment, checking behind doors and in closets, but there were no signs that anyone else had broken in.

Grabbing my cell phone out of my pocket, I called the building supervisor about the patio door. After a string of expletives, he promised to be upstairs within the hour to take a look.

I walked over to Amy's door and knocked on it.

"Later, okay?" she called out. "I just want to get settled."

I opened the door and stepped in, and she looked up in surprise. "Really?"

"I need to talk to you."

She was sitting on her bed with her phone in her hand, and she frowned, waiting for me to go on.

"Someone broke in this morning."

She blinked, but she didn't say anything, and I walked closer to the bed.

"To my—" I cleared my throat. "To *our* apartment. Someone broke in."

Still no response.

"Did you see the broken glass?"

"No."

"When you walked in, right now, you didn't see—"

"No," she said again. "Did you call the cops?"

"Yeah, of course—"

"Okay," she said. She looked back down at her phone.

"Are you kidding me? You can't take it lightly, Ames."

"I'm not taking it lightly. But if you called the cops, what exactly do you expect me to do?"

"I need to go back out. Maybe you can go to a coffee shop?"

"I just got here, and now you're trying to get me to leave?"

"Just until I get back," I said. "You could go stay with my friend Cam for a bit, actually. Let me just give her a call—"

"Are you kidding me? I'm not going anywhere. Just lock the—"

"It was locked the first time," I said.

"Look, I appreciate what you're trying to do here. I really do," she said. I couldn't tell if she was being condescending on purpose, but I suddenly felt embarrassed. "But I'll be okay."

"You can't stay here with the patio door bust—"

Before I could finish, someone banged loudly on the front door.

"Who is it?" I called out as I went back into the living room.

"Frank! I'm here about tha door!" It was the building manager, and I walked over to let him inside. He stood there holding a bunch of tools and stared past me toward the patio door. "You gotta be kiddin' me!" he said, shaking his head. "You all right?"

"Yeah. Thanks, Frank," I said, stepping back. I turned to see Amy standing in the hallway.

"See? You can go," she said. "I'll be fine." She walked back in her room and closed the door.

Frank smiled and gestured toward the shut door. "Oh, your little girl's here, huh?"

"Yeah, she just got in."

"Francis the pop, huh?" Frank said, patting me on the back hard enough to make me take a step forward. "Neva really pictured you as much of a dad."

"Thanks," I muttered.

"Well, if you really need to go, no problem. I'll look out for her for a while."

I glanced at Amy's door and then back at Frank.

"Really?"

"Yeah, it's no problem."

I hesitated for a moment but finally nodded. I walked over to the coffee table and shuffled through some old mail until I found a relatively blank envelope. Grabbing a pen, I turned it over and wrote the word "Emergency" along with Cam's name and phone number. I walked back to Amy's room and shoved the note under her door.

I stood up and turned back to Frank. "Thanks a lot," I said. "I really appreciate it." I walked quickly to the door. I'd met Frank when I first moved back to Lansing; he'd jump off the balcony before he'd let anything happen to one of his tenants or their guests. But, of course, he couldn't be there all day. I needed only a few more hours to figure out what the hell was going on with my father.

Just a few hours, and then I'd come back, and we'd have time to catch up.

To have dinner.

To talk.

I jumped into my car and headed to my father's apartment. He lived a few blocks away from the *Lansing News* office, which caused Cam to hound me at least once a week to go visit him.

"How can you drive by his apartment every day and not stop?" she'd asked. "It's crazy, even for you, Francis." I didn't tell her that I deliberately drove an extra five minutes out of my way each day to ensure that I didn't drive by his place.

It was, to be fair, a remarkably ridiculous standoff, one that even I was surprised had gone on this long.

In the eighteen months that I'd been back in Lansing, I hadn't seen my mother at all, and I'd seen my father only once, completely by accident. I'd been in Lansing for about eight months and was checking out at a Target about ten minutes from home when I turned and saw him file into line, two people behind me.

It had taken a few moments for his face to register, but when it had, my first instinct had been to hide. I'd whipped around quickly, facing the front of the line, and swiped my credit card without a glance at the total. I couldn't have borne it—the questions about where I'd been, or why I hadn't called, or what had happened with Reba. I just couldn't.

As I'd made my escape, my shoulders hunched over my shopping cart, I'd snuck a peek back at the line. I'd almost crashed into a family of four when I'd seen what my father was doing.

He was in the same place, but he'd picked up a magazine. Not just any magazine—from the collage of faces on the cover, I could tell it was *Us Weekly* or *People* or something else he'd had no business holding.

Which could have meant only one thing.

As he positioned the magazine in front of his face, I'd realized he'd seen me too.

And he was avoiding me as much as I was avoiding him.

And as much as I didn't deserve to feel sorry for myself, I did. Until that day, I'd been telling myself I'd go by to see him at some point, but all those empty promises flew out the window the day I saw him ducking behind a picture of Taylor Swift.

About ten minutes after I left Amy in my apartment, I pulled into the parking lot of my father's aging apartment complex. The grounds were dingy and unkempt, the light coat of snow unable to hide the bits of trash that littered the premises. Stealing an assigned space, I jumped out of my car and jogged quickly over to the front door.

A handwritten *Apartments for Rent* sign was taped to the inside of the glass, the scribbled phone number barely legible. I pressed the buzzer to Alex's fourth-floor unit.

Nothing.

I waited a few seconds before pushing it again, letting my finger linger on the buzzer.

Come on, Alex.

The last time I'd come to visit—*hell, had it been six years?*—I'd pushed the buzzer for nearly five minutes before he'd answered. He'd been "in the shower." When I'd gotten upstairs, the place had smelled like a disgusting mixture of rotten food and weed, and it had been clear that Alex hadn't taken a shower in days.

I was about to push the buzzer again when I saw movement. Through the glass, I watched the elevator at the end of the hallway open and a tall, muscular woman walk out.

In full Lansing Police Department uniform.

I drew in a breath and pulled back from the glass, spinning around to face the parking lot.

Shit.

Without giving myself time to hesitate, I walked back down the stairs, hoping I was walking neither too fast nor too slow. I imagined the cop's eyes trained on my back, watching me, wondering where I'd come from and why I was rushing away from the building.

Slow down.

I walked back to my car and opened the door as casually as possible. I could see out of the corner of my eye that the cop had opened the front door and was now standing on the front steps, peering in my direction. I started the car and pulled out of the parking lot. At the first stop sign, I made a right, hoping the officer wasn't still watching me.

Delroy had cops at my dad's place.

Which meant that Alex was probably nowhere around.

"I'm not sure why people hate us so much," I'd heard my father say to my mother one evening when I was ten or eleven.

"They don't hate you. They don't hate cops. They hate that you have the ability to stop them from going about their lives, to speak to them when they don't want to be spoken to, to judge them."

"To protect them. Do they hate that part too?"

"No, but they hate what comes with that."

I turned into the alley behind my father's building, staring straight ahead as I navigated through the overflowing garbage bins. If I let my eyes rest on them for even a second, I knew the itchy feeling of disgust would come over me, and I didn't have time for an episode.

It took me a moment to recognize the back of his building, and when I did, I hit the brakes. Pulling into a space across the alley, I shut off the car and stepped out onto the gravel. With my head down, I moved quickly and deliberately up the staircase of a neighboring building, making sure to keep my eyes straight ahead.

"If you don't want to be noticed, just move with purpose." It was one of the tips my father had doled out during my "awkward year" in middle school. "Nothing sticks out like a person who lingers, who hesitates. You'd be surprised at how much you can get away with just by moving quickly, talking louder, and pretending you know what you're doing."

I continued up the staircase and stopped, turning to look casually at the back of my father's building. Shielding myself behind a large column, I scanned his back door for any signs of the cop I'd seen out front. The steps outside my father's apartment stood out like a sore thumb on an already bruised hand. He'd hung faded, light-blue sheets around the perimeter of his small deck for privacy, but as the wind blew them apart, they exposed a cluttered, crowded space that was obviously being used more for storage than anything else.

I had to find a way inside.

I could come back later, but what if the cop was still there? Besides, I had plans with Amy, and I needed some time to convince her that she had plans with me. My gaze dropped down to the third floor and the second, in search of anything or anyone who might be out of place.

There.

The thing about being around cops so long is that you know how to spot them. A man in a faded black leather jacket and ripped jeans stood between the second and third floors of the staircase, leaning over the side, his elbows braced on the railing. In his hand, he held a Big Gulp, and he let the straw dangle in his mouth as he cased the alley. I pulled back even farther.

Two cops?

For a "person of interest"?

Delroy was a lot more concerned than he'd pretended to be. I walked back down the stairs and into the alley again. Crossing it quickly, I hugged the garages behind my father's building, praying the cop couldn't see me from his vantage point. There was no way Delroy had three cops watching my father's building, right? The apartment itself *had* to be empty. Waiting for an opening, I peeked around the corner of the closest garage. I saw almost instantly what it would be. The cop was in the same place, but he'd begun to move. A slow bob, back and forth, shifting his weight from one foot to the other.

I knew that dance.

I'd done it many times: after too many beers at a concert, or in the middle of a crowded bar when the bathroom was just too far away.

Come on…

After a few minutes, the cop straightened, turned, and walked quickly down the stairs. He looked over his shoulder in my direction, and I darted back against the garages. I counted slowly to ten and leaned forward again. The cop was walking between a pair of parked cars toward a shaded corner of the alley. He'd already started unzipping his pants.

I moved toward the staircase of my father's apartment building. The cop couldn't see me, but he would be able to hear me if I made too much noise. Without letting myself think about the absurdity of what I was doing, I slipped out of my shoes and walked in my socks up the stairs. I held my breath the whole time, and when I got to the top, I breathed carefully out of my mouth, listening for any sounds.

Nothing.

I pushed past the billowing blue sheets and stepped onto the small deck.

Navigating the chairs, boxes, and piles of junk, I went over to his kitchen window. Bending down, I peered inside. Nothing. I tried the back door and wasn't surprised to find it locked, but maybe…

On the ledge outside of the kitchen was a small, empty planter, which my father had left there to hide his backup key. He'd told me about it the last time I'd visited.

"I've locked myself out so many times, Francis," he'd slurred, shaking his head. "Landlord charges me $75 each time. Each time!"

"Why don't you give me a spare set," I'd said. "That way, I could—"

"Could what?" he'd asked sullenly. "Fly here from New York to let me in? Hell no. You don't need to be able to come in here anytime you want. Besides, I fixed the problem. I hid a key out on the deck."

I hadn't felt the need to tell him he'd just given me access through that admission. I'd seen the key under the planter on the way out. Somewhere between the whiskey and the wine, he'd gotten sloppy with things like that. If I was honest with myself, I knew the moment I saw it that one day I'd have to use it to let myself into my father's apartment, and it wouldn't be a good day when that happened. Though, to be fair, I'd suspected more of a "locked up for a drunken bar fight" scenario than a "kidnapping of a nine-year-old child."

I lifted the planter, and my heart skipped a beat when I saw the key was still there. The old key and cold lock took some finessing, but I was finally able to open the door and quietly step inside.

I slipped my shoes back on and walked slowly into the kitchen, letting my eyes adjust to the dim interior. My stomach flipped as I walked through the rooms. There was junk everywhere, piled on top of itself. Paper towels and plastic bags. Trinkets and garbage, all littering the kitchen table and the hallways. I stepped into the living room and froze when I saw a large suitcase on the couch, half-empty.

He'd been packing?

I balled my hands into fists as I walked farther into the apartment, letting my gaze rest on the dingy furniture, the musky smell of dust and old food filling my nostrils.

Damn it, Alex.

The place was a mess, but it was clear the cops had done a number on it too. Desk drawers were open, the cushions on the sofa tossed aside. They were looking for something, and I had a feeling they hadn't found it.

But I knew one place to look that they didn't.

When I was a child, my father always hid things in one place, and one place only.

"I want something heavier," I'd heard him say once to my mother as he inspected a large oak dresser at a furniture store.

"Heavier?" she'd asked. "What's the point of that?"

"It'll just...look nicer, believe me. You know, more expensive," he'd said, turning and giving me a wink. He knew I'd seen him hiding some cash under his dresser a few weeks earlier, and it had become our little secret, one I found exciting to keep from my mother.

It was worth a try.

I walked into the bedroom and was immediately overwhelmed by the feeling that I wasn't supposed to be there, in his most personal, private space. Taking a deep breath, I put both hands on my father's dresser before digging my feet into the carpet and pushing.

It didn't move an inch. I took a deep breath and tried again, lifting just one corner, then the other, until I was able to shimmy it back along the wall a few inches.

There.

A small, perfect square had been cut in the carpet. I knelt down and tugged. Beneath the carpet, there was a hole in the floorboard, not much bigger than my hand. Steeling myself, I leaned forward and put my hand inside.

My fingertips brushed against what felt like crumpled papers, and I pulled out the contents.

A stack of cash—not much.

A few crumpled receipts.

And an address book.

I flipped open the book and scanned the pages. There were only a few addresses and phone numbers listed, one for Raymond Banks, the prosecutor in my brother's case. I also found an address for a place listed only as "Cabin," in Swatchport, Illinois.

Swatchport?

I'd heard of the small town; it was just thirty miles or so outside of Chicago.

I left the money but picked up the receipts and the address book. As I stood up, I unrolled one of the receipts and peered down at the boxy, blue-and-white logo at the top of it—it looked like the letters *C* and *S*, framed by a thick rectangle.

I squinted at the small text and began to replace the carpet with my foot when I heard the sound of a door opening—followed by footsteps as someone hurried into the apartment.

Shit.

Chapter Six

The footsteps were fast and confident, and my mouth went dry. There wasn't enough time for me to move the dresser back into place. I finished pushing the carpet down and moved quickly against the wall, shielding myself from the hallway outside the bedroom door.

"Yeah, that's fine," a male voice said loudly. "I'll do one more walk-through, and Lewis will stay out front."

Damn.

It was one of the cops, probably Big Gulp, and there was a good chance Delroy was on the other end of the line. I couldn't decide if I was relieved or disappointed that it wasn't my father. The cop's footsteps got louder as he neared the bedroom, and I flattened myself against the wall.

Was he coming in here?

What would I say?

And what would Delroy say when he found out?

I panicked, sliding down onto the carpet. I rolled to the side of the bed farthest from the door. With my body flat on the musky, filthy carpet, I waited, blood pumping furiously through my body.

A second later, I heard another sound.

Urine—hitting the toilet bowl.

Again?

The cop was humming to himself, and I knew it was my only opportunity before he did his final check. I stayed low to the floor and crept around the bed. Peering into the hallway, I could see the man standing with his back to me in the bathroom, since he'd left the door wide open. I crept slowly out into the hall.

Creak.

The floorboard squealed beneath my foot, and I froze, my gaze fixed on the back of the cop's head. My mouth was open, and I continued to take in short, shallow breaths, praying he wouldn't turn around.

But Big Gulp didn't move, didn't even stop his stream. I took a deep breath before continuing. I hit the kitchen just as the toilet flushed. I slipped quietly out the back door and navigated the stacks of junk on the back porch before racing down the stairs, not stopping to look back as I bolted toward my car.

On the way home, I sent Amy a text, asking her what she wanted for dinner. It took her a few minutes to respond.

Not hungry.

The fridge was packed with the groceries I'd purchased the day before, but I knew I had a better chance of getting in some quality time if I brought home something quick and easy. I took a detour and stopped at Duo's Pizzeria, a small mom-and-pop shop that doled out a free two-liter with every large pizza.

I walked through the front door of my apartment around eight o'clock, more exhausted than I'd been in a long time. My attention immediately went to the patio door, which was patched poorly with a large piece of heavy-duty plastic. It did nothing to stop the cold evening air from whipping around the living room.

There was a handwritten note from Frank on the counter, promising he'd be back the next day for a more permanent fix.

I put the pizza down and opened the box. I'd tried to call Amy from Duo's, but she hadn't answered, so I'd gone with half meat, half veggies. It seemed like a safe bet in case she didn't eat meat anymore.

Hell, I didn't even know whether or not she ate meat.

I walked through the apartment to her room.

"Hey, you here?" I called out when I reached her door. I could hear what sounded like a radio. I knocked gently on the door, and it partially opened.

Amy was sitting on her bed, her computer in her lap.

"Hey," I said again. "I brought some dinner home."

"I'm not hungry," she said, not looking up from the computer. She took a moment to angle the screen away from me, just slightly.

"Oh..." I said, standing at the door. "Well, come on out and try it anyway. I got pizza. I didn't know what kind you liked, so I got half sausage and pepperoni, half green peppers."

I felt like I was talking a lot.

"Amy."

"What?" she asked, looking up again, pressing a key as she peered at the screen. "I'm really not hungry. Besides, I don't eat pizza anyway. Thanks, though."

"You don't like pizza?" I asked, frowning. "I didn't know that."

"No, I just don't eat it."

"Okay..." I said. I lingered for another moment and finally stepped back out into the hallway. I pulled the door gently behind me and was almost back in the kitchen when I heard a voice.

"*Sto bene.*"

The voice was mechanical, and it wobbled out of the computer, making me pause. I'd inched back closer to Amy's door when I heard her repeat the phrase quietly.

"*Sto bene.*"

I walked quickly to her door.

"What?" I said, pushing the door open slightly.

She looked up at me, her face covered in annoyance, and the voice on the computer spoke again: "*Di dove sei*?"

Amy reached out and pressed something on her keyboard, and the sound stopped. "What's up?" she asked.

"I thought you said something."

"Nope, I didn't."

I hovered by the door for a moment. "Was that Italian?"

She blinked, and I got the sense she was uncomfortable all of a sudden. "Yeah, I'm just…just doing a little practicing," she said.

"Oh, okay," I said, stepping forward. "When did you start doing that?"

She shrugged a little, and it was clear she wanted the conversation to be over. "I don't know, Dad," she said. "Just a couple of weeks ago. I've always wanted to learn a new language."

"I thought you were taking Spanish at school."

"Dad."

"Yeah, no, I mean, that's great," I said. "You're going to need it when you go to stay with your mom. I get it." I cleared my throat. "Hey, by the way, since tomorrow's really the only day we'll have to hang out before school starts, I thought maybe we could do something fun. Maybe go play mini golf like we used to. You're not a kid anymore, so I don't have to let you win though."

She didn't laugh, but she nodded. "Sure, sounds cool."

I waited for her to say something else, but finally she just shrugged and spread her arms slightly. "All right, great. Well, let me know if you get hungry, and I'll order something else," I said before walking away.

"Thanks, but I'm not hungry," she called out.

And so went our first five minutes of bonding.

I went back into the kitchen, grabbed a slice of pizza, and slumped against the counter to eat it, my eyes glued to the patch in my patio door.

Chapter Seven

Sunday, 10:45 a.m.

The next morning, I woke up and called Vincent Jeffries, the cop I'd seen at the station the day before. After a few minutes of chitchat and an apology for brushing him off, I got him to look up Sam Farr's address for me.

"What are you going to do?" he'd asked in a stage whisper. "We all know Alex didn't have anything to do with this."

"I'm just going to talk to him, that's all," I said. "Thanks, Vince."

Sam and Miranda Farr lived in a small home on the northeast side of Lansing. When I first pulled up to the house, I sat there for a moment, gazing out at the modest structure, which seemed, somehow, to blend into its surroundings. It was a ranch-style home with large windows, pale-green siding, and a rust-colored roof.

As Miranda Farr opened her front door, I saw the flash of dread in her eyes, even as she squared her shoulders.

"You're going to press charges," she said, her face stony, her hands down at her sides. "That's why you're here."

"No—" I started, but she cut in.

"I know it was a bad idea, I knew it going into it, and I knew it when I left your apartment yesterday. But you have to understand that I didn't have any other choice. I needed to know, for certain, if you knew where he was. I couldn't handle any more runaround or empty promises about what's going to be done to find him. I just needed to know."

If she was scared, she didn't show it, and she stood there waiting for me to say something.

"That's not why I'm here," I said.

She stepped forward and crossed her arms in front of her chest, letting the screen door swing against her body. "No?"

"No. I came here because I want to find my father as much as you do," I said, and her eyes narrowed, but she didn't say anything. "And I think I'm the best chance you have of actually finding him." She still didn't respond. "Please. I want to help. That's it."

She was still hesitant, but finally, she nodded before moving back to let me inside.

I stepped into the dimly lit foyer where a row of bath towels had been placed on the floor in lieu of a floor runner, and a pile of snow- and salt-covered shoes were bunched against the wall by the door. "Should I…" I started, gesturing toward the pile.

Miranda shook her head. "It's okay."

We took a single step down into the living room. The ceiling felt low, and even though it was still several feet above my head, I instinctively hunched my shoulders. The room wasn't gorgeous by any means—the brown carpet was worn, and the mismatched couch and love seat had obviously been bought secondhand. The walls were painted a nauseating sea-green color that had chipped in several places, revealing a much darker color underneath. The room smelled like a mixture of cigarette smoke and a cloyingly sweet air freshener.

But all things considered…

It was nice. It felt like a home; Sam and Miranda had managed to build something for themselves, however outdated and mismatched, and there was a *normalness* to the place I never would have expected.

"What now?" Miranda asked, turning back as I stopped.

I shook my head quickly. "Nothing," I said. "Nice place."

She hesitated before nodding her thanks and kept walking, leading me through the room, into the dining area, and finally into the kitchen.

"Can I get you something?" Miranda asked, and she pointed to one of the chairs.

It wasn't really an offer, just a formality, and I shook my head as I sat down. "No, I'm fine, thanks."

She shrugged, grabbed a coffee mug, and filled it with steaming coffee before turning back to me. "So what do you want to know? Let me guess, you went to see your cop friends, and they told you to fuck off?"

It was only then, in the bright light of the kitchen, that I saw the deep bags under her eyes and the pure exhaustion on her face. "Something like that. They told me a little bit about what happened, but they want me to stay out of it."

"Why just a little?" she asked. "I mean, I get the whole conflict-of-interest thing, but if they don't think you had anything to do with Matthew's kidnapping, then why not fill you in? At least see if you have anything to add. Or are they worried you're going to print something in…what is it, the—"

"*Lansing News*."

"Yeah. Why the radio silence?"

I didn't want to let on how much those were the same questions that had been plaguing me since she'd first shown up in my apartment. It seemed like more than she needed to know.

She was crazy, but she didn't seem stupid.

And she was right. It didn't make any sense that Delroy hadn't asked me for the slightest bit of input. It could mean only two things: they had way more on my father than they were letting on, or they didn't fully trust me.

Or maybe both.

"Where's your husband?" I asked, changing the subject indelicately, and she frowned and let it hang there for a moment before answering.

"He's in the bedroom, resting." She looked back toward the entryway and fidgeted with the handle of her coffee mug. "I'll really need to go check on him in a few minutes, so what can I tell you, Mr. Scroll?"

"Clarke."

"What?"

"It's Clarke now. Francis Clarke."

"Oh, right."

I cleared my throat. "You said my father was following you? When exactly did that start?"

"I wish I could tell you," she said, rolling the coffee mug in her hands. "I only know the day we first noticed it. Sam came home one day… It was a Saturday, so it must have been three Saturdays ago. He told me there was a car following him. Brown, old, loud, not discreet at all. He saw it at first in the FreshMart parking lot and then later on at the post office."

"Did he see the person in the car?"

"Not at first. But when he saw it at the post office, he tried to get closer to see if it was the same car, and suddenly, the driver made a U-turn and drove away."

"When is the next time he saw the car?"

"We never saw him in the car again. I think your father got scared that day when Sam tried to approach him, and he switched things up. But maybe three or…no, four days after that, because it was a Wednesday, Sam saw him again, following him."

"Where?"

"When he was leaving work."

"On foot?"

"Yes. Sam works only about a mile away. Sometimes he walks there."

"Where does he work?"

"At the Citgo station on Foster."

"Foster and what?"

"Lincoln."

"Was Sam alone both of those times?"

"Yes, the first two times. Matthew was with me on the first day, and he was at school the second time."

"And how many times did you see him after that?"

She paused to think about it. "Three," she said. "Sam saw him another time, and then we both saw him two times after that. The last time, I confronted him."

"Where was that?"

"At the grocery store again."

"What exactly did you say?"

She shrugged. "I just walked up to him and told him if he didn't leave my family alone, I would single-handedly separate his head from the rest of his body." She stared at me with angry, watery eyes, and I didn't doubt she'd used those exact words, and meant them too. "And that's when he told me it wasn't fair. I asked him what he was talking about, and he just left."

"So what happened on Wednesday? When Matthew went missing."

She took a deep breath, the mug still spinning between her palms. "Matthew and Sam go to the park every Wednesday after school," she said. She smiled a little as her eyes became unfocused, and she stared past me out the back window. "Rain, sleet, or snow. They've been doing that for a few years now, and they both absolutely love it."

"Which park?"

"Warren, on Torrence."

"What time?"

"They go right from school, so it was about three fifteen."

"And what happened?"

She shrugged, her gaze on the floor. "One minute, Matt was there, and the next minute, he wasn't."

"He just vanished? Sam didn't see my father? Or anyone else?"

"No," she said. "But Matthew would never run away, if that's what you're thinking. Someone took him, we know it."

I paused as I watched her, and even though I knew the answer to the next question, I had to ask it. "I appreciate you taking the time to talk to me about this," I said, "but it would be much better for me to get the details of that day from your husband. Do you think I could go in and talk to him?"

Her eyes widened, and she shook her head. "Not now. I'm sorry, but he really needs to rest."

"Why?"

She didn't say anything, and I leaned forward.

"What do you mean, why?" she asked. "He needs to rest because he's tired. Obviously."

"From what?"

She took another sip of her coffee, her hands shaking.

"I'm sorry, but…" I swallowed. "Is your husband ill?"

She frowned. "No, he's not," she said as if I'd insulted him. "But his son is missing, and he's having a very difficult time. I'm really tired of people bothering him."

I was going to press her a bit further about these "people," when a loud noise from the hallway stopped me. We both looked up sharply, and her expression changed.

A door had opened and closed, and loud footsteps moved quickly in our direction.

It sounded like…high heels?

The person who turned the corner was *not* Sam Farr. It was a woman, tall and slender, with thick curls of hair that fell past her shoulders. She carried a notebook in her hand, and there were two pens placed delicately behind both ears, holding her hair back from her face. It took me a moment to recognize her and the oversize animal-print glasses. She stopped short when she saw us in the kitchen.

"I'm done for now, but I'll be back later," the woman said to Miranda, but her eyes were on me. She frowned slowly as she put the notebook in her purse, not breaking her gaze. "You're Francis Scroll."

"You're the reporter," I said quickly. "From Channel 3. How did you know—"

"I know exactly who you are." She reached out her hand, and I hesitated before shaking it. "I'm Kira Jones."

"Nice to meet you, Ms. Jones." I gestured to the pens behind her ears. "Two of them? Just in case…"

"One runs out of ink, yes," she said levelly, without flinching.

"What are you doing here?"

"Kira is doing some research about Sam and his family," Miranda said, and there was a defensiveness there she couldn't quite hide. "She was just leaving."

There was an awkward moment of silence, and as I opened my mouth to ask another question, Kira spoke up.

"Well, it's nice to meet you. I'll be speaking with you soon." She said this deliberately before turning to walk out of the room. "I'll see myself out."

I turned back to Miranda, who still stood with her back to the counter.

We didn't say anything as the reporter opened the front door and left. When she was gone, I raised both eyebrows at Miranda.

"Research?"

"Yes," she said, squaring her shoulders and staring me in the eye. "Sam and I have hired her to ghostwrite a book. To tell Sam's story, once and for all. I'm sure you have your own opinion about that, but it's our decision, and he needs it." She shook her head and looked down at the floor. "We both need it."

I had a million questions for her, but she cut me off before I could begin.

"Listen, Mr. Scroll, I'm glad you came. I really am. I believe you don't know anything about where my son is and you're here to help. But I need to know what you're going to do differently to find Matthew. What are you going to do that the cops aren't? You must know somewhere your father may have gone."

Immediately, my mind went to the address book I'd found in my father's apartment and the cabin in Swatchport. The pain on her face was so intense that I wanted to tell her about it—to let her know I was trying as hard as I said I was. But I needed to check it out first.

"No, I don't know anything else," I said, and I winced as the lie tumbled awkwardly from my lips. "But I'll let you know as soon as I do."

"Promise?"

I cleared my throat as I stood. "Yeah, sure. I promise."

Chapter Eight

Sunday, 11:30 a.m.

I stepped out onto the Farr's front porch and tried to wrap my mind around everything Miranda had just told me.

I liked her, I had to admit.

She was a handful, sure, but then who wouldn't be losing it if their child was missing, they thought they knew who did it, and nobody had been able to do anything about it yet?

Still, the whole thing with Sam Farr and the reporter could be described only as odd.

Why wouldn't Miranda let me see him?

As I headed toward my car, I was surprised to see the woman who'd just breezed by us waiting for me. She was perched on the driver's seat of her bright-blue Toyota RAV4, her feet barely touching the ground. She toyed with a cell phone as I walked across the porch and down the stairs. As I reached the bottom step, she looked up and dropped out of the car, closing the door behind her gently.

I nodded to her.

She stepped forward, nodded back. "I figured I would just wait for you instead of trying to follow up later. I didn't know you were involved in all of this," she said, gesturing to the Farr's house. "I'd love to get your take on things, if that's okay."

"My take on things? You mean, for your book? Yeah...I'm not really interested in that since—"

"No, of course not. The book is about Sam Farr and his family. It's *their* story." She'd managed to reject me for something I'd just told her I wasn't interested in. She stepped a bit closer. "No, I'm interested in your thoughts about the accusations against your father."

She said it so plainly, and I stumbled for a response. "My thoughts?" I repeated. "I don't mean to be rude, but I would think that's pretty obvious. My *thoughts* are that we need to do any and everything we can to find Matthew, and that should be our only focus. Everything else seems pretty unimportant right now, don't you think?"

"Yes, of course," she said. "Now, have you—"

"Hey, is this on the record or something?" I asked. "For your show? Because I don't want to be on that either. No offense, but being on one of your little 'segments' is probably the last thing I'd want to do right now."

She chuckled and shook her head. "You can't just say 'no offense' before you say something offensive. It doesn't really work. Let me guess, you feel pretty proud of yourself for working at a community newspaper, huh? Salt of the earth, journalism at its core, inverted pyramid and all. What's your circulation like these days?"

She'd waited to chat but was prepared to fight. I was surprised, not because of the insult, but with how much she seemed to know about me. "A lot smaller than your show's viewership, I'm sure. Look, Miranda told me why you're here. I assume you'll be putting your book on hold, given what's happened?"

"Miranda and Sam would like me to work on both," she said, her gaze cutting into me. "The fact that the Lansing Police Department is not adequately addressing their son's case only highlights the injustice Sam Farr and his family have faced for twenty years."

"How did you get involved in all of this?"

"They contacted me," she said. "Miranda stumbled across one of my old articles online and asked if I was interested in ghostwriting a memoir. Too many years have gone by, and it's time for the truth to be told about what happened that night. That's why I'm here."

"Nobody knows what the truth is," I said. "That's the point. Maybe Sam Farr, but maybe not. He was just a kid. I'm trying to let it go, and I think most people have already."

"It's easy for you to say that. You haven't had to go through Sam Farr's life. He can't 'let it go.' It's not that easy."

"Has he really been talking to you?"

"Yes," she said, crossing her arms in front of her. "Sam is very involved."

"What are you talking to him about?"

"Everything. His childhood. That night. The aftermath. Miranda wanted me to be very thorough. I'm recording every single one of my sessions with Sam," she said. "It allows me to get very nuanced in my storytelling."

"Why not take a break?" I asked. "With everything that's happened?"

"It's terrible, of course," she said. "And don't take this the wrong way, even though I'm sure you will, but it makes my work all the more relevant, if you ask me. If I didn't know any better, I'd say the Farrs orchestrated this. That they have Matthew tucked away somewhere. To make people actually listen when the book comes out."

"And what's to say that's not the case?" I asked.

"I know too much about them," she said. "I've been here every day for the past few weeks. It's not possible."

"Maybe Brian Farr and his wife took him."

"His grandparents? Are you really going down that path after everything we know about your father? He was *stalking* them, Francis."

"I'm just saying there are other options—"

"Of course there are. And I hope the Lansing Police Department is looking into every single one of them."

"They are," I said. "I don't know what the Farrs have been saying, but I've known Keith Delroy my whole life. He wouldn't put a child's life in jeopardy. Ever." I knew it was true, but why did it sound like I was trying to convince myself?

We were quiet for a few moments, so I moved on. "When will it be finished?"

"What?"

"The book. When will it be ready?"

"Oh, I'm polishing a few chapters and have a few left to write," she said. She brushed a strand of curly hair out of her face. "This town is so weird. I grew up nearby, in Midlothian, and I felt it. Nobody wanted to talk about it. It's like Lansing's ugly secret. And Sam Farr has *all* of the wounds to show for it. His side of things deserves to be told."

"But it doesn't help bring Matthew Farr home."

"Yes, but hopefully, we'll find him. And his abductor must be shown for who he really is. I'm not going to stop until the Sam Farr story is told."

"Is that what it's called?" I asked incredulously. "*The Sam Farr Story*?"

"Well, I'm still working on a title..."

"The title is the most important part, right?"

She shook her head. "You can laugh at me as much as you want to, Mr. Scroll. But *I* abide by the ethics of our profession, and that's to expose the truth." She shrugged and turned to get in her car. "Whatever that truth turns out to be."

Chapter Nine

The Sam Farr Story (new title? needs a better hook)

By: Kira L. Jones (use K. L. Jones in credits?)

DRAFT v.3—Not to be shared without express permission of author, K. L. Jones

<insert a map of Lansing? early photos of the family?>

On the afternoon of December 30, 1992, Sam Farr was getting ready to go to a party. The ten-year-old stood on the worn carpet of his bedroom in front of his full-length mirror, his arms out to his sides.

He didn't want to sweat.

Sweating meant pit stains.

He'd been saving this shirt—a pale-green T-shirt with a picture of a frog wearing shorts—for the past three weeks. It was a cool shirt, and it had been neatly folded in his dresser since he got it, because he wanted it to be crisp and new for the party, not already worn and faded by their centuries-old washing machine in the basement.

But just his luck, he'd ruin it with pit stains.

Sam put his arms down and took a deep breath. He would just have to calm down. He couldn't keep his arms lifted from his body all night—if he did that, Lucas would think he was even weirder than he already did.

Sam dragged his thumb across each of his knuckles, one at a time, moving from his index finger to his pinkie and back again. He was so excited that he was having trouble keeping still, which was bad for his whole sweat problem.

He was really hopeful about tonight. Lucas was one of the boys at school who wasn't so bad, at least not all the time. Sure, he teased him a little bit, but it was only when the other boys were around. When Lucas was by himself, he was actually sort of nice. He'd even picked up Sam's sketchbook when he'd dropped it as they were coming out of church one morning.

"Thanks," Sam had said, shocked. "I didn't even realize I'd dropped it."

"You're welcome," Lucas had responded. "I know it's hard."

"What's...hard?"

"Just like, keeping up with stuff."

"Oh, yeah, I guess so. Well, thanks."

Sam took a step closer to the mirror and peered at his hair. It wasn't that bad. He'd asked his mother for something else, something that made his head look less long and also less wide, but this is what he'd ended up with. When he pushed it really hard to the right side, it lay in a way that didn't look so goofy.

Sam heard a sound behind him, and he turned to see his mother walking into the room.

Elizabeth Farr was smiling as she always did, and she breezed over to him, running her hand quickly through the hair he'd just put in place.

"Tonight's going to be fun, right?" she asked.

"Yeah," he said, smiling too big and resisting the urge to straighten his hair again.

He didn't want her to know how nervous he was. It would make her sad if she knew he was worried about being bullied. He knew his mother thought he was one of the more popular boys at school, and Sam wanted it to stay that way.

Once, she'd said something about him not inviting any other kids over, because if he invited one, he'd have to invite "them all," and of course their home couldn't hold that many people. Sam had actually started laughing, giggling almost hysterically at his mother, and she'd just frowned, sweetly, as she always did.

"What's so funny?" she'd asked.

"Nothing, Mom," he'd said.

He did have a friend, sort of. Gerry Brandon Lee. But the kids made fun of Gerry way worse than they did Sam because Gerry had a bit of a limp and spent most of his time lost in his thoughts. Sam talked to Gerry if he had to, like when he needed a teammate for a school project and there was nobody else around.

Sam looked at his mother, who clasped her hands in front of her.

"It's going to be great. And I made your favorite—chocolate pie."

Sam had been smelling the pie all morning, but he smiled again, just as she expected him to. "You did?"

"Yup. And I had some extra filling, so I made a small one so you'll have some here when we get home. In case the Scrolls eat it all up."

Sam forced a smile and then turned back to look at himself. He tried not to grimace as he saw the small, circular stains forming under his arms.

"You look great," his mother said, catching his eye in the mirror. "I love that shirt. Okay, we'll be ready to go in ten minutes."

Sam nodded, and she walked out of the room. Then he walked quickly over to his closet and pulled out a shiny silver briefcase.

He'd gotten the case from his great-uncle, and the minute he'd seen it, he'd known it was perfect. He carried it over to his bed and set it down, running his fingers along the smooth top.

His mother had said he could take them with him, and he'd still been debating if he should.

He wanted to show them off, sure, but there were going to be a lot of people around.

A lot of people meant accidents.

People simply weren't careful with things that weren't their own.

But he was going to have to chance it. It would be his first time taking them outside of the house, and though he was nervous, he couldn't deny how excited he felt to show them off.

Sam took one final look at himself in the mirror and then turned and walked out of his bedroom, shutting his light off as he exited.

He walked purposefully down the stairs, the silver case in his hand, careful not to let it bump against the stairs or the railing.

When he got to the bottom, he turned into the living room, where his father was sitting on the couch, pulling on a pair of his shiniest shoes.

Brian Farr would never admit it, but he was nervous too. Sam could tell. They all were, even his mother, who'd been smiling ear to ear all morning as she baked her chocolate pie. It wasn't every day they got invited to parties.

And at a place like the Scrolls'...

Sam had seen only the outside of it, and he'd been blown

away by all of the levels and trees and windows. It was a beautiful home, and Sam couldn't wait to see the inside.

Neither could his mother, it seemed. She had been talking about it all week, about how Kate Scroll had invited her, about what she would make and what she should wear.

But Brian Farr hadn't seemed nearly as eager. He frowned as Sam entered the room.

"Are you sure you want to bring that?" he asked, gesturing to the briefcase "Why don't you just play some games with the other kids? Kate said Lucas might invite another friend over too."

"Mom said I could bring it," Sam said defensively, grasping the case with both hands and pulling it closer to his body.

"I'm not saying you can't. I'm just asking if..." He sighed as he pulled on his other shoe. "Not a lot of kids will understand it, that's all. Kate told me Lucas is really into soccer these days. That might be fun, right?"

"Not really," Sam said. Brian Farr opened his mouth to say something else, then he shook his head and closed it. Sam shifted uncomfortably, still holding the case against his knees, unsure of how else to respond. He watched as his father's expression changed, and finally, Brian Farr stood up and walked over to his son, ruffling his hair.

They always went for the hair.

"Hey, I was just making a suggestion," his father said, and Sam could see the disappointment on his face. "If you want to bring it, that's perfectly fine. You're just as great as Lucas and his friends, and if he doesn't see that, well, he's not worth your time. Right?"

Sam nodded and reached up to fix his hair back the way he liked it. His dad was always saying things like that, and Sam wished he wouldn't. It wasn't the kind of thing you said to a popular kid, and he knew Lucas's father never had to say anything like that to him.

No, parents said that only when their kid was a real loser. Sam turned away and walked toward the window.

He knew his dad got along with the Scrolls well enough—he occasionally watched a game with Mr. Scroll or met up with Mrs. Scroll for coffee—but Brian Farr seemed mostly annoyed by tonight's party.

"They're just regular people," Sam had overheard his father say to his mother when she'd first told him about the dinner party invitation. "You don't have to go buy something new. You have plenty of nice dresses."

"There's nothing wrong with wanting to look nice," Elizabeth had said.

Sam and his father waited silently in the living room. Before they could speak, Elizabeth Farr breezed around the corner, and just like that, it was time to go.

Sam turned and watched as his father's expression changed quickly. He smiled, but it didn't reach his eyes.

"You ready to go, honey?" he asked too cheerfully, but Sam could tell that his mother didn't notice. She smiled back happily as she balanced both the pie and her purse in her hands.

"Yep, how about my boys?"

"We sure are," Brian answered for both of them, and he gave Sam a meaningful look.

Sam smiled slightly and nodded, his fingers curving around the handle of the metal case.

Now or never.

They piled into the car, and Sam sat in the backseat, buckling his seat belt. He picked his briefcase up off the seat beside him and placed it on his lap. He let his mind wander to his presentation tonight.

He'd kept messing up in practice, but he wasn't too worried.

He'd get it right.

He'd never performed in front of a group of people before. Only his parents, and his grandmother once. They all loved it. But then again, that's what parents and grandmothers do.

He didn't know what the Scrolls were going to think. Especially Lucas. But he was going to do his best.

That's what his mom would say.

"Just do your best, and everything will turn out great."

It was going to be an awesome night.

Chapter Ten

Sunday, 12:30 p.m.

When I arrived home on Sunday afternoon, Amy was in her room with the door closed. I knocked on it gently.

"Yeah?"

She looked up as I opened the door and stepped inside. "Hey, so I was thinking we could leave soon. For the mini-golf place."

I could see the excuse coming even before she opened her mouth. "You know, I'm still feeling a little tired from my trip, and with school tomorrow and everything—"

"Oh, come on, it will only take an hour or so. And then I thought we could grab something to eat. You used to love mini golf."

"I did," she said as she stood up, pulling her hair up into a ponytail. "I mean, I do. Just maybe next week or something?" She walked over to her mirror and leaned forward as she finished wrapping her hair. She turned back when I didn't say anything, and finally, she sighed. "Okay...what if we just do lunch?"

She was throwing me a bone, and I resisted the urge to pump my fist in the air—it was better than nothing. "Yeah, sure, that's fine," I said. "We'll go down to Vinny's. And we'll do golf next week. Or whenever we can fit it in. Let me know when you're ready. It's just a couple of blocks away."

"Okay," she said with a forced smile, but I didn't *care*. I'd scored a lunch.

Twenty minutes later, we were seated across from each other in Vinny's, a twenty-four-hour diner that smelled of coffee, french fries, and recycled cooking grease. We both held the menus in front of our faces like shields, unprepared to just dive right in.

I lowered mine first.

"So tell me, honestly: I know you haven't seen much, but what do you think of Lansing?"

Amy put her menu down and stared at me for a moment before looking down at the table.

"It's cool," she said. "Not bad."

"You can handle a couple of years, right?" I asked with a small smile, and she forced one back.

"Yeah, of course."

"I emailed you all the info about your first day of school. You got it, right?"

"Yep, I'm all set."

The waitress appeared with water, and I took a deep breath, grateful for the break. We both ordered burgers with fries, and I made a mental note that Amy still ate meat.

"So you've been practicing your Italian, huh?" I asked as I unwrapped my straw and stuck it in my water.

I looked up when she didn't respond and found her staring off at something behind my head.

"Amy?"

I turned slightly to see what she was looking at. I drew in a deep breath when I saw what had her attention.

The small, mounted television above the counter was muted, but the image on the screen made my heart leap into my throat. It was a still shot of Sam and Miranda Farr, taken from the interview I'd seen yesterday while I was at the police station. Beneath their picture was a simple hashtag: #WheresMattFarr

"It's so tragic," Amy finally said, her eyes still on the screen.

I cleared my throat. "What's that?" I asked, and she finally looked at me.

"Matthew Farr? You know, the kid of that guy from the trial… back in the nineties?" She spread her hands wide. "The one who's all over TV?"

I blinked. "Of course. Wow. I didn't know you knew about that."

"Are you kidding? It's the only thing on the news. You were living around here back then, right?"

"Yeah," I said, clearing my throat. "That was a terrible case."

She stared at me intently, expecting me to tell her more, and my throat was suddenly impossibly dry. I took a drink of water and stared at the ice cubes as they knocked into one another when I placed the glass back on the table. I looked up, and she was still watching me, waiting for me to say something, and I searched for a response.

Actually, honey, I know a lot about that case.

The boy who died? That was my little brother.

Yep.

Your uncle.

And the man now accused of kidnapping Matthew Farr—you know, Alex Scroll? Well, funny story: my name was once Scroll too.

And that guy, Alex, he's your grandfather.

Yep.

The dead one.

Amy kept staring at me, and I knew there was no way I could tell her now. Not like this.

"Dad?"

"Yeah, no, I was here, but I was pretty young. But it was a… big deal."

As soon as the lie came out of my mouth, I regretted it.

Now it wasn't just that I hadn't told her *yet*; I'd lied, and she would never forgive me if she found out.

She frowned but leaned back as the waitress approached with our heaping plates. I snuck a glance back at the television and saw that the news station had moved on.

We walked home in silence. Amy thanked me for lunch and headed up the stairs as soon as we reached the building.

"I'll be back in a little bit," I said to her back as she let herself inside. I got in my car and pulled out my GPS. I typed in the location for the cabin I'd found in my father's address book.

5337 Crystal Lake Drive, Swatchport, Illinois.

The voice on the GPS sounded confident, and I followed her directions to merge onto I-57, heading south, away from Chicago.

As I drove, I thumbed through the address book until I reached the entry for the prosecutor in Sam Farr's trial. I'd heard he'd since left to start his own private practice somewhere on the east side of Lansing. I didn't know if he and my father still kept in touch, but it was worth a try. Grabbing my phone, I keyed in the number listed with his name.

"This is Raymond Banks. Sorry I can't take your call right now, but leave a message."

"Mr. Banks," I said, clearing my throat. "This is Francis…Scroll. I'm calling because I was hoping to get some information from you about my brother's case. Lucas Scroll. If you could give me a call back, I'd appreciate it."

I left my phone number and hung up.

It was probably a waste of his time, and mine, but he and my father had been close once. He might have some ideas about where Alex could be.

About twenty minutes later, the traffic on the highway began to thin, and I saw a small sign for Swatchport. I'd passed the town once or twice on my way out of the city, but I'd never had any reason to stop. I probably still didn't.

I exited and turned as the GPS led me down a gravel road consisting of two narrow lanes. A lone car moved toward me, and when it passed, I suddenly felt very alone, out in the middle of Nowhere, Illinois. Within minutes, the highway became a distant memory as the barren trees on either side of the road seemed to multiply around me. With the setting sun as my backdrop, I gripped the steering wheel and peered ahead, scanning the land for any signs of the cabin, or any life at all, really.

I made another turn as directed, and the gravel crunched indelicately beneath my tires.

"You have reached your destination on the left."

What?

She said it so calmly, and I wondered if she was mocking me, since the only thing I could see "on the left" were clusters of massive, crumbling trees.

I parked the car and got out. Even though it was cold, I felt warm under my jacket, and I unbuttoned the top button. I stepped away from the car and moved deeper into the woods. The dense brambles poked and prodded my face, and as I put up my hand to block a pointy branch as it headed for my eye, it occurred to me that I was wasting my time.

Not only my time, but also my father's. And Matthew's.

I was seconds from giving up when I stepped into a clearing and saw the first sign that my trip may not have been so futile after all. Past the open space, there stood a small, rustic cabin, buried in the dense woods.

No shit…

The small structure was haunting and beautiful at the same time, and on any other day, I may have appreciated the perfectly placed logs or the intricate roof. As I moved through the clearing, I scanned the front and sides of the building for a vehicle, but there was none. I reached the massive front door and took a deep breath before pounding on it with my fist.

I dropped my hand and waited.

Nothing.

After a couple of seconds, I pounded again.

Silence.

I stepped away and walked along the side of the building. My gaze landed on a sliding glass door. Pressing my face against it, I peered inside; I could make out a large kitchen and the adjoining living area. I grabbed the patio door handle and pulled.

No such luck.

I took a few steps toward the back of the cabin and stopped when a small window caught my eye. It was ajar, just slightly, and I knew immediately it would be my way in. It was going to be an incredibly tight squeeze, but I had no other options. I used both hands to lift the window as far as it would go before leaning forward to look inside.

The cabin was dank and musky and modestly decorated in shades of brown and black. The living area contained a dated, ripped black leather couch, a worn suede recliner, and a tall oak bookshelf that was filled with all sorts of things that weren't books.

I leaned back out into the fresh air. Though the window was at eye level on the outside of the cabin, it was located about seven feet up in the sunken living area. I could get in, but it wasn't going to be pretty. Going in headfirst would end in disaster. I pushed myself up until I was kneeling awkwardly on the windowsill. Rocking from side to side, I swung each of my legs through the window and held on to the top pane with both hands.

All that was left to do was to let go and let gravity do its work.

I'd spotted a small table just to the left of the window, but other than that, I was in the clear. Taking a deep breath, I tucked my arms close to my body.

And let go.

I crashed down into the cabin, my leg striking the side of the table as I fell, and I cried out in pain. The noise was deafening, and I pushed myself up quickly, my heart racing.

Silence.

If there was anyone inside, this would be the time to come out, but there was nothing.

No running, no footsteps, no sounds at all.

The late-afternoon sunlight streamed into the cabin, illuminating the thick layer of dust that covered everything, and I struggled to breathe normally in the stale space. I walked farther into the cabin, toward the kitchen, and stopped in my tracks.

In contrast with the rest of the cabin, the kitchen was beautiful—rustic and large, overflowing with maple cabinets and a gorgeous stacked oven. It looked out of place, as if the previous owners had put too much money into it, while ignoring the rest of the cabin.

But it wasn't just the beauty of the kitchen that made me pause.

It was something else.

I'd seen this room before.

I stood in the entryway, probing the sense of déjà vu, trying to understand why the room was familiar. Why I knew it, and where I'd seen it before.

The photo.

I'd seen this kitchen before in a picture…

It was one my father had brought home one day from one of his golf trips with his buddies from work.

In Indianapolis.

As I stared at the room, my mind went back to an argument my parents had had many, many years ago.

"Another golf trip?" my mother had asked as she stirred something in a pot on the stove, the anger and frustration pouring out of her. "That's already three this summer. Sometimes it feels like you'd rather be anywhere but here with us."

"Oh, come on," my father had said. "You don't have to make a big deal out of everything. It's not like we were doing anything that weekend anyway."

He'd come back from the trip and flashed a few photos of himself and some of the other cops, smiling in their rented apartment, supposedly three hours away in Indianapolis. My mother had barely looked at them.

This was where he'd been going?

All that time, my father had been here?

Just thirty miles away from home?

And probably more important—who had he been coming with?

I walked into the bedroom and tried to push the old memories out of my head. The room was small and dingy, and it contained only a queen-size bed, a nightstand, a wardrobe, and a large, light-blue floor rug. There was a single blanket on the bed, and it was pulled aside, exposing the stained mattress beneath.

I walked over to the dust-covered nightstand and opened up the top drawer. It was filled, almost completely, with condoms. Or condoms and condom wrappers, to be fair. Old and crumpled in the drawer, remnants of stolen moments and secret meetings.

I wondered how much my mother had known.

Probably enough.

I closed that drawer and tugged on the bottom one, pausing when it moved slightly but didn't open. It wasn't locked, but instead seemed to be caught on something. I shook the drawer to move the items inside around and tried again. The door scraped slowly open, and I frowned when I saw what was inside.

Books.

Large, hardcover books. I pulled the top one out and read the title.

The Methodical Mind by D. B. James. I flipped through it and paused on a line in the introduction.

"A collection of essays on ways to maximize brain power."

I pulled the drawer out even farther and saw more books by D. B. James, as well as a few by other authors I'd never heard of.

What the hell?

My father did a lot of things, but he rarely read for pleasure. If I'd found newspapers or old financial magazines, it would have made sense. But psychology books?

I put the book back and stood up. Walking around the room, I searched for any sign that my father had been here more recently than twenty years ago. I opened up the small walk-in closet and found a few old shirts hanging there, dingy and worn. One immediately caught my attention, and I sucked in a breath. It was an oversize, faded, black-and-white Chicago White Sox T-shirt. I grabbed the hem of the shirt and pulled it closer, my eyes resting on the nickel-size hole in the collar.

"Why do you insist on wearing that shirt?" my mother had asked my father almost every Saturday morning when he pulled it on. "It's disgusting. One day you're going to look for it, and you know where it's going to be? In the donation bin at church."

"Leave it alone," my father had said, and even though she'd been joking, he'd obviously been annoyed.

I let go of the shirt and sighed, stepping back. Besides the shirts and a few pairs of shoes on the floor, the closet was mostly empty.

As I backed out of small space, a protrusion on the wall caught my eye.

Pushing the shirts all the way to one side, I moved back into the closet and squeezed myself toward the far end. Against the wall, there was something else…

A door?

I put my hand against it and felt a draft coming from the crack in the doorframe.

What the hell?

I dragged my fingers against it until they hit a metal latch holding the door closed.

Was it real?

Or just an old fixture that had been built over at some point?

I was reaching to open the latch when I first heard the sound.

It was the briefest of tapping noises, and it came from out in the living room.

I spun around quickly, bumping my head against the tight, sloped ceiling.

Suppressing a curse, I bent my head and walked out of the closet, moving quietly into the bedroom. The noise had been soft—it was so light, it could have been nothing at all: a squirrel running across the deck, or the wind slapping the tree branches against the window.

The next noise ruined that theory.

As I stood with my neck craned toward the living room, I suddenly heard the loud sound of something breaking, followed by a deep thump as someone or something entered the cabin.

Chapter Eleven

I'd only ever had one thing broken into in my entire life. I was seventeen, and I'd left the windows down on my '84 Buick Skyhawk outside of a gas station as I went inside for a bag of chips. So I guess it's not fair to say my car was "broken into" that day. More that someone reached into the open window and grabbed my backpack off the front seat.

The fact that someone was breaking in on me for the second time in two days was just too coincidental.

I covered the distance between the closet and the bedroom door in seconds and stood behind it, waiting for another noise. I didn't have to wait long. I heard the sound of footsteps crunching on the broken glass and then one of the kitchen chairs scraping against the floor as the intruder bumped into it.

Alex?

He probably still had a key and should have no reason to break in, even if he'd seen me come inside.

No, this was someone who had no right being there—probably even less of a right than I did.

I clenched my fists and struggled to breathe normally. Who would be bold enough to break into the cabin that loudly, without even a hint of discretion in case there was someone else inside?

As if to answer me, I suddenly heard another loud thump, a groan, and then a woman's voice: "Shit! Stupid plant."

I sighed and stepped out of the bedroom.

"Miranda, what the hell are you doing here?"

She stood in the middle of the living room, staring down at a dead plant on the floor that had just toppled over and covered her pants with dirt.

She looked up at me and blinked. "Is he here?"

"No. What are you doing here?" I asked again. "What's with you and breaking and entering?"

"Are you sure?" she asked, ignoring my question and walking farther into the kitchen. She spun around and walked back into the living room, then through the passageway toward the front door. I followed closely on her heels and watched as she opened up the large walk-in closet.

"Miranda—" I started, but she moved quickly past me again and walked into the bathroom.

"I told you, I'm the only one here," I said, standing in the doorframe as she ripped back the shower curtain. "How did you get here?"

"The same way you did," she said, pointing toward the side of the building, out into the woods. "I followed you. I saw you come in. What is this place? Is this your father's?"

I opened my mouth and then closed it, not wanting to tell her anything I didn't need to.

"Yes," I finally said. "He owns it, but it doesn't look like he's been here in a while." I bit my tongue as I thought about what I'd just found in the bedroom closet.

"Why didn't you tell me about this?"

"What—"

"At the house. When I asked you if you knew anything else about where Matthew could be. You lied to me. You looked me in the eye and said you didn't know anything."

"I didn't know what I'd find here," I said. "Really."

"But what would have been your first reaction if you did find something? To call me? I doubt it."

"Look," I said. "I'm sorry I didn't tell you about it. I needed to come on my own. But you have to believe me—all I'm trying to do is find Matthew."

"Why?"

"What?"

"Why? You keep saying that, that you want to find him, that you're here to help. Make me believe you. Why are you so concerned with finding my son?"

"Well, I think it's obvious—"

"It's not."

I cleared my throat. She stared at me with a pained expression, her back against the windowsill in the bathroom.

"What's my other choice?" I asked her. "To just forget about it and go to work? To write a story about a new wing at Harvey Memorial? To just walk away because it's not my problem, not really?" I shook my head. "I can't do that anymore."

Her jaw softened, but she didn't say anything.

She sat down on the edge of the tub and looked up at me. "You know, I told Sam we should move away from here, anywhere else. Somewhere warm. I said San Francisco, but I would have been happy with something south, even Florida, since Sam didn't want to go west. Said it felt too far away from home, which really just meant too far away from his parents. Sam refuses to even consider the idea of going somewhere without them."

She rested her forehead in the palms of her hands and then

pushed hard against her face with closed fists. "I can't believe I let this happen."

"It's not your fault," I said, stepping closer. "You've got to know that."

She looked up again. "Isn't it, though? As a mother, your job is to protect your children. That's it. Protect their bodies, their minds, their hearts, their teeth. It's a terribly hard job, of course, but in a way, it's pretty simple. Make them better, not worse. Keep them safe." She shook her head. "If I don't get him back, what's the point of anything else?"

I fumbled for a response, sure I should tell her we'd definitely find him but unable to form the words.

She sat patiently, waiting for me to say something, and finally, she stood.

"I'm going to ask you this again. Will you promise me you'll call at the first sign of your father? Please?"

"Yes—"

"No, I mean, really promise. Last time, you lied. I'm losing my mind here. Can't you see that? I'm losing it. Tell me you'll help me. Please."

"I will," I said. She stood there, waiting for me to say something else, and I nodded hurriedly. "I promise. Really. I'll let you know if I find anything that will lead to your son. You have my word on that. But you can't keep following me, okay? You have to trust me."

She took a deep breath and nodded as we walked out of the bathroom and back into the living room. She went closer to the patio door that she'd busted and grabbed the handle. "I'm going to forgive you for not telling me about this," she said, gesturing to the cabin, "but if we're really working together, I need you to keep me in the loop."

Working together?

"Okay," I said.

She stared at me for a moment, and I could tell she was still trying to convince herself that it was okay to leave. "All right."

She turned and walked through the patio door, stepping out onto the small deck before walking off toward the woods. I stayed rooted to my spot until she'd disappeared completely.

When I couldn't see her anymore, I looked down at the broken glass that littered the cabin floor.

I'd just lied to her face—again.

I waited a few moments and then turned to head back into the bedroom. I walked quickly toward the closet, imagining that when I opened the door again, what I'd seen earlier would be gone.

That it was just a figment of my imagination, and that Miranda Farr wasn't the only one losing it these days.

But when I opened the closet door and pushed the few pieces of clothing aside, there was the small door again, still latched tightly.

The bedroom was obviously some sort of add-on, and it had been built around the door.

But where did it lead?

After a final check over my shoulder to make sure Miranda hadn't returned, I turned back to the door and lifted the latch. It opened easily. The door creaked, and I had to move back to open it fully, squeezing myself tightly into the small space. The closet door was still open, but my heart rate increased as the space inside shrank. I tried to ignore my building panic as I pulled the hidden door all the way open and stepped forward.

The light from the bedroom only let me see about five feet or so in front of me. The door opened onto a narrow staircase that led down into a pitch-black room, which, judging by the musky smell, was some sort of basement.

What the hell?

Before I could freeze up at the sight of the tight, dark space, I took a deep breath and started down. The stairs creaked under my weight, and I peered into the darkness around me, knowing I should stop to go back and look for a flashlight, but sure that if I left the cramped stairwell, I'd never come back. I could see nothing, and I let each foot dangle slowly to find the step below as the little light from the open closet door diminished the farther down I went.

As I reached the last step, something soft brushed against my face, and I took a startled step backward, almost landing on my butt on the stairs.

But it was too thick to be a spider web. I reached out with my hand and felt around in the air, my fingers connecting with a thick rope cord that hung from the ceiling. Pulling down and praying it was what I thought it was, I released a sigh of relief when a single lightbulb flickered on, illuminating the room in a dim, yellow glow.

It was definitely a basement, and from the direction I'd walked, I guessed I was somewhere beneath the bathroom and the kitchen. I stepped forward into the large room, my gaze darting about.

What was this place?

There was a dark pool of water in the center of the room, near a drain blocked with old newspaper. I stepped gingerly around it as I peered even farther into the room.

I moved past a bunch of junk—tables and chairs pushed against one wall, old, soiled cardboard boxes, pots, trash. It shouldn't have surprised me that Alex had a secret room of junk beneath his cabin, but I still had to force down my nausea.

I kept walking, my gaze on the wall in front of me. A corkboard had been mounted on it; it was completely covered in photos. My stomach turned over when I stepped closer and saw who'd been captured on the film.

Sam Farr.

And a young boy who couldn't have been more than ten years old.

Matthew.

There were at least two dozen photographs of Sam and Matthew pinned up side by side. In some, they were laughing and talking; in others, they looked serious, but they all had one thing in common: the pair obviously had no idea they were being photographed. The candid photos had been taken from different angles, some from the inside of a car it seemed, others through a window.

This proved it.

My father *had* been stalking Matthew and Sam Farr.

But why?

And could he really have been planning on taking Matthew?

I walked over to a shelving unit on the side of the corkboard and picked up a stack of photos—more pictures of Sam and Matthew, held together by a large paper clip. Placing the photos in my coat pocket, I flipped through the other items on the shelf.

More books by D. B. James.

Who the hell *was* this guy?

And why did Alex have so many books by him?

Was he exploring his "academic" side these days? Surely, not that much could have changed in the last six years.

Though things had started to change the night Lucas had died. Every single moment after that—every single thing my parents did and did not say—humanized them in a way that was hard for me to understand at first. Before Lucas died, they were parents, and after, they were just people, a difference it had taken a long time for me to come to terms with.

I don't know exactly when my father became Alex to me—maybe it was when I saw him sitting in his bedroom, unshowered, filthy, and soaked in whatever it was he'd been drinking that day, unable to do little more than call Delroy to take me away.

I was reaching for another book when I suddenly heard a loud noise behind me. I dropped the book and spun around at the sound of a door shutting—the passageway to the closet?—followed by heavy footsteps moving down the stairs.

The booming steps made me jolt backward, and I cried out as my back slammed into the shelving unit. My throat tightened, and a wave of fear rushed over my entire body as I caught a glimpse of a large figure barreling down on me.

"Hey..." I started, the sound nothing more than a strangled croak.

Before I could finish, the person leaped up, clean into the air, and yanked the string to shut off the single, flickering bulb.

And then we were down there—me and someone who I had a feeling knew a lot more about me than I knew about them—together in complete and total darkness.

Chapter Twelve

In an instant, the air in the room became thick and heavy, as if a warm blanket had been tossed over my head and body, trapping me against the basement wall. I opened my mouth and gasped for a full breath, suddenly feeling thirsty, and drained, and hot. My fingernails immediately went into my palms, and I pushed so hard that they sliced into my skin. The dark room was spinning impossibly, and I was trapped, cornered…

Just breathe, Francis.

Count to ten.

It was a trick I'd learned in my early twenties, and it never worked very well, but I always went back to it when I started to panic. It was a last resort, and even just trying to count took my mind off what was happening for a while.

I struggled to form the numbers in my mind.

One…two…three.

What the hell is going on…?

I struggled to see in the dark space, and I tried to remember the room I'd walked through only seconds earlier. I shivered as the darkness seemed to take on a life of its own, holding me hostage. It wasn't fear of the dark itself, so much as the inability to see the space around me.

To know my limitations, my constraints.

But I couldn't afford to be paralyzed now.

There was someone else there.

I went through the room quickly in my mind, trying to remember every step I'd taken. The bookshelves pushed against the north side of the basement. The large puddle of water in the middle of the room.

What else?

"Hello?" I called out. "Who's there?"

But it was silly, futile. The person who'd just run down the stairs hadn't been quiet about it; he knew I'd heard him. He knew exactly who I was. And he hadn't come downstairs to reveal himself to me.

No, he wanted me in the dark.

But why?

I reached in front of me, and my hand hit the corner of something, most likely the metal shelf I'd just walked around. It clanged loudly, the sound echoing in the room like a beacon, and I gasped in the darkness.

"Hello?" I said again, grabbing the shelf and holding on to it, grateful to have something to steady myself, even for just a few moments.

I stepped back, bumped into the shelving unit again, and cursed at the noise it made. I hurried away, as quietly as possible. I felt clumsy and out of control, milling from side to side in the same space, while the person who'd just joined me stayed completely silent.

Completely still.

I'd just identified where I was, and I needed to move. As I scrambled away, I heard the first noise—footsteps coming in my direction. Shit. I moved quickly along the wall, running to the far side of the room. The person clanged into a few items and barreled toward the part of the room where I'd just been. As I ran in the darkness, I tried to convince myself to slow down, that it wasn't going to work this way.

I needed to be *quiet.*

To orient myself and to figure out where the stairs were.

That was it.

I had to find the stairs.

I crept along the wall, feeling the curved edge of the cool, exposed bricks. The jagged edges cut my hands, but I moved along, slowing my pace just enough to quiet my movements. My eyes wouldn't adjust. I was still struggling to breathe normally.

You have to get over this. You have to get over this, Francis.

I was tempted yet again to call out, to ask who was there. But I couldn't ask what I really needed to—if, by any chance, the person in the basement with me was the owner of the cabin.

Alex Scroll.

My father.

I stopped in my tracks and waited, and it didn't take long for me to realize that my attacker—if that's what he was—had the same idea. We both stood silently, waiting, hoping for a fault, for someone to give up. I thought about making a mad dash for the stairs, but it seemed so far away. Plus, I was too turned around. For all I knew, I could be heading straight toward another wall.

I reached around for anything I could use as a weapon. My hand landed on something rectangular and wooden. Plywood? That could work. I picked it up and crept farther along the wall.

I needed to act—to do whatever I could to get the upper hand. Whoever was down here with me hadn't thought this through all the way. As much as I'd been thrown off guard, they were now trapped in the basement with me in the dark, and they were in the same position I was.

Except for one key difference. He seemed to know who I was and what I was doing here.

I didn't have that privilege.

My fingers brushed something else on a shelf beside me—a

book?—and I picked it up with my free hand as a plan began to form.

You can't stay down here forever.

I tossed the book about five feet to my right, and it clattered on the floor. Immediately, footsteps moved toward the sound. There was a pause, a silent heartbeat, and I knew he was searching for me.

This was my chance.

I let out a roar and rushed in the direction of the book, swinging the piece of wood in front of me. I connected with absolutely nothing, but the motion took me down to the floor, and I heard a grunt as the man stepped backward, or forward, to avoid me. I reached out as I fell and grabbed something—the edge of his shirt, or coat—and we both went down.

The room was so dark that I could not see him, though he was only inches from my face, but I knew he was there, felt his presence, heard his breathing, smelled him. Suddenly, I felt pressure on my foot as he kicked me, and then I was kicking too, my foot connecting with his shin, then his thigh. He cried out, and I felt hands on my chest, then my neck and face, and I scrambled forward on the cold concrete, letting my fingers rip into any skin and flesh I could find that was not my own.

He groaned in pain, and I dug in harder. His blood coated my fingertips. "What—" I started, but I was cut off as his hand connected with my chin, and he began to push. He was taking care not to speak, but even in the darkness, I was convinced this man wasn't my father—it couldn't be.

I hadn't seen him in years, and yet it seemed I would know him. *Right?*

He pushed his hand into my face, forcing my head back against the concrete, and I struggled to breathe. We were roughly the same size, it seemed, and I fought viciously. But he had the upper hand.

He knew why he'd come down there.

And what his end goal was.

While I wanted to get free and get away from him, I still didn't know what he was doing, whereas he was very clearly trying to accomplish something. Was he trying to hurt me? Kill me? His knee pushed into my stomach, and I gasped. I used my fingernails again, grabbing on to his knee and clawing through the fabric of his pants, twisting until I heard him cry out. It was a low, guttural sound, and it wasn't at all recognizable.

It couldn't be Alex.

It couldn't be.

He whipped his leg away, and I took a deep breath and rolled onto my side as his hand came down near my face. I had moved just in time. His knuckles smacked the floor, and he groaned again. My eyes had finally adjusted enough that I could see a hint of his shape, but I couldn't make out any of his features.

He was still bunched over, groaning, and I used the opportunity to push him onto his back. I kicked into the darkness, hoping to connect with something. I missed, and he grabbed me around the waist, pushing me backward yet again into the dirty water. It coated my scalp as I struggled to get free.

I rolled to try to grab his free arm, and that was my mistake. He propelled me forward and then turned me over so I was lying facedown in the stagnant water. I sputtered as it went into my nose, my mouth, my eyes. Then he grabbed me and lifted me off the floor before lowering me back into the sludgy pool. He pulled me up, and I coughed violently, wiping the dirt out of my eyes and gasped as the room spun. In my search for air, I forgot to fight, and my body gave out. I sputtered, expelling the water from my lungs as I searched for a clean breath. He lifted me high one more time, and I knew, deep down, that this was it. The motion was so rough, so quick, that I had only a second to swing my arm out to block my face as I hurtled toward the floor for the final time.

I tasted the water once more before everything went black.

Chapter Thirteen

I yanked at the sweater that was itching every part of my body—even the parts it wasn't touching. Dinner had been as boring as expected, and the Farrs seemed content to stay around as long as possible.

I wished they would just leave.

They weren't all that bad, to be honest, but I was tired, and I wanted to go upstairs. I wanted to go finish my book or stare at a wall or do anything that didn't involve being around anyone else. But I didn't have that option.

"Hey, look alive, Francis." My father was always catching me drifting off, and he shuffled past me into the kitchen, a glass of wine dripping from his fingertips. "It's not so bad, is it?"

"Yeah, it is," I said. I was thirteen years old. It was my life's mission to make sure that everyone knew exactly how miserable I was.

"What's the matter?" He walked over to the fridge and pulled out the bottle of red wine they'd been drinking with dinner. He took out the wine stopper—a beautiful silver rose settled into the top of the bottle—and poured himself another glass. "Seriously, you can't be that upset that we have guests. You used to like our dinner parties."

"No, I didn't," I said, and I felt whiny and defensive at the same time. I did used to enjoy them, back when I was Lucas's age. I knew it, and yet, I didn't want to admit it. I wanted him to know he was practically killing me, making me sit there in the hot sweater and pretend like I cared about their conversation. I didn't feel the need to try to make everyone else feel comfortable when I wasn't.

"All right, fine," he said. "Maybe you didn't like them. But you didn't hate them this much. You're walking around here like somebody stole your puppy. Did somebody steal your puppy, Francis?" He walked closer and poked me lightly in the neck. "Huh, did somebody?"

"Quit, Dad," I said, moving away. I could tell he wanted to keep teasing me, but he sighed and stepped back.

"Look, I'm just saying, it wouldn't hurt to brighten up a little bit. Your mom put a lot of hard work into this, and she's upset because she thinks you're having a horrible time. She can't even enjoy her party. You could go a little easier on her. You know what she's doing right now?"

"No."

"She's upstairs, looking for Clue, because she knows it's your favorite board game. I bet you won't even play it, and nobody else wants to, but she's looking for it because she thinks it's going to make you happy. Can you at least give it a try?"

"Playing Clue? I play it all the time. I don't need to give that a try."

"No, smart-ass. Give a smile a try. Make it seem like being here with your family is not the very last place on earth you'd like to be right now. Okay?"

I took a drink of my milk without saying anything, pretending it prevented me from responding, but my father leaned in closer and waited for me to finish my gulp.

"Okay?" he asked again.

"Yeah," I muttered with a shrug. "Okay."

"You'll try?"

"Yeah. I'll try."

When I opened my eyes, I was far away from the warm kitchen I'd so disapproved of some twenty-three years earlier. I would have given anything to be back there, bantering with my father, only an hour or so before the downward cycle of my life had started.

Instead, I was lying on my stomach, my neck twisted painfully to one side, my cheek submerged in a pool of putrid water that also soaked my scalp and mixed with my blood as it rolled down my forehead and into my eye.

There are memories of people that stay with you—smells, sounds, images. Those few that I kept of my father from the last time I'd seen him were of the drink he'd sloshed around in his hand, the smell of his cheap cologne.

And it wasn't enough.

It wasn't enough for me to say, with any certainty at all, that the person whom I'd just encountered in the basement of the cabin had been him.

Or *not* him.

The scary truth was that it could have been Alex. The last time I'd seen or spoken to him had been six years ago in his filthy apartment. When I'd tried to take a bottle of whiskey away and he'd thrown a pot at my head.

Yes, it could've been him.

If it wasn't him, there was only one other person who it could have been.

Sam Farr.

Miranda Farr had been there only minutes earlier. In the brief moments between when she'd left the cabin and when I'd been attacked, someone had managed to sneak inside.

He hadn't said a single word, which led me to believe that he'd known who I was, what I was doing, and exactly where I'd been in the cabin. Miranda had claimed she'd shown up alone, but what if Sam had been in the car with her? What if she'd sent him back in after she left?

There were so many what-ifs that could be solved simply by sitting down with the Farrs. I pushed myself up and stumbled up the stairs and out of the cabin, gulping in fresh air and letting it linger in my lungs. I raced through the bushes in the direction of my car, feeling a rush of relief when I spotted the red roof.

I opened the car door and dropped inside. I rubbed the back of my jaw, which was starting to hurt—I hadn't realized how tightly I'd been clenching my teeth. The pain was so severe, it created flashes of bright, white light in front of my eyes. I stared out at the thick, wiry branches that covered the hood of my car, and suddenly, the anxiety began to swell again.

Breathe, Francis.

I'd put the key in the ignition and was about to start it when I heard a shrill noise. I reached in my pocket and pulled out my cell phone.

"Yeah?"

"Hey," Cam said. "Where are you?"

I looked out at the thick brush that surrounded me. I was nowhere.

"I'm at home," I lied.

"Did you find Alex?"

"No, he wasn't home."

She didn't say anything for a moment, and I almost heard the words before they spilled from her lips. "Do you think he did it?"

Immediately, my mind flashed to the photos I'd taken, and the shadowed figure who had beaten me senseless. "I don't know," I said. "I really don't know what to think."

"Is Amy there with you?"

I coughed and glanced around the empty car. "Yeah, she's in her room."

"Look, I don't want to sound like a broken record, but did you—"

"Yes," I said, leaning forward and resting my forehead against the steering wheel, my eyes closed. "I talked to her. I told her everything."

"That's good, Francis," Cam said softly, and the gentleness of her voice made the lie feel even worse. "I know that must have been tough, but it was the right thing to do."

I wished I could tell her about everything that had just happened, but it didn't seem right. For the most part, Cam and I kept our relationship strictly professional—if you don't count one slipup about a year ago during an overnight work trip.

We'd gone to Milwaukee for a media symposium and had spent the evening having drinks with a group of writers and editors. After dinner, we'd all walked together to the lobby, where I'd frozen as someone had pushed the button for the elevator.

"What floor are you guys on again?" an editor at the *IndyStar* had asked.

"I'm on nine, and Cam is on ten," I'd blurted out, feeling trapped as the heat rose in my face. I couldn't suddenly excuse myself and make my way to the stairwell. Usually, I'd prepare for such a situation by darting off to the bar or coming up with some reason to stay behind until I was alone and able to take the stairs. But the wine and the company had thrown me off, and I had no choice but to get in the tiny box of terror with them. Cam had watched me carefully as the doors closed slowly behind us.

"I really think we should all try to get together for breakfast tomorrow morning before heading back to our respective corners of the world," the woman standing closest to the buttons had said without pressing anything, and I clenched my fists tightly as we stood there, staring at one another in the stationary elevator.

"You want to hit nine and ten?" I had croaked out, and the abrupt request had made everyone turn. The woman had finally shrugged and nodded, pressing her floor as well.

They all got off by the fifth floor. When we were alone, Cam had turned to me. "You okay?" she'd asked. "We can get off on the next floor and walk the rest of the way."

"No," I'd said, though I'd felt beads of sweat dripping from my armpits. "I'm fine."

"You don't look fine," she'd said, stepping closer. "You look like you're about to shit."

A strangled laugh had escaped me, and for just a second, I hadn't felt so trapped as she'd given me the classic Cam smirk.

By the time the elevator doors had opened on the ninth floor, we'd been all over each other, and I remember that she tasted like steak and Merlot, a ridiculously sexy combination. When I woke up the next morning, she was back in her room.

We haven't spoken about it since.

Now, on the phone with her outside of my father's cabin, I desperately wanted to share more with her, to let her know I needed her, but I couldn't bring myself to speak.

"Francis?"

"Huh?" I said, jolting back to our conversation.

"I said that Cynthia Green is covering the missing Farr kid case, but we've already had a conversation about what is and isn't off-limits."

"Thanks, Cam," I said. "I appreciate it."

"Get some rest."

"Yeah. Thanks."

We hung up, and I started the car, heading toward Miranda

Farr's house. As I sped along, I dialed my mother, but the answering machine picked up.

"Mom, it's me. Can you give me a call back as soon as you have a chance? It's really important." I hung up and thought about the message I'd just left. It didn't give her much reason to call me back. Not after all this time. It had been almost eight years since our awkward dinner with her boyfriend and my classmate, Jimmy Calloway. I honestly didn't know what I wanted to talk to her about, or what I would say if she did call back. I just needed someone to tell me that, as crazy as things had been—as they still were—there was no way Alex could have been the one in the basement.

I was approaching the Farrs' house when I heard my cell phone ring again. I slowed, not wanting to answer it while sitting in their driveway, so I swerved and stopped the car about half a block down.

The number on the phone was not my mother's; it was one I didn't recognize.

"Hello?"

"Hi, Mr. Scroll, this is Patricia Smith-Bilks," a woman's voice said. "I'm a teacher at Matthew Farr's school."

I frowned at the use of my real name. I pulled the phone away, looking at the number again.

"Yes?" I said, putting the phone back to my ear. "How can I help you?"

"I was wondering if you have a few minutes to talk. I got your number from the *Lansing News*."

I shifted into park and took my foot off the brake, trying to concentrate on what the woman was saying.

"Okay," I said. "What's this about? Matthew's disappearance?"

"Yes."

"And you called the *News* to talk to me in particular? Why me?"

"Because there are certain things you don't tell a mother

whose child is missing unless you're absolutely, one hundred percent sure you're right," she said. "I called her, but I just couldn't tell her—"

"Tell her what—"

"—and she mentioned that you were helping her, so I called your office, because I don't want to talk to the police. I don't need to be involved in all of that—"

"Tell her *what*?" I asked again, and she stopped talking. She was completely silent for a few moments.

"Look, I'd feel a lot more comfortable talking in person," she said. "It's about...well, a pretty delicate matter."

"Okay," I said. "But is it something concerning his whereabouts? Because the sooner I know about it, the better."

"Well, yes or...no, I mean." She stopped, and I could hear her take a long, deep breath. "I guess I don't know. It's just something I think you should know. Can you come by the school?"

"You're there today?"

"Yes, we have rehearsals for the school play, so a bunch of us are here all weekend."

I wanted to push her harder, get her to tell me right then and there, but I knew that strategy could backfire.

"I'll be there in about forty-five minutes," I said. "Will you still be there?"

"Yes," she said. "Thank you."

She gave me the intersection, and I hung up. I pulled away from the curb and drove up to the front of the Farrs' house.

As I did, I cursed. Kira Jones was standing on the front porch, a notebook in her hand and a frown on her face. She was turning away to head to her car when she caught sight of me.

"Where are they?" I asked as I stepped out. My entire body was shaking as memories from the last couple of hours hit me again, and I searched the front of the house for any signs of life.

"I don't know. Not home." She frowned and walked forward, peering at my face. "What happened to you?"

I reached up to my temple, where I felt a thick crust. When I drew my hand down, my fingers were covered in the drying blood that was, at the least, no longer dripping into my eye.

"Nothing, I'm fine. What do you mean they're not here?"

"Are you sure you're…?" She was examining the rest of my body, the wrinkled, damp clothing, the dirt on my hands.

"I'm fine. I really need to speak with them."

"Are they expecting you?"

"No," I said, looking over her shoulder and walking past her toward the door.

"What, you don't believe me? I just told you they weren't here," she said with annoyance. "Sam told me I could come back for another meeting today."

"A meeting?"

"Yes, we have some more interviews lined up, and I have a few more chapters to polish."

I walked up the steps to the porch and rang the doorbell, listening as the chimes rang inside the home. I peered through the front window, but couldn't see much. I could make out some of the shapes of the furniture in the living room, but there didn't seem to be any motion. If the Farrs were there, they weren't answering.

Kira followed me back onto the porch and watched me with a curious expression. "I know you don't like me very much, but there's no reason to assume I'm lying."

"I didn't say you were lying," I said. "I just really need to talk to them."

"About what?"

I moved past her and down the steps again. "I told you before, I'm not interested in being your next interview subject."

"You know, your little holier-than-thou act is getting old," she said, following me. "Especially considering your history."

I spun around. "What's that supposed to mean?"

"I made a few calls," she said, and when I narrowed my eyes, she shrugged. "It's the journalist in me, I couldn't help it. Why did you move back to Lansing?"

"What?"

"You changed your name; you were living in New York. So why the hell did you come back to work for the *Lansing News*? Don't tell me it's the pay."

I swallowed. "I like working there—"

"I'm sure you do. Since it's, quite literally, the only place that would hire you," she said, and at that moment, I could tell she knew it all. "Tell me, why were you fired from the *Queens Gazette*?"

"For none of your damned business."

"For completely and utterly making up a story!" she spat. "Who does that? How dare you talk down to me? No wonder you had to come back home. Let me guess, you got the job through an old connection? Do they even know why you've been blacklisted in New York?"

I felt every defense coming to my lips, but I faltered. "I don't need to explain myself to you," I said quietly. The shame and humiliation of my last few weeks at the *Gazette* rushed over me, and I tried to keep my composure. If anyone had told me during my days as a young reporter that I would end up going all Jayson Blair, I would have laughed in their face. But I'd underestimated the pressures of being a young journalist in New York and had quickly fallen into the trap of overpromising and under-delivering. The minute I'd clicked Send on the story with the fake quote from the fake resident of a very real apartment complex being torn down on Ditmars and Thirty-Fifth Street, I'd known my days were numbered.

She stood at the bottom of the steps, waiting for me to say something else. I turned, heading toward my car.

"Where are you going?" she called out. "Don't you think he's paid enough?"

She asked it quietly, and I froze, unsure if I'd heard her correctly.

"What?" I asked, spinning back around. "Think who has paid enough for what?"

She blinked and swallowed, and for just a moment, she looked uncomfortable.

"For...everything that's happened?"

"No, I want to know what you mean. Don't I think who has paid for what?"

I could see the hesitation in her eyes, but she squared her shoulders and held my gaze. "For what happened to your brother."

It was as if she'd slapped me. "You think he did it," I exclaimed. "Why, Kira? Has he told you something?"

She blinked rapidly, and I could tell she wanted to backtrack. "No, no, he hasn't. And I don't, not necessarily. But even if he did..." She shook her head and stepped closer to me. "Nobody can take that pain away, but think about what Sam Farr has been through. Even if he lied, even if he made something up—he was *ten years old*. He was a child too. You know that, right? Whatever happened, at worst, was a horrible accident. I don't see how you can't understand that. Sam's life was taken that day too."

"How can you say that?" I asked, gesturing toward the house. "A lot of lives were taken that day, but Sam Farr seems to be doing all right."

She shook her head. "That's just it. He's not," she said simply. "Sam's not doing all right. Somebody has made damn well sure of that, haven't they?"

Chapter Fourteen

The Sam Farr Story

By: K. L. Jones

DRAFT v. 6—Not to be shared without express permission of author, K. L. Jones

<insert a map to show distance from Farr house to Scroll house>

The Farr family pulled up to the Scrolls' house at about six on that fateful night of December 3, 1992.

From the backseat of the small car, Sam Farr's eyes widened. The house was ordinary in size for the upper middle-class neighborhood—a large two-story home with an expansive lawn flanking it—but to Sam, it was almost magical. He'd seen it from afar, many times, but up close, it looked like something out of a film, and he wondered if a butler would come rushing out to help them with their things. Sam giggled at the thought, and he saw his father look at him in the rearview mirror.

Sam took in a deep breath.

Here we go.

He wished his cousin Cory could see him now. Cory always

liked to tease him when he came to visit, saying his family was poor, which was relatively true, Sam guessed.

But even Cory would have been impressed by this.

They stepped out of the car, and Sam's mother walked quickly around to the backseat to get her pie.

He was so excited, he wasn't sure he was going to be able to eat much tonight anyway.

His mother smoothed down her coat while juggling the pie in her hands. He thought it would be nice to be a grown-up. Grown-ups were friends with whoever was around. It wasn't like school, where people had a whole class of people to be friends with, so they only chose the best, or the coolest.

Grown-ups simply weren't around that many people, what with work and taking care of their families and all. So they got to be friends with people nearby. His mother and Kate Scroll had met at a church meeting, and just like that, they'd become friends.

Sam hoped that when he was an adult, he'd be able to make a lot more friends too.

They walked up the path toward the front door. It was such a cold day, and they bundled together, shivering, nervous, and excited.

Sam was happy to see the door open just seconds after they pushed the buzzer.

Kate Scroll stood there, smiling, her pretty brown hair hanging around her shoulders. The sounds of a pop song floated from the living room, and Sam wondered what kind of stereo system they had. Probably something fancy. Kate danced in place a little while, holding something in her hands.

"Hi, guys! Come on in out of the cold. Sorry it's still chilly in here." She reached forward and took the pie from his mother, handing her a pair of something that looked like fuzzy socks.

"Alex said I was crazy for bringing these out, but you may need them."

"Thanks," Elizabeth said. Sam watched as his mom shifted awkwardly out of her shoes and pulled the thick, plush socks—which were really more like slippers, Sam could now see—over her own socks. She'd made a point of wearing "good ones" that morning, and she took her time putting on the new ones, covering up the socks she'd taken out of the package for this occasion only.

Sam shifted, realizing he'd have to take his shoes off too, and he wondered what kind of socks he'd put on. He was pretty sure there was a hole just over the big toe on the left one.

His mother and Kate stood aside, giggling about the socks and talking about the music, which seemed to swell all around them. "I made this mix especially for tonight," Kate said, and Elizabeth nodded emphatically. "A little R&B, a little jazz. I'm not sure what you listen to."

Sam's mother rarely ever listened to the radio, but she tapped her fingers against her thigh in time with the rhythm. "That's perfect. I love it!" she said with a smile and a small shrug.

As the women walked away, Kate looked back over her shoulder. "Boys, why don't you head upstairs to Lucas's room, and we'll call you downstairs for dinner."

Sam turned to see who else she was addressing. He was startled to see Lucas standing there, not far from the entrance, his eyes on Sam.

"Okay," Lucas said cheerily enough, and he bounded up the stairs. Sam took a deep breath and quickly stepped out of his shoes, using his right foot to pull the sock with the hole forward and tucking the hole away, beneath his toes, out of sight. He followed Lucas, heading up the stairs slowly, his briefcase still in his hand.

"Hey, you want me to take that for you?" Sam's father asked.

Sam looked back and shook his head. "No, Dad, it's okay." He paused when he saw the expression on his father's face, a mixture of disappointment and exhaustion. "Dad?" he said, but his father shook his head and turned to walk away.

Sam watched his back for a moment before turning to trail Lucas up the stairs. As he did, he tried his best not to marvel too much at the pictures on the walls, the smiling family in them, or the ornate rug that ran up the middle of the long stairwell up to the second floor. He didn't want to seem uncool; he wasn't rich, but that didn't mean he needed to gawk over Lucas and his cool house or his cool family.

They walked into Lucas's room, and Lucas picked up a magazine off the floor. He sat on the edge of his bed and began to read it. Sam could see from his place by the door that there were pictures of trucks in it.

"What's that?" he asked.

Lucas looked up, and he shrugged. "Just *Vintage Trucks*," he said and looked back down at the magazine.

Sam wasn't sure what to do. The bass line from whatever song Kate Scroll was playing downstairs floated up into the bedroom, and it seemed to only highlight the silence between them.

Stop being weird, Sam thought. It wasn't like they had to talk every second he was there. He walked over to the bed and sat on the edge of it, attempting to look at the magazine with Lucas, but the boy didn't move.

"That one's cool," he said, pointing to one of the trucks in the magazine, but Lucas didn't respond. Sam cleared his throat.

He leaned over again, arching his neck to see just a corner of the magazine.

"Oh, and that one comes apart. I saw a commercial for it."

"Yeah, I know," Lucas said as he continued reading. "How long do you think your parents are going to be here?"

"Huh?"

"How long do you think you're staying?"

"Oh," Sam said, blinking. "I don't know. I think not too long."

Lucas didn't say anything but went back to his magazine, and Sam suddenly felt very hot. He pulled at the neck of his T-shirt and looked around the boy's room. There were so many cool toys that he wished he had. There was never enough money for them, according to his mother.

Maybe Lucas would let him borrow some of his old toys. He was really good with things and wouldn't mess them up.

"Hey, everything going okay?"

Lucas looked up from his magazine. Kate Scroll was leaning in the doorway, her hair fluttering around her face. Sam tried not to stare at her, but she was so pretty, almost like a movie star, and he wondered if he had walked right into a film set, since that would explain the beautiful house.

"Yeah, things are great," Lucas said.

Sam frowned. The sudden smile on Lucas's face seemed odd, since just a minute ago, he'd seemed sad or upset. But Sam forced himself to smile at Kate Scroll too.

"Good," she said. "Well, the food won't be ready for a little while. Some of the other boys are outside. If you bundle up very tightly, you can go outside to play for a little while."

"Yes," Lucas said excitedly, jumping off the bed and heading out the door.

Sam followed quickly behind, his briefcase in hand.

He didn't want to go. Not really. The "other boys" probably meant Lucas's neighbors, a couple of boys from school who were mean to him sometimes. But he couldn't very well just sit inside. Who would he talk to? Lucas's older brother, Francis, was downstairs somewhere, and he wasn't so bad, but he was older, and he didn't really talk to anyone.

No, he would go outside. He would just go watch. He wasn't really into their games anyway.

By the time he got downstairs, Lucas was already outside with the other boys. Sam bundled into his coat, put on his shoes, and opened the patio door. He stepped outside, his fingers tightening around the handle of his briefcase.

The boys grabbed a soccer ball and began kicking it around in the cold, crunchy grass.

Sam shivered and took a place on the side of the lawn. He tried to pretend to look interested in the game, but really, he wondered if they were all thinking he was weird. It was freezing outside, and he balled his free hand into a fist. He considered going back inside to start preparing for tonight's show, but he knew his dad would want him to at least try.

"Who's your new friend?" one of the boys asked Lucas. There was a long pause while Lucas looked at him and Sam looked back, a half smile on his face, unsure about whether he should do something. After a moment, he lifted his arm and waved slightly.

Lucas didn't move.

"He's, like, the son of my mom's friend or whatever," Lucas said. "I think he's kind of retarded or something."

The other boys looked at Sam, and there was a long moment of silence.

Sam wondered if he should say something or protest against Lucas's idiot choice of words.

"I—"

A giggle escaped one of the boys, who bounced the soccer ball off his knee. "He probably rides the short bus," he said, and they all laughed.

Lucas nodded and reached for the ball. "Yeah, probably," he said. "He brought that briefcase with him from home, and he's been hugging it all night. Super weird."

Sam inhaled sharply and took a step back. As he did, he stumbled and fell on the grass. The boys looked over again, and he immediately pulled himself up, pretending nothing was wrong. But the tears that had rushed to the surface were overwhelming, and he bit his lip, looking off into the distance, wishing he could run inside and tell his mother he wanted to go home.

But he wouldn't ruin it for everyone.

His mom would be so sad if she knew he was upset. He would get through the dinner and go home and forget all about trying to be friends with Lucas Scroll.

He'd never make the same mistake again that he'd made tonight.

Chapter Fifteen

Sunday, 6:00 p.m.

I pulled away from the Farr house, my gaze on Kira Jones in my rearview mirror.

She was at least five years younger than me, which meant she couldn't have been more than eight or so at the time of Lucas's accident. Still, I'd seen in her eyes a passion I'd witnessed many times as a kid. Sam's trial had created two distinct camps—on the one hand, there were people who had empathized with my parents. Much of their anger had centered around the fact that Sam wouldn't say anything about the moments that led up to the drowning. Had the boys been in the same room? Did Sam see what happened? Were they playing together or alone? My parents' supporters had felt that Sam's refusal to talk was a clear indicator that he'd done something wrong, and that regardless of his age, he should be punished.

On the other hand, there were those who had sympathized with the Farrs. They weren't always decided about what had happened upstairs on the night of the party, but they were certain about one thing: a child shouldn't—couldn't—be held accountable for it.

"Why were these beautiful children upstairs alone in the first place?" Sheridan Porter, a popular newspaper columnist had written. "Aren't the real ones to blame the parents, who were downstairs, drinking wine, playing games, and doing who knows what? Aren't they the ones who let this happen?"

Few people had taken the middle road. That's what happened in a small town like Lansing. Everyone had an opinion and took care to make it known.

I sped through the streets of Lansing toward Sam's school. I pulled into the parking lot just after six p.m. and wedged myself into a narrow space. The school sat at the end of a residential block, and there was a small playground out front where a couple was walking their dog. As I turned off the car, I leaned forward and looked at my forehead in the rearview mirror, cringing at the sight of drying blood. I opened the glove compartment and rifled around, pulling out a few takeout napkins. Using a bit of saliva, I wiped at the gash on my head and tried not to think about the germs, filth, and dirt that were working their way through my system at that very moment.

As I got out of the car, I straightened my clothes and headed toward the main doors of the school. I was surprised to find them unattended, and I felt like an intruder as I walked inside the building. No one was in sight, but the sound of laughter and children's voices came from a room down the hall.

I passed a classroom as a man with a neat haircut and friendly smile walked out. "Can I help you?" His smile waned when he took in my appearance, but he didn't say anything.

"Yes, my name is Francis Scroll. I have an appointment with Ms. Smith-Bilks."

The man crossed his arms. "Are you a parent? Rehearsal won't be done until seven."

"No, I'm not. She called me and asked me to come by..."

He seemed to want to probe, but he finally nodded. "You can wait here, please."

I waited as he walked down the hallway. I turned toward a large bulletin board on the wall and scanned the pictures of smiling kids for any signs of Matthew Farr. The pictures of him and his father burned a hole in my pocket, and I wondered how I'd explain them if they fell out.

"Are you waiting for someone?"

I spun around, my hand instinctively going to my pocket. I was eye to eye with a woman in a pantsuit, her hair combed into a low bun. She assessed me quickly and boldly, and I shifted uncomfortably under her gaze.

"Yes, I'm meeting with Ms. Smith-Bilks."

"I'm Principal Erin Murray. And you are?"

I cleared my throat. "Francis Clarke."

Something about the woman's stern gaze made the name slip off my tongue.

The woman nodded. "Are you a parent?"

"Oh, no," I said. "Just a…friend."

She raised her eyebrows. "Ms. Smith-Bilks knows better than that," she said, but she smiled knowingly and leaned closer. "I'm sure she'll be here soon."

I nodded. "Thanks."

"Do you have children?"

"Uh, yeah. A daughter. She's fifteen."

"Ah," she said, smiling. "Too old for us. Well, if you know anyone who is looking for a good grade school or junior high," she said. "We're working on enrollment. Our numbers just came out."

"Not great?"

"Better than most in the area, but our head count is still low. We're always on the lookout for great students and families."

I nodded, unsure of what to say next.

"Mr. Scroll?"

I turned around, and the man I'd met earlier approached us. "Ms. Smith-Bilks is ready to see you now."

I followed him, turning back to smile at the principal. She was watching me with a curious expression.

"Scroll?"

I shrugged pathetically before following the man down the hall.

A door near the end opened, and the voices of a choir swelled as a petite woman stepped out and closed the door.

"There she is," the man next to me said, pointing, and the woman raised her hand in my direction.

"Thanks," I said. The man turned away, and I kept walking.

The woman waiting for me couldn't have been more than five feet tall, with a short, blond bob, a round face, and a nervous, twitchy demeanor.

"We can talk in my classroom," she said, leading me around another corner and down the hall to a cool, dark classroom. She flipped on the lights as we walked inside.

"Sorry, I'm earlier than I thought I'd be," I said.

"It's okay," she said, shifting back and forth. "What happened to your face?"

"It's nothing," I said. "A little accident. I hope you don't mind me getting straight to the point—"

"No, not at all," she said, spinning around and walking to her desk. She sat in the chair and then stood again. "Did you want to sit?" she asked, gesturing toward the desks, and I shook my head.

"No, thanks." She still didn't say anything, and I fought the urge to move around her desk and shake her. "Ms. Smith-Bilks, what's going on? Please, if there's something you know about Matthew Farr, now would be the time to tell me."

She nodded. "I have been trying to think of the best way to tell you this," she said. "I guess there is no other way than to just come out with it. I am concerned about…"

"About?"

"The relationship Matthew had with someone on staff at the school."

I froze, staring down at her. I wasn't sure what I'd expected—maybe something about his performance at school, or the way he got along with his parents.

But a relationship?

"Who?" I asked.

She hesitated again, and her gaze darted over my shoulder toward the door. "Our principal. Principal Murray."

Wait—the woman I'd just met?

"Why do you say that?"

"Principal Murray hasn't been… Let's say, she's had some accusations brought against her in the past."

"By whom?"

"By a parent. The parent of one of our seventh graders. It wasn't anything public, just a buzz that went around in some internal circles. And then one day it stopped, that kid was transferred, and that was it."

"What were the accusations about?"

"Well," she said, eyes widening, "I'm sure you can imagine."

"No, actually. Imagining is the worst thing I can do in my job."

"Well, the seventh grader—his name was Todd King—he was spending a lot of time with Principal Murray. There were all sorts of after-school projects and things like that."

"So there were accusations of abuse."

"Yes."

"How long ago was this?"

"About two years."

"And what is the connection with Matthew Farr?"

"Well, there are always rumors, you know. Like I said, nothing public, just internal chatter. There was another boy about six months ago, but I don't think that was anything, just teachers being teachers, especially after what happened with Todd. But then I heard a bit of chatter about Matthew Farr."

"A third grader?" I asked incredulously.

She grimaced. "Like I said, rumors."

"And nobody said anything? I mean, to his parents? To anyone?"

"Well, that's the thing," she said, looking down at her hands. "And that's why I wasn't sure I should say anything to you. It's not like we knew it was going on. At all. Believe me, if I'd had any evidence that something was going on, I would have said something. But it seemed like gossip after what happened with Todd."

"Then why do you think it's something more than that now?"

"Well, I don't—not necessarily. But now that he's gone missing…"

"That's a pretty big allegation you're making."

Her eyes narrowed, and she shrugged. "That's why I didn't want to make it. But if I don't, then…" She shook her head. "I don't know. It came to mind when I heard someone joking about how horrible it would be if that were the case, and I realized we were joking about something so horrible, and nobody had thought to…" She shrugged.

"To tell anyone?"

She nodded. "It's one of those things that sounds completely insane until you see yourself on the news, and the journalist is asking you, 'Well, Ms. Smith-Bilks, if you had these suspicions, why didn't you say anything?' and you're watching that woman on TV, and you're like, 'She's such an idiot! Who does that? Who doesn't say something?' I don't want to be that woman, Mr. Scroll."

"Have you noticed anything suspicious about the way Principal Murray has acted over the last couple of days?"

"Not really," she said. "She's been in and out. She's working on a fund-raiser or something like that for her church."

"Well, thank you for telling me," I said. "You did the right thing."

"I hope so. And I'm sorry I didn't say anything before. It's not the kind of accusation you throw around unless you're desperate. We have to find poor Matthew. He's such a sweet little boy."

I left moments later and peeled out of the school's parking lot with no clear direction in mind. As I drove through the streets of Lansing, my head throbbed mercilessly, and I felt short of breath. What Smith-Bilks had told me hadn't changed my mind, not completely—there was no denying what I'd seen in the basement of Alex's cabin.

Still, I couldn't ignore an accusation like that.

What the hell was going on here?

I pressed down on the gas pedal and moved quickly through the streets. Driving fast, letting the windows down, the cold air rushing past my face—this always helped clear my head.

I was about fifteen minutes away from home in a part of town I rarely visited. I turned again, looking for Torrance Avenue—the main road that would get me back to the south side of Lansing—when the bright lights of a hospital caught my attention.

I blinked against the lights, the glare making me squint.

I almost kept going.

On the surface, there was nothing special about the hospital.

But on the north side of the street, there was a large sign that made me pause.

It wasn't the name of the hospital that caught my attention, but the logo beside it: a large box that contained the letters *C* and *S*.

There was nothing more than a bright blue box around the two letters, which were mashed together in a jumble of curves.

C and *S*.

Cove Sparry Hospital.

I'd seen that logo before.

I racked my brain about where exactly I'd seen that treatment of those letters.

C and *S*.

And then it hit me. I stopped the car suddenly, eliciting a loud honk from the car behind me. The driver sped around, shaking her fist as she tore off down the street.

I put the car in park and jumped out, stumbling to open the back door and diving inside. I tore through the items on the backseat, looking for the things I'd taken from beneath my father's dresser.

Come on…

I'd tossed the address book back there, but I needed—

The receipts.

I picked up a handful, uncrumpled them, and immediately found what I was looking for.

Cove Sparry Hospital.

Same logo.

That *C* and *S*.

3N Café.

What the hell?

I opened a few more receipts—about half a dozen were from the same place.

I turned to look at the building. It was a small community hospital on the other side of town; it wasn't impossible that Alex would go there, but also was not likely.

What had he been doing there?

Why had he been coming to this hospital on a regular basis?

I looked at the dates and the times on the receipts, but nothing stood out. Each day he'd visited, he'd purchased something small. A coffee and a muffin. A cup of tea. The receipts were spaced out about a week apart.

I pulled out my cell phone to get a better look at the dates.

I fumbled clumsily as I scrolled through to find the calendar, my breath coming out in short bursts.

Thursdays.

Every single date on the receipt was a Thursday.

My father had been visiting someone at Cove Sparry Hospital every Thursday for the past month.

I got back into the driver's seat and drove ahead, following the signs for visitor parking.

Chapter Sixteen

Sunday, 7:15 p.m.

The doors to the hospital opened, and I stepped into a large atrium.

Everything about it felt hospital-like—the pristine common area, the healing images on the walls, the friendly but stern security presence. Like most people, I hate hospitals, since they always seem to hold more despair than they do hope or healing.

What had my father been doing here?

I walked up to the main desk, and a bored-looking twentysomething tilted her head to the side but said nothing.

"I'm looking for Three North."

"Elevators to the third floor and across the bridge." She barely looked at me, but I thanked her before moving on. I walked over to the elevators and scanned the wall for the stairwell door. I paused in front of the elevators for a moment—I could have done it, if the doors had been open right then and there was no one else around. But a family of four joined me by the elevator doors, laughing, talking, and waiting, and another couple walked up a few seconds after that. I immediately headed for the stairs.

Not today.

I stepped out onto the third floor and crossed a bridge over the street where I'd first stopped my car to look at the receipts. I walked into what felt like an older part of the hospital and approached the sign for 3 North.

Mental health services.

What?

My father had been visiting a psych patient?

I knew it could be completely unrelated to Matthew and Sam Farr, and yet, I didn't have much else to go on. As I moved through the main doors of the wing, I turned a corner and entered a small waiting area. A woman sat in one of the chairs, watching television. An image on the screen caught my eye, and I slowed. It was a boy's face, and I recognized it as an old picture of Sam Farr.

"...has been missing since Wednesday afternoon when he and his father were enjoying themselves at a local park," the reporter said.

I froze, my gaze fixated on Sam's face.

"Alex Scroll, the man who accused Sam Farr of being responsible for his own son's death back in 1992, is a person of interest in the case."

The picture of Sam disappeared and was replaced by a pleasant news anchor who couldn't have been more than twenty-five years old.

"Matthew Farr is just under five feet tall, and he was last seen wearing a blue down coat, a light brown hat, and red-and-blue-striped mittens. If you know anything, anything at all about the disappearance of Matthew Farr or the whereabouts of Alex Scroll, the Lansing Police Department is asking that you step forward. You can also join the search and spread the word on social media, using the hashtag #WheresMattFarr."

I grimaced as the large hashtag appeared on the screen, directly under the anchor's face.

The woman in the waiting room shook her head.

"Social media, huh?" she said.

I nodded before walking away.

I turned down a long hallway and saw the sign for the café, which was no more than a few chairs and tables pushed up against a long counter at the end of the corridor. Two people were working in the café—a boy of about seventeen, stocking a small cooler, and an older man at the counter, who smiled as I approached.

"Welcome to the Three North Café," he said. "What can I get for you today?"

"Actually, I just had a question. How late are you open during the week?"

"We stay open until nine o'clock," he said with a smile. "One of the latest spots open in the whole hospital. A lot of our visitors stay here pretty late."

"My dad has been a visitor here, and he loves coming to this café."

"Really?" he said proudly. "Well, that's great to hear. Which dish is his favorite?"

I looked up at the chalkboard and pretended to give it some thought.

"I think he likes the ham sandwich…or maybe it's the turkey…"

He nodded. "It's probably the turkey. It gets ordered the most. I add cranberry jam to it. I really think that's what wins people over. You have to take something traditional and add a new spin to it."

"Yeah, you're right. I think that's it. He's mentioned the cranberry. I'll take one of those."

He nodded with a smile.

"My dad comes every Thursday night. You must know him—Alex Scroll?"

The man frowned. "Sounds familiar, but I can't say I know all of my customers by name."

"Really? Well, he's here every Thursday night, and he raves about the food." I felt conspicuous, like I was pushing too hard, but he didn't seem to notice.

"Well, I do most of the cooking myself, so I appreciate that."

"It's funny you don't remember him," I said. "He comes to visit one of the patients every Thursday night. He even mentioned you, I think."

"He did?" the man asked, his eyes lighting up.

"Yeah, besides the food," I said, deciding to go all in. "He said the service here was incredible, and I think he was talking about you. Here, let me show you a picture."

I reached into my wallet and pulled out a picture of Alex.

He reached for the glasses around his neck and put them on, leaning forward.

He stared at the picture for a moment.

"He looks familiar, for sure, and that name..." He shook his head. "I just can't place it, but I'm sure I've seen him around here." He straightened. "Now, let me go get that sandwich for you."

I smiled, disappointed and not at all hungry.

I placed money on the counter for the sandwich and then moved aside as he went to the back to fix the food.

"Excuse me."

I looked up, and the kid who'd been stocking the cooler was staring at me. He picked up a dish towel off the counter and whirled it around quickly. He didn't break eye contact as he snapped the towel, making a loud, popping noise.

"Yeah?" I said.

"Why'd you make that up?" He snapped the towel again, and I looked over my shoulder.

"Excuse me?" I asked.

"Why'd you make that up? About your father. The whole coming-to-visit-a-patient thing."

"What are you talking about? He comes here every Thursday."

Was I missing something? Had I been mistaken about what the receipts meant?

The boy spun the towel around again in his hands and stared at me. He seemed to be looking for something in particular, but he didn't speak for a while.

"Who are you?" he asked.

"I'm his son," I said again. "Do you know him?"

"Yeah, I do."

He didn't say anything else, and I stepped closer. He was watching me too carefully, with too much suspicion, so I tried to gauge my next words.

"I'm just trying to find him. He hasn't been home in a few days." It wasn't a lie, but it wasn't quite the truth either.

"Okay, but why are you acting like he's a visitor and not a patient?" he asked. His expression didn't change as he waited for me to respond. I couldn't tell if he was trying to help me or if he was suspicious.

"Because my dad can make up things sometimes, and I wasn't sure how he'd identified himself," I said, surprised at how quickly the lie came to me.

"Hmm..." the boy said with a smile. "Now there you go lyin' again. What's going on here?"

"Look," I said, leaning forward, deciding honesty might be my best bet with this kid. "My dad is missing, and I found some receipts that said he'd been here. But how can he be a patient here?"

"He's not," the kid said. "I mean, sort of. He comes in every Thursday night, but old Max doesn't see him because he's usually in the back, cooking. I'm the one out here."

"So you see him?" I asked, my heart speeding up. "Was he here last Thursday?"

"Yeah, of course. He doesn't miss it."

"Why did you say he's sort of like a patient?"

"Because he comes here to meet with Dr. Christine after her clinic is over."

"Dr. Christine?"

"Yeah, the health psychologist. They meet here for coffee on Thursday nights. But nobody calls him Alex. It's Al."

"But still, why 'sort of'?"

"I don't know, okay?" he said. "I don't know all the details. But I know he ain't visiting no patients. Dr. Christine does that. She's real nice. She'll meet with you just to talk if you get uncomfortable in the office setting. But they're not kidding anyone. He's messed up."

"Why do you say that?"

"Why you wanna know?" he asked, peering at me, and I sighed, reaching into my pocket. I pulled a twenty out of my wallet, and he took it quickly, slipping it into his pocket.

"Because he's my dad," I said. "And I worry. Come on, help me out."

He nodded. "Well, he's always coming to talk to her, but to be honest, he doesn't really talk that much. Sometimes, he just stares at the table, and she talks to him. Other times, he's whispering in her ear, real close like," he said. "It's a little nasty, if you ask me, because she's a doctor and he's a patient and whatever," he said.

"Where can I find this Dr. Christine?"

"Fourth floor. Four North, directly above us. She's probably there now. She works Sundays, Tuesdays, and Thursdays, and she's usually here pretty late."

I didn't say anything for a moment. "Anything else weird about the whole thing?"

The kid slung the dish towel again and turned away. "Naw, that's it. Maybe next time, just ask for what you want instead of making stuff up."

"Yeah," I said. "Thanks for the advice."

I was halfway to the elevator bank when I heard a voice call out, "Your sandwich!"

But I couldn't stop. Seconds later, I was back in the stairwell, skipping stairs up to the fourth floor.

Alex hadn't been coming to visit a patient.

He'd been coming to visit a doctor. A psychologist.

One who'd seen him just six days before the kidnapping.

Dr. Christine, whoever she was, might be my best bet for finding him.

I came out onto the fourth floor of the hospital and found myself in a large reception area. A woman was sitting behind a desk in front of a wall of closed office doors. I walked over to her, and she smiled professionally.

"May I help you?"

"Yes, I'd like to speak with Dr. Christine."

She tilted her head. "You mean Dr. Christine Sharpe? Dr. Sharpe is in with a patient right now. Is she expecting you?"

"Not quite," I said. "I'm the son of one of her patients. Alex Scroll."

If the woman recognized the name, she didn't show it. She uncrossed her legs and rolled closer to her desk, setting a stern expression on her face. "Well, you can leave a message for her, but she is in with a patient, and she needs to leave right after."

"I only need a couple of minutes—" I started.

"I'm sorry, she's very busy," the woman said. "She has to go straight from here to her Orland Park office."

"She has an office in Orland Park?" I reached over to pick up one of her business cards. On it were two office locations—the one in the hospital, and one out in Orland Park, a suburb about thirty minutes northwest of Lansing.

"Yes," she said. "Look, I can ask her to give you a call." She reached for a memo pad and a pen before looking up again. "Your name?"

I was considering how to answer her when the door to one of the offices opened and a couple walked out.

A tall woman followed them, carrying a file folder in her hand. I always find it weird when women are described as handsome, but it seemed fitting. The woman was nearly six feet tall, with long, gray hair pulled into a loose braid, kind eyes, and a stern jaw. She was attractive but not pretty, gentle but not delicate.

"Set up your next appointment with Linda," the woman said with a smile as she shook hands with the couple. She was about to turn to walk back into her office when she caught sight of me.

Her eyes widened, and she paused.

"Sir, your name?" the woman sitting in front of me asked again.

At the same time the tall woman breathed out, "Holy hell."

I walked around the desk, and Linda began to stand as though to stop me.

"Are you Dr. Christine? Or rather, Dr. Sharpe?" I asked as I approached her. "I'm sorry to bother you, but I really need to talk to you."

Her eyes didn't leave mine as she spoke. "Linda, please sign the Johnsons out." She took a deep breath and squared her shoulders as she gave me a slight smile of resignation. "Yes, Francis, I'm Christine Sharpe. And of course we can talk. Now seems as good a time as any, doesn't it?"

Chapter Seventeen

I walked into her office, and she shut the door.

It was a nicely appointed room, with plush purple couches and a soft rug that had no business being walked on. She motioned to one of the couches, and I sat down as she folded herself into a chair.

"How did you know who I was?" I asked, the question coming out more bluntly than I'd intended, and she smiled slightly.

"I've seen pictures of you, of course. From the trial, but more recently, from your father. But that doesn't really matter. You look a lot like him."

I'd never heard that, and I wondered if she was making it up. I hadn't seen my father in a while, but I had a feeling it wasn't a compliment.

"Can I get you some water?" she asked.

"No, I'm fine," I said. "Thank you."

"You sure?" She nodded toward my lap. I looked down and realized I'd been tapping my hands nervously against my things without noticing. I stopped and looked up at her.

"No, I'm fine," I said again, and we both knew it wasn't true.

Dr. Christine—it wasn't her name, but it seemed fitting—leaned forward. She was watching me so carefully, and I wondered if she was doing it on purpose, just to make me nervous.

"How did you end up here?" she asked. "Did your father tell you about me?"

"No," I said. "I found a few old receipts from the café, and I stopped by there and talked to a very helpful employee. After that, I put things together."

She paused, and then she burst out laughing, which took me completely by surprise. She didn't seem like a woman who laughed loudly very often. Dr. Christine shook her head. "Alex is quite the hoarder; I bet he keeps all of his receipts. Of course that's how you found me. I shouldn't have expected anything less." She took a deep breath. "So I'm guessing you're here because of the missing boy."

"Yes," I said, noting the casual, controlled way she said this.

"The missing boy."

As if it were nothing at all.

Or, as if she wanted to pretend like it was nothing at all.

I wasn't the only one who was nervous here. I was just worse at hiding it.

"How do you know my father?"

She rocked back in her chair. "We're friends. I've been helping him out now for about a year."

"Helping him out? Is that your way of saying you've provided treatment to him?"

"I'm sure you know I can't tell you anything like that," she said. "But you made it this far, so I have to assume you know I was meeting with your father on a regular basis."

"Off the books."

She didn't flinch. "Not at all. I don't do things off the books, Francis. Your father wanted to meet with me in the café. He said it made him feel more comfortable. So I met with him in the café. I always took proper notes."

I glanced quickly at the laptop on her desk, and she smiled slightly. "They're not on the computer," she said.

I cleared my throat and tried to keep the conversation moving. "So he's a patient of yours."

She frowned slightly and didn't respond.

"I'm just trying to find him," I said. "Really, that's all. How long have you known him?"

"About a year," she said, her tone even, and I realized she'd just said that. "We met at a conference."

"About?"

"Does it matter?" she asked, and I continued staring at her. "I don't know, gardening."

I tried not to react. It was her way of telling me she wasn't going to answer my questions, at least not the ones she didn't want to.

"What did he need to talk about?"

She smiled wryly. "But you know I'm not allowed to answer that."

"Even if it will help find a missing child?"

"Especially since that's why you're asking. Now that you're here, I expect the police will be making their way by sometime soon too," she said. "Believe me, patient confidentiality isn't something I'm inclined to break."

"So he is a patient."

She continued without acknowledging me. "Also, I'm not convinced your father had anything to do with that boy."

"But you think it's possible."

"I think he and the boy are the only ones who know that. You don't seem as convinced as I am," she said. "Is that right? You think your father had something to do with Matthew Farr's disappearance?"

"I don't know," I said. "I'm here to try to find some answers. Look, I know you're not allowed to tell me what you and my father talked about. But can you tell me this—was my father in any kind of trouble? Was he telling you about something that was bothering him? Please, it could be important to finding both him and Matthew."

She seemed to think it over for a while, and I could tell she was debating how much she should tell me.

"Look, your father was battling a lot of things, but if you're asking me if there was one specific thing he was worried about these days, the answer is not really." She shook her head. "But I'm unable to address that any further. I hope you can respect that. It's at the core of what I do."

I nodded, even though shaking her was at the core of what *I* wanted to do.

"You know, the fact that you're so worried about him… Alex would be thrilled to know that."

"What do you mean?"

"Your father… I tried to tell him that it was the circumstances. That you would have been there for him if you could've."

Jab.

"What?"

"He wasn't sure you cared about him anymore."

Cross.

"He told you that?"

"He told everybody that."

Uppercut.

The words stung, hitting me in the face. She shook her head. "I can't believe I'm saying all of this, but it seems you should know. And you should know he felt like it was his fault. That he'd lost you, and you'd made the decision to let him go. So to see you here, to see how worried you are, I just…I wish I could talk to him, tell him. It would matter to him. It would matter a lot."

I bit my lip and was surprised by the emotion that had welled up. I cleared my throat and stood.

"I should get going," I said. "But thanks for your time."

"Of course," she said. "I'd be lying if I said I wasn't worried about him. I hope you'll keep me informed if you hear from him." She reached over and grabbed a card from her cardholder. She walked around the desk and handed it to me. I took it, hesitant to tell her that I'd already taken one from outside. I glanced at it and was surprised that it only had her hospital address and phone number—the Orland Park address wasn't listed.

I looked up, and she was still staring at me, waiting for a response.

I nodded. "Of course. I'll let you know if I hear anything, and I hope you'll do the same. We need everyone on board to find Matthew Farr."

"Of course," she said quickly. Too quickly.

We were lying, and we both knew it. She wouldn't contact me, and I wouldn't contact her.

As I turned to leave, it occurred to me that Dr. Christine Sharpe was hiding a hell of a lot more than she wanted me to know.

And I had a feeling that the more she had to hide, the more my father had to hide.

I arrived home that night to a silent apartment.

I cracked open Amy's door and saw her curled up on one side of the bed, fast asleep.

Her laptop was lying on the bed beside her, still open. I walked over and picked it up.

As I did, my thumb brushed the touchpad, and the screen lit up the room.

I froze and looked down again at Amy's sleeping figure. She didn't move, which was refreshingly familiar—since the day she was born, she'd had the uncanny ability to sleep like a log, no matter what was going on around her.

I walked the laptop over to her desk and put it down. With one hand on the lid to close it, I—for reasons I wouldn't have been able to explain if she *had* woken up—let my eyes linger on the screen for just a moment.

I sucked in a breath when I saw what she'd been doing.

Her screen was open to her Facebook page, and at the very top of her feed, she'd posted a link to a broadcast story about Matthew Farr: *Some people want to give up, but we can't stop until we find him. #WheresMattFarr.* Her post had been liked by fifteen people, and a quick scroll through the comments let me know that they were mostly friends of hers from New York.

Super tragic, ugh. Miss you, Ames.

Ew. Come back. Civilized society misses you.

I sighed and closed the laptop, pushing it back farther on the desk. I took one more glance at Amy before walking out of her room and pulling the door closed behind me.

I didn't have days or weeks or even hours anymore. I had to tell her. It was going to be the hardest conversation of my life, but there was no more time for excuses.

I'd tell her in the morning.

For sure.

Chapter Eighteen

Monday, 7:15 a.m.

I tried; I really did.

Before I went to bed, I set an alarm to wake me up at six thirty—plenty of time to talk to Amy and help her get ready for her first day of school.

But when I opened my eyes a little after seven, certain I hadn't heard an alarm go off, I leaned over to find that I'd set it for six thirty at *night*.

And that Amy had already left.

I walked to her door and pushed it open, peeking inside. Empty. I sent her a text.

Hey u ok? Sry I missed u. U should've woken me up. Would've dropped u off.

I was halfway back to my bedroom when my phone lit up.

Yeah tks no worries. I'm here, it's super close.

I sighed, staring at the text before walking into the bathroom to get ready. When I got out of the shower, I noticed a little envelope on my cell phone, alerting me that I had a voice message. The man's voice that filled my ears was gruff and to the point, his drawl instantly familiar.

"Francis, this is Banks. I got your message and...well, I'm not too sure how I can help you, okay? I don't mind if you want to come by, but I mean...I can tell you what I know, but it's not a lot. Anyway, I'll be at my office until about three o'clock this afternoon, if you want to stop by. Okay."

Banks left his address and hung up.

I pulled up in front of Banks's office around nine thirty. It was small and nondescript, in the storefront of a narrow plaza. It was flanked by a taco joint and a nail salon.

The front door was open, and I walked inside. The room was outdated, with ripped tan leather chairs and a worn, dark-gray rug. A desk near the front of the office was covered with papers. I walked past it and peered toward the back, where there was a cluttered corridor.

I was about to call out for assistance when I heard a noise, and a figure suddenly appeared in the passageway. I recognized him immediately.

"Mr. Banks," I said.

His eyes widened when he saw my face. "Francis Scroll. I didn't hear you come in." He stepped closer and reached out his hand. "I didn't know if you were actually going to come."

"I appreciate you taking the time," I said.

"Oh, don't worry about it," he said.

Raymond Banks was a tall, portly man in his early sixties, with shrewd, gray-blue eyes and a lilt in his voice that gave him an air of the South, even though I was pretty sure he'd never spent any real time there.

"I have to admit, I was intrigued when I got your message, but like I said, I don't have much to tell ya that you don't already know." He turned and walked toward his desk. "I guess we'll just..." He grabbed a large stack of papers and placed it on the floor. "Can I get you something? Coffee?"

"No, I'm good," I said, sitting in one of the empty chairs as he took the other.

"So, what exactly can I do for you?" he asked. "I didn't think I'd have to talk about this again for a long time, or ever, really."

"I was hoping you could tell me a little bit about my brother's case," I said.

"Now why would you want to know a thing like that?" he asked. "There wasn't much of a *case*, to be honest. Now that I've had some distance, you know, a little bit of space...I can see that clearly. It was two sets of parents, desperate to find justice for their children. Nothing more than that, nothing less."

"But you represented my father. You believed the same thing he did, that Sam had something to do with my brother's death. Didn't you?"

Banks didn't say anything for a moment. "You do know that not every lawyer defends cases they truly believe in, right?"

"Well, yes, but I thought—"

"No, you're right. I mean, I don't know if I can tell you what I think happened that night, because like everyone else, I really don't know." He shook his head. "People think lawyers have some sort of magic wand that can dig up the truth. Get ready for this knowledge bomb, Francis: we don't! We look at the same things everyone else does; we just have more experience in where to look and what to look for."

He leaned forward, resting both hands on the table. "Sometimes, it comes down to the most educated guess you can make based on the facts you seem to have, and I mean it when I say 'seem to.' Because in a case like this, nothing is really 'factual,' not when you don't have much to go on. You got a dead kid, no offense, a lot of possible scenarios for what could have happened, and only one other person on earth who may—and I do mean *may*—have seen something or been involved. And that person was a shy little ten-year-old who, let's face it, wasn't going to win any congeniality awards, that was for sure. So a case? I guess you could call it that. It was more like an unfortunate set of events that weren't ever supposed to have any sort of satisfying ending, not for anyone involved—"

"Until Matthew Farr went missing."

He stopped and stared at me before sitting back in his chair. Then, he began to nod slowly.

"So *that's* why you're here." He ran his hand over his mouth and down his chin. "Yeah, I heard about that, and I don't really know what to make of it, I'll be honest witcha."

"I do," I said. "I need to get inside my father's mind, and the only way I can do that is to go back to what's been driving him all these years. Can you help me with that?"

"I can try." He shook his head. "What a trial. Did you follow it? You went away for school, right? I remember that. When did you get back?"

"About a year and a half ago."

"Oh, wow. Did you follow it while you were away?"

"Some," I said, clearing my throat. "I mean, it was impossible not to. But I was in a new place, and I think it was good for me to stay away from—"

"Oh, I'm not suggesting it wasn't," he said with an understanding smile. "You were just a boy back then too. They wanted to keep you out of it as much as possible. But I'm assuming you looked into it at some point, right? I mean, you had to be curious."

"I'm curious now." It came out more curtly than I'd planned, and his expression changed slightly before he nodded.

"Well, what can I tell you? I'll help you as much as I can." He frowned. "But you should remember the details of the night better than I do. Seeing as how you were actually there."

"Yes, but I'd like to hear what a jury heard," I said. "Please, it will be helpful." I felt dangerously behind everyone else, and I couldn't help but think that getting to the heart of what my father *thought* he knew about Sam Farr was the key to helping us find Matthew.

"All right," the lawyer said. "Well, as I recall, and correct me if you remember differently, but you guys finished dinner that night around eight?"

"Yeah, it was something like that."

"Nobody ever talked about the dinner that much. Just that eight o'clock was when everything started. For the sake of the trial, that's when the night really began, I guess."

"Yeah, I guess it did," I said, my mind reeling back to that cold night more than two decades ago.

It was amazingly quiet now, in contrast with the bass-ridden pop songs my mother had been playing all night, and the uproar following Sam's soaking-wet appearance in our living room. I stared at the backs of Rudy and the detective as they continued to throw out words like "tragedy" and "useless" and "reports."

Then Rudy stepped aside, ungluing his shoes from the bottom of the tub.

I didn't realize how much his large frame had been blocking, and suddenly, I caught sight of that tie-dye shirt Lucas had been wearing. Immediately, my stomach lurched. I threw up again, and the sound attracted the attention of both men.

"What the—" the detective said as they turned and caught sight of me. I stared at them, scared of getting in trouble and also scared I'd see him.

Lucas.

In the tub.

Floating.

"Oh, it's the older one," the detective said. "Kid, you shouldn't be in here."

I heard him, but now they'd both shifted in my direction, and there was that shirt again, and I knew that at any minute, I'd see his face or his hair, and I was certain that if I did, I would die too.

"Son?" The two men glanced at each other uncomfortably, and then the detective walked closer and put his hand on my shoulder. "C'mon, let's get you outta here, okay?"

And then his body was in the way, blocking my view. I felt sad, because I knew it was the last time I'd ever see Lucas, except for maybe in a picture, but I was also happy, because I couldn't stand the thought of even a glimpse of his lifeless body.

He ushered me out of the bathroom, onto the landing, and looked around for someone to hand me off to.

"Lucas..." I said, his name coating my tongue, and I stared through the open door at the edge of the bathtub. "I can't—"

"Hey," the detective said, crouching down, and I could see he wasn't as hardened or detached as I'd thought he was. Like Rudy, his eyes were watery, and he clenched his jaw tightly as he knelt in front of me, grabbing me by both arms. "It's going to be okay, you know. I know you can't understand it now, but it's going to be okay."

"But he's..." I struggled to get the word out. "He's d... He's d..."

"He's dead," the detective said, still watching me carefully. "And I'm so sorry. But you're going to be okay. I promise you."

He stood up and searched the halls again for someone else to take me. But everyone had pulled away, retreated, and I was left alone. That's the thing about death. We're taught so long how to live correctly, how to act properly while we're alive, but when somebody dies, we're taught nothing except that it is okay to act as we feel. It was okay for my parents to leave me standing there, alone, scared on the landing, with all of the ghosts in the small bathroom next door, and nobody around but a detective who seemed ready to unleash me on the first capable adult he could find.

That adult turned out to be my grandfather, Grandpa Zach, who was coming up the stairs at that very moment, looking for something, when his gaze landed on me. He almost seemed not to recognize me at first. When he did, he nearly toppled over himself in his haste to get to me.

"Come on," he said. "You don't need to be anywhere near there, Francis."

That's when I lost it, lashing out, kicking and screaming, desperate to go back into that bathroom, because as much as it scared me, this couldn't be it; this couldn't be the end.

"Francis, come on, shhh, please!" my grandfather cried out as he dragged me down the hallway and away from Lucas for the very last time.

"Francis?"

I blinked and stared into the face of Raymond Banks, who was watching me closely, waiting for me to respond to something he'd said.

"Sorry?"

"I asked if you heard the argument Lucas and Sam had after dinner."

I shook my head. "No, I was in the kitchen, I think."

"Your father really thought that would seal the case, you know? Catching the boys fighting like that, just an hour or so before the accident."

"What exactly did he hear?"

"According to your father, he was standing at the bottom of the stairs when he heard screaming from up in Lucas's bedroom. It was hard to make out over the music, but he was pretty sure it was Sam who was yelling at your brother, calling him all sorts of names…"

"But Brian Farr heard it too, right?"

"Yeah, he did. He went upstairs to calm his son down. Farr tried to downplay it at first, but he later admitted that Sam was the aggressor, throwing things around and everything. That boy was quiet, but he had a temper. We never found out what that fight was about."

"That Sam and Lucas got into a fight doesn't prove anything," I said.

"No, it doesn't. It didn't back then, either, obviously."

"Was there ever any sort of explanation given for why Sam Farr was soaking wet when he came downstairs?"

"His parents and lawyers came up with the story that he probably leaned into the tub to try to get your brother out, ya know, tried to save him. But the boy never said it himself."

We sat there silently, and I floated back to that night and the peculiar, thick, grainy moment when everything stopped.

Footsteps pounding down the stairs.

Sam Farr's face as he appeared in the living room, drenched in water, his entire body shaking.

"What's wrong?" his father had asked, launching from his seat.

I heard my mother say, years later, that she saw Sam's expression, and in an instant, she knew her youngest son was dead. I think she said it for the sake of the media, but I don't doubt there was some truth to it. The quote had been plastered across newspapers for an entire week. She said she knew, right then, what she would find when they got upstairs, and for that reason, she hadn't wanted to move.

She didn't want to know.

Sam had stood in front of us, frozen, and it seemed that everybody had started to hurt at the same time, the pain oozing out, everywhere, and then the wineglass had slipped from my mother's fingertips, and the last traces of the evening's thick, joyous red wine had coated the carpet like blood, staining it forever.

"How did they explain the silence?" I asked Banks. "Why Sam never talked..."

"Well, as you know, the boy didn't talk much anyway. A psychologist said the tragic event could have caused a complete shutdown. I just wish the one statement he did make hadn't been ruled out, you know?" He shrugged. "That might have been the real turning point in the case."

"Wait, what statement?"

"The..." Banks frowned. When he saw my expression, he tilted his head. "What Sam said to your father that night, while everyone was upstairs. Of course you heard about that..."

He watched my confused expression, and his eyes grew wide.

"Wow, I guess you really were young," he said, a look of confusion on his face. "But didn't you hear anything about the case afterward?"

He wasn't trying to drive a point home, but it felt that way, and I tensed up again.

"I read a few things here and there, but I finished out the school year on the East Coast," I said, my jaw clenched. "That's why I'm here now. What are you talking about?"

"The boy apologized—"

"What?"

"Yeah..." Banks said, sitting back and shaking his head. "I can't believe you didn't know that. The boy apologized to Alex while everyone else was upstairs. Not another soul in sight, which you can imagine made things difficult for the case. The boy didn't talk after that night, but according to your father, he said more than enough that evening." Banks leaned forward. "If I remember your father's words correctly, Sam said, and I quote, 'I'm sorry it happened, and I'm sorry I have to lie.'"

Chapter Nineteen

He said that?"

"If we're to believe Alex, then yes."

"But..." I sputtered. "The whole case rested on the fact that he never said anything about that night! A kid of that age was sure to break, but not Sam Farr. How come this was never brought up at the trial?"

"Sam's lawyers got it thrown out. They denied it ever happened. And they made it clear that if we pushed it, they would be forced to put more weight on what happened right after that."

"Right after that?" I struggled to put the pieces together. "In the foyer? You mean, when my father pushed him—"

"Yep," Banks said. "Bad news is that there was no one else around to hear Sam say that he had to lie, but everyone showed up as this thirty-seven-year-old man rushed a ten-year-old boy, knocking him over." Banks chuckled and shook his head. "I know it's not funny, but it was certainly a shit show. There wasn't much we could do about that. It was your father's word against Sam's, and no jury was going to find fault in a young boy who had just seen his best friend die in a horrible accident, only to be attacked by the friend's father."

"It sounds to me like you thought Sam was guilty too. At least, somewhat?"

Banks blinked and looked at me as if he hadn't expected such a question. "Well, that's a tough one. I don't know that I ever came to a conclusion of guilt. Now, if you're asking if I think the boy was responsible for what happened to Lucas, then you know what? Probably. Does that make him guilty? I don't know. He was a kid. We don't say that when babies do things wrong, they're guilty. This is a ten-year-old. I don't know. It's a tough one. Certainly didn't give people the right to do what they did, harassing him and everything. But I do think he was hiding something."

"Why?"

"Because you and I know that the normal reaction for anyone, of any age, to being accused of doing something they didn't do is to deny it. Whether you scream and shout it or whisper it quietly, you deny it. He never even tried."

"Who else spoke at the trial?"

"Oh, all sorts of people. A scene-by-scene analyst who testified to all of the possible accident scenarios that could have led to Lucas's death. All speculation, really. There was the on-the-scene detective who interviewed Sam first. He made it pretty clear that he thought Sam was guilty. Then there was the expert who testified that yes, Sam Farr, with enough anger in him, could have pushed Lucas hard enough to make him fall and hit his head. A real shit show, I tell you. We all had an expert who showed how things could have happened. But nobody had any real proof." He shrugged. "Nobody except one person. I think he's taking the truth with him to his grave."

"Do you keep in touch with anyone? Other than my father?"

He frowned. "No, there's no reason to," he said.

"Do you know if Alex did?"

He thought for a moment. "He was pretty close with the detective. Younger was his name, I think."

I thought about the tall man who'd practically dragged me out of my parents' bathroom. He didn't look like a "Younger."

We were silent for a few moments, and finally, I stood up to leave. "I guess that's it then. Thanks for your time, Mr. Banks."

"Oh, anytime. That case," he said, shaking his head as he stood with me, "I'm sure I'll never be able to let it go. There are just some of them that stick with you forever."

"You're telling me." I shook his hand and left his office. While we'd been talking, I'd been forming a plan. There was so much about my brother's case I didn't know. So much my father had been living with for years. Some of those insights had to point me in his direction, and maybe—just maybe—Matthew Farr's.

I knew one person—a tall, striking health psychologist—who had some of those answers, but she didn't seem willing to share them with me. She said she kept all of her interview notes at her other office in Orland Park.

So I'd have to get them myself.

What I was about to do was wrong.

Unethical.

Risky.

Against the law.

And borne out of pure and utter desperation. Christine obviously knew more than she'd let on when I'd gone to meet with her, and as far as I knew, she'd had the most regular contact with Alex for the past few weeks.

When I made the decision to break into her Orland Park office later that night to find her notes about her sessions with Alex, I'd underestimated all of the time I'd have to think about what I was doing before I actually got there. As I punched the address from her business card into my GPS, I battled with the voice of reason that told me this was too much, too far, too ridiculous.

I distracted myself during the drive, listening to talk radio, zoning out, and ignoring the overwhelming urge to turn the car around and head home. When I finally parked the car, my hands ached as I released my grip on the steering wheel.

Here we go.

Christine's suburban office was a storefront on a quiet downtown street. The streetlights were on, but there was no one around. A few of the storefronts had apartments above them. I waited for a few moments, searching for movement. When the silence continued for a full three minutes, I opened my car door and stepped out. I shivered and pulled my collar up around my face, wishing I hadn't left my scarf at home. I inched toward the front of the building, my gaze darting all around me. I couldn't afford to be surprised by Miranda Farr again, not this time.

The sign out front of the modern brick building contained just her name. Christine Sharpe, Psy.D.

I moved closer to the front door and peered through the window. Darkness. I could see the outline of a neat waiting area just past the door. I tried the handle without any expectation and sighed, stepping back.

Of course not.

I walked away from the front door, my head down, weighing my next move.

I walked toward an alley alongside the building, navigating between two large, overflowing Dumpsters. I swallowed, holding my breath as the scent of trash wafted into my nostrils and made my stomach roil.

Don't look at it, Francis.

Do not look at it.

There had to be a back door, right? All buildings had back doors for the purpose of breaking and entering, second only to escaping fires and trash disposal.

As I moved slowly along, a sudden motion near the end of the alley caught my eye, and I stopped.

What the…?

Standing at the end, near what must have been the back door to Christine's clinic, was a man.

I moved quickly behind one of the Dumpsters and pushed myself against the side of the building, my back flat against the hard, cold, and rough bricks. The smell of the trash was overwhelming now, and alarms went off in my head as I fought the urge to flee. A creeping sensation began to take over my body, and I pushed it down, determined to ignore it as I craned my neck forward to peer around the large bin.

I couldn't make out the man's face, but his hands were stuffed in his pockets, and he shifted back and forth, looking nervously in every direction.

Who was it?

Was he waiting for someone?

I was about to step closer to get a better look when the man suddenly moved.

He slipped his hands out of his pockets, walked up to the back door of the office, and knocked on it with the palm of his hand.

Bang, bang, bang.

Three slow knocks.

A pause.

Then he reached up and banged his palm one final time.

Bang.

I crept closer, squinting to try to catch a glimpse of his face.

What the hell was going on here?

As I inched around the Dumpster, I heard a noise, and seconds later, the back door opened.

I couldn't see who opened the door, but the man in the alley stepped closer and began to speak. After a moment, he stepped inside, and the door shut quickly behind him.

The dark alley seemed even quieter now, the weight of what I'd just seen making me freeze in place. It didn't look like I was going to get my hands on my father's file, at least not tonight. But that seemed less important now. What was Christine up to? Had she been the one who answered the door?

I turned to head back toward the front of the building and then gasped.

Standing just a few feet away from me, his eyes trained on me, was another man.

He was shorter than me but stockier, with sunken eyes and a relatively fresh bruise on his cheekbone. He wore a hooded sweat suit beneath a dirty, light-gray jacket, and he kept both hands in his pockets.

"Is that the place?" he asked, not moving.

It took me a moment to find my voice.

"Uh, what?"

"I said, is this the place?" He stayed where he was but leaned slowly to one side to look around me to the end of the alley.

He scratched the side of his neck and stepped closer.

I held my breath, watching him, waiting for him to act.

"Yeah, I think so," I said quickly when he didn't do anything. "Pretty sure it is, yeah."

"What's the code?"

I blinked. "The code?"

"Yeah," he said, his gaze darting down the alley and back to me. "Black rock or something, right?" He scratched again.

"Yeah," I said. "I think that's it."

He tilted his head to the side and then began to shake it slowly. "Naw, man, it's black something, but it's not that. Shit. I been tryin' to remember it all day."

"Black...moon?" I said, taking a stab in the dark.

He frowned. "Was it moon? Naw, I don't think so, it was like rock, but not rock, you know?"

I struggled for something to say that would make him believe that I had any idea at all about what he was referring to.

"Oh yeah, you're right," I tried. "Black...wasn't it, 'stone'?"

He shook his head. "Naw, man. Shit. Black..." He closed his eyes for a moment, and I prayed he would get it right. "Box!" He opened his eyes and nodded. "Right?"

I nodded. "Shit, man, you're right. They should've made it something easier."

"You going in?"

"No, I have to wait here for a friend. I'll be in soon."

"All right," he said. He gave me what felt like a nod of approval and walked past me.

What the fuck was going on?

He walked down the alley toward the door, and with one quick glance back at me, he raised his hand and knocked on the door.

Bang, bang, bang.

He paused and looked at me again before lifting it again.

Bang.

Immediately, the door opened.

The man spoke to the figure shielded by the door for a few moments. I couldn't make out what he was saying, except for one word.

"Box."

Then he walked inside.

I knew it wasn't the best idea, but I knew immediately what I had to do.

I had no other choice.

I could go home and come back tomorrow to find her notes. But Christine was up to something tonight that she didn't want anyone to know about.

If she was the one answering the door, I'd confront her right away. If not, I'd try to find out what was going on, maybe even find a chance to slip away to find my father's file.

I had nowhere else to look, and not much else to lose.

I took a breath and walked down the alley, toward the back door, glancing over my shoulder for any other late arrivals.

As I approached, I saw a dim light beneath the door.

Bracing myself for whatever was on the other side, I raised my hand and knocked on the door three times.

I paused, looking once more for any other guests, but I was alone.

The voice that had been pulling me back home all night shrieked like a car alarm, but I planted my feet on the ground and took a deep breath.

Before I could talk myself out of it, I reached up and knocked once more.

Chapter Twenty

I have a recurring dream where I'm running through a public place in search of a bathroom. Each one I find has a serious problem: sometimes it's covered in filth, or the stalls have no doors. Once, every single toilet was taken up by someone I only sort of knew—the barista at my favorite coffee shop, a neighbor I barely spoke to—and they all stared at me brazenly while taking care of their business. I didn't stop for coffee for weeks.

Still, the thing about dreams is that as awful as they feel in the moment, there's a fuzziness to them that always lets me know something isn't quite right, that it isn't actually real.

As I stood in the alley outside of Christine's office, waiting for someone to answer the door, it all felt too real.

Incredibly, painfully, unavoidably real.

I'd been standing there for a full thirty seconds when I realized nothing was going to happen. Had I knocked too quietly? Were they expecting anyone else?

The cold air swirled around my face, and I looked over my shoulder again.

I'd regret it if I didn't try one more time. I raised my hand and went through the process again, this time banging loudly.

Bang, bang, bang.

Pause.

Bang.

Almost immediately, I heard a noise on the other side of the door, and my stomach flipped over.

Then, the door opened, and behind it stood the largest man I'd ever seen.

He towered over me, and his shoulders almost touched either side of the doorframe. He was wearing a turtleneck, and in the dim glow behind him, I could see a rough scar that trailed from his ear, across his jaw, and down his neck.

"Yeah?" he said, startling me, and I drew my gaze away from the scar, back to his face. His eyes were piercing, and he watched me carefully, waiting for me to respond.

My throat was suddenly dry, too dry to speak, and the words that came out of me weren't much more than a whisper.

"I'm here about the black moon."

It sounded so ridiculous, and I half expected him to laugh in my face, turn around, and shut the door.

"The what?" he asked.

I blinked.

Wait, what did I say?

Did I say "moon"?

Shit.

Was that it? I pictured the man I'd just spoken with near the Dumpsters.

I cleared my throat. "The black box."

His expression didn't change.

"Who sent you?"

Shit, shit.

A logical question. I should've asked the junkie before he went inside.

"He didn't tell me his name," I said, and the man's eyes narrowed. "Look, can I come in or what? It's cold, and I got other places to be."

The man looked past me into the alley, and after a moment, he nodded and stepped back. I almost toppled over in relief, but I squared my shoulders and walked inside.

It had worked.

Un-fucking-believable.

The back part of Dr. Christine's clinic was nothing like her office at the hospital or the neat waiting room I'd seen through the window out front. It was cold, worn, and dirty. We walked through a long hallway, which was flanked by doors. The halls were virtually empty—no paintings on the walls, no floor runner, barely enough light to see in front of me.

The man turned, and we went toward what I imagined must be the front of the building. I kept a lookout for Christine, wondering if she was here and how much she knew about what was going on in her clinic after hours.

The man slowed down in front of a door on the right side of the hallway. He stepped forward and opened it before moving back.

"Wait in there."

As he turned to walk away, he looked at me again. "Do I know you from somewhere?"

I paused, my body turning to enter the room, and I looked back at him. "I doubt it," I said. I waited, staring at him, just long enough for him not to get suspicious, before walking into the room.

What could that mean? Had Christine showed him a picture of me?

Did he know my father and think I looked like him too?

In the room, I saw I was not alone. The other men I'd seen in the alley were sitting there, along with two more who must have arrived before I did. They looked up at me.

Judging by their appearance, I could tell that at least two of the four men were homeless. The man I'd talked to in the alley was still scratching furiously, and he gave me a slight nod as I sat down.

"Where's your friend?" he asked.

"My what?" I blinked, and then I remembered my lie from the alley. "Oh, he decided to go home," I said with a shrug. "Whatever."

We sat in black plastic chairs around the perimeter of the room. No one spoke, and everyone seemed okay with that. I was dying to ask them why they were there, but I held back, tapping my finger against the armrest and hoping I looked bored rather than nervous.

What in the hell was going on here?

The door opened again, and a woman came into the room. She paused and looked around before walking over to me.

"If you'll come with me," she said. "They're ready for you."

I stood and locked eyes with one of the other men, who frowned.

"Why does he get to go first?" he asked. "I been waiting here an hour!"

"Your turn will be up soon," the woman said before walking through the doorway and stepping aside to let me exit before pulling the door closed behind us.

The woman moved quickly, and I soon lost track of where we were in the building. She walked swiftly through a maze of hallways and doors, and I shuffled along behind her.

"Here we are," she said as she approached a room. She opened the door and stepped back to let me enter. "Please undress and put on the robe," she said. "Someone will be with you shortly."

The door closed behind her, and I stood in the middle of the room. Did they really expect me to take off all my clothes?

Just what were they doing here?

I knew I didn't have a choice if I really wanted to see this thing through. Quickly, I undressed and wrapped the robe around me. Then, I sat down on the exam bench and waited. I crossed and uncrossed my legs as I tried to get settled on the elevated perch.

I was seconds away from getting up and walking back into the hallway when the door opened and the man who'd let me in from the alley came inside. He strode over to me and asked me to stand.

"I need to check for wires," he said, motioning for me to put my arms out.

He patted me down through the gown, and when he was satisfied, he nodded for me to sit back down.

"Do you have any sensitivity to light?"

I blinked, surprised by the sudden and direct question.

"Well?" he asked. "Do you?"

"Uh, no, not really."

"Do you ever experience dizziness or anything similar?"

"No."

"Do you have any problems with anxiety, panic attacks, or similar conditions?"

I swallowed. Now why would they need to know that?

"No," I said softly.

"What?"

"No. I don't."

The man nodded. "Okay, good." He took a key out of his pocket and went over to a small cabinet above the sink. Opening it, he pulled out a bottle and turned back to me. "As you know, you'll need to take these pills before we get started."

He poured two pills into a paper cup and then opened a cabinet under the sink and took out a bottle of water. He handed me the pills and the water bottle.

"You'll need to take these while I'm standing here, and then we'll get started."

I took them from him and was about to respond when he cut me off.

"And make sure they go all the way down, okay?" he said. "I'll be checking."

Chapter Twenty-One

Stop shaking, Francis.

I stared at the cup in my hand. The two pills seemed to stare back at me defiantly, and they started to rattle against each other. I switched the cup to my other hand, hoping Scarface wouldn't pick up on how nervous I was.

"Is there a problem?"

"No," I said, pouring the pills out into my palm and juggling them around.

Think.

The man took a step closer to me, his face scrunched in a frown. "What the hell are you waiting for?"

I unscrewed the cap on the water bottle and held it in my hand, gripping the cap firmly against the pills.

"Look, I don't have all day," the man said, shifting even closer and peering over into my hand. "Are you going to take them or what?"

He was watching me so carefully, as if he knew, and I wondered if he could hear my heart racing.

"What are they?" I asked as casually as possible.

"What does that matter?"

"I'm just asking," I said. "It could be anything."

"No questions, remember?" he said. "If you don't want to take 'em, you don't have to be here."

"No, no problem," I said, the pills still rattling in my hand.

Do something.

Taking a deep breath, I leaned my head back and dropped the pills in my mouth, opening my hand out wide for him to see that it was empty.

I lifted the water bottle up to my mouth and filled it with water. As I did, I carefully slipped the two pills beneath my tongue.

Now.

Pressing down as hard as possible on the pills, I began to swallow the water, letting it slide down the back of my throat before opening my mouth and expelling the majority of it into the man's face.

"Ugh!" he cried out, stepping back and putting his hands up to shield himself. "What the fuck is wrong with you?"

I pretended to choke, and soon, the charade turned to reality as the water continued to drip down my throat, and I coughed violently. I bent over, the coughs shaking me as I pressed down even harder with my tongue. Putting the water bottle to my mouth again, I pretended to take another swig, but this time, I pushed the pills into the opening of the bottle before screwing the top back on. I opened my mouth to take in big gulps of air.

"What the fuck, man?" he asked, peering at me. With his eyes still on me, he backed toward the sink and unrolled a few paper towels. He used them to wipe at his face and chest. "That's some nasty shit."

"I'm sorry," I said between heaves, and I sat in the lone chair, placing the water bottle on the floor beside me. "I've always had a really hard time swallowing things. They always want to come back up."

He glared at me angrily as he continued to wipe his face. After a moment, he reached behind him and grabbed another paper towel, handing it to me. "Open your mouth," he said, leaning forward, but he was careful to keep his distance.

I stood and positioned myself so my body completely shielded the water bottle. I opened my mouth wide. "Not this time, though," I said. "I think they're going to stay put."

He didn't say anything. For good measure, I turned my head to the side and coughed again, and he finally took a step back.

As I turned, I caught a glimpse of the water bottle. I couldn't see the pills, but the water had turned a dull, murky white.

Shit.

"Sorry about that," I said again, searching for a way to distract him. "Hazards of the job, huh?" He stared at me for a moment but didn't say anything, so I kept going. "How long have you been working here?"

His eyes narrowed, and he crossed his arms in front of his beefy chest. "Why?"

"Just making conversation, man."

He watched me carefully. "About a year."

"Wow. So a year of late nights and idiots like me choking in your face," I said. "I hope it's worth it."

He took a step closer and snarled. "Look, I know you're here just to make a few bucks, but you can be assured that there is nothing more important than the work we're doing." We stared at each other, and the tough-guy facade broke, just a bit, and I saw there was more to the man than his gruff responses or scarred face. He wasn't just muscle. Maybe, just maybe, I could get a little bit more out of him.

"And what's that?" I asked, shrugging when he narrowed his eyes. "Hey, man, I'm just curious."

"You should keep your curiosity to yourself."

"Oh," I said casually. "So you don't really know what's going on, huh?"

"What?"

"I mean, they probably don't give the details to just *anybody*."

I could see the annoyance flit across his face. "Good thing I'm far from just anybody," he said, and I could see he was rattled. He covered it quickly. "You may want to sit down," he said, and the conversation was over. He turned and headed toward the door.

"What?" I asked, but he walked out of the room and closed the door.

The pills he'd handed me had to be some kind of sedative...but why? I sat back in the chair and used my foot to push the water bottle as far beneath it as possible.

I scanned the ceiling for signs of cameras but didn't see anything. Still, they could be watching me. I closed my eyes and leaned back in the seat.

Less than a minute later, I heard a light, barely noticeable knock on the door, and it opened. The woman who'd led me to the room came in and stared at me for a second before frowning.

"How are you feeling?"

"A little dizzy," I said, praying it was the right response.

She nodded. "You seem to be holding up pretty well."

"Yeah, I...I don't know." I took a chance and leaned forward, placing my head in my hands.

Too much?

Too little?

The woman placed a hand on my shoulder, and I looked up. "If you'll please sit here," she said, gesturing to the exam table.

She walked to the wall and pulled down a blood pressure cuff. As she lifted my arm, she peered into my face. "Are you sure you're okay?" she asked.

I nodded. "Yeah, I'm just... I'd like to lie down."

"Okay, no problem," she said, nodding. "Do you need some water?" I saw her glance around the room.

I cleared my throat loudly. "No, I'm fine. No more water. Just… lying down would be good."

"Sure," she said, helping me recline back onto the table. She continued taking my blood pressure.

"What were those pills I took?" I asked.

"Oh, just a mild sedative, but it doesn't seem to be affecting you too much, so that's a good thing," she said with a smile. "You're a big guy. I guess you can handle it."

I smiled and nodded. "Yeah, sure."

"Now I need you to relax." She was silent as she read the dial. "Blood pressure is normal." She lowered the cuff and grabbed a penlight from her pocket. She shined the light into my eyes and looked closely.

"Are you a nurse?" I asked.

She smiled again. "Something like that."

I was about to ask another question when a noise made us jump. She turned to a phone on the wall, which I hadn't noticed when I'd walked in. The woman picked it up, her attention still trained on me.

"Hello?"

As she listened to the person on the other end of the line, her eyes widened, and she stared at me for a moment.

"Okay." She waited a few minutes, and then she frowned a little. "Okay," she said again. She hung up the phone and came back to me. "It's time for you to move on to the next stage."

"What was that call about?"

"Nothing," she said quickly. Too quickly. "There was a problem with one of the recruits in the waiting area, so they've sent him on."

Recruits?

I nodded. "Where are we going?"

"You're going to see the doctor now."

"The doctor?"

"Yes."

I wanted to ask her if she meant Christine, but I bit my tongue. I looked down at the flimsy robe I was wearing. “Like this?”

“Yes, that’s fine,” she said. She seemed to be in a hurry. She opened the door and waited for me to get off the table to follow her. She wasn’t nearly as gentle as she had been before.

What had changed?

I pretended to feel a bit woozy and stood slowly, following her out. But she wasn’t wasting any time. She walked down the hallway, and I moved quickly to keep up with her.

Did I even need to pretend anymore?

Had they figured me out?

She turned down another hallway and stopped. I was again surprised at how big the space was compared to the outside.

She pushed opened a door, and I was greeted with another waiting room, this one empty.

Across from where we stood, on the far wall, was a single office.

“You can head into room three,” she said, pointing. “Whenever you’re ready to begin.”

With that, she walked out. When I heard a soft click, I spun around, reaching for the handle.

Too late. She’d locked it.

I banged on the door, but there were no sounds from outside.

What the hell?

Why had she locked me in?

Was this really part of the “experiment”?

I walked slowly toward room three, my eyes searching for cameras. The rectangular waiting room contained only a few pieces of furniture: an old desk with stacks of file folders on it, two armchairs, and an empty, floor-to-ceiling metal bookcase near the door against the far wall.

When I reached that door, I put my hand on the handle and waited.

Taking a deep breath, I pulled it open.

And froze.

Standing in front of me, hands at her sides, was Christine Sharpe.

I walked farther into the room. "What the—"

Before I could finish, two hands were on my back, pushing me roughly to the ground. I choked on my breath as I hit the floor.

Groaning, I rolled over slowly and stared up into a man's face.

Scarface.

"Oh, hi again," I said as I began to push myself up, but he stepped forward and placed a foot firmly on my chest. "Oh—okay, got it. I'm supposed to stay down here—"

"What are you doing here, Francis?" Christine asked, and I looked back and forth between them. This room was even smaller than the one I'd just left, but it was filled with filing cabinets and overstuffed bookshelves. "Why'd you come?"

"I don't know. I think a better question is what are *you* doing?" I said. "What are you hiding here?"

Christine didn't answer my question but continued to stare down at me. "Why did you sneak in?"

"Because you're hiding something, and we both know it," I said again. "Do you know where my father is?"

"No!" she said quickly.

"Look, all I want is to find Alex and that kid," I said. "I came here tonight to talk to you, and I saw the men coming in through the alley. What's going on here?"

"It's none of your business, Francis," she said. "You had no right sneaking in. It wasn't just to talk to me. I saw you on the cameras the minute you entered the premises, but I wanted to see what you were up to."

"You know what *I'm* up to," I said, cursing myself for having missed the cameras. "I just told you. But that's a lot more than I can say about you."

"I said it's none of your business!"

She locked eyes with Scarface and made a small motion toward the door, communicating something with her eyes that I couldn't understand. He said something back, a whisper under his breath, and she shook her head. I watched them debating their next move, and I knew it might be my only opportunity to act.

Without giving myself time to overthink it, I reached up and grabbed Scarface's ankle firmly, pulling toward me as hard as I could.

He looked down at me, startled, but it was too late.

As he lost his balance, he reached out to brace himself on a filing cabinet. He missed, the underside of his arm striking the corner of the cabinet, and he cried out in pain. As he landed, gripping his arm, I pushed myself up and bolted toward the door.

"Francis!"

I reentered the waiting room and immediately stepped to the side, flattening myself against the wall near the door.

Christine rushed out behind me. "You can't get out that way," she said as she walked out. "I had Giselle lock it so we could speak."

As she turned back toward the office door and caught sight of me, I quickly pushed the door shut. I rushed forward and grabbed hold of the tall metal bookcase on the other side of the door. I breathed in and yanked as hard as I could, toppling it. The crash it made was deafening, and we both froze.

Christine blinked as the sudden separation between her and her scar-faced friend settled in.

"I know," I said. "And it's time for us to do just that."

A loud breath escaped her, and then she turned, rushing for the other door, but I was right behind her. I grabbed her by the waist and pulled her down with me. We fell backward, and she kicked and pushed, struggling to get free. I pinned her on her back, her arms on either side.

"What the hell is going on here?" I screamed into her face, and we both breathed heavily as we stared angrily into each other's eyes.

"Tell me, Christine, or I'll go to Delroy, and we'll turn this place upside down. You know we'll find out anyway."

She'd stopped struggling, and she shook her head from side to side. Tears were forming in her eyes, and they began to creep down her cheeks, pooling along her chin.

"It's not my fault, Francis, please," she said, and she closed her eyes for a moment. There was a loud banging noise as Scarface tried to open the office door. Christine took a long, slow breath and then opened her eyes again. "It's not my fault."

"What are you talking about?" I asked. "What's not your fault?"

"I…" She let her head fall back against the floor, and I could see the resolve leaving her. The banging continued, but we ignored it. Christine stared at me, and her next words were as heartfelt as they were chilling.

"Nothing was supposed to happen to the boy."

In that instant, everything stopped.

"What?" I asked, leaning closer to her face. "Christine, what are you talking about?"

The expression on her face was one of resignation and defeat.

Then the words began to spill out of her.

"Nothing was supposed to happen to Matthew, I promise. We were going after Sam Farr. He was the one we were supposed to take, not Matthew! We never meant to hurt anyone." Her voice broke, and a sob escaped her. "I don't know what happened, Francis. I don't know what your father did, I swear. But we have to find that boy *right now*—before something really bad happens to him."

Chapter Twenty-Two

I scrambled off her in shock, and we sat there for a moment in complete silence.

"What are you talking about?" I finally asked. "What did you *do*?"

She didn't move, but I could see her swallow. "We weren't going after the kid," she whispered. "I would never, ever be a part of that."

"But you would take part in the abduction of an adult?" I was spiraling, and as much as I pretended to be calm, I could barely think straight.

Sam Farr had been the target?

Dr. Christine and Alex had planned to…

"Look," she said. "When I told you I've known your father for a long time, and said it was about a year, well…it's more like five years. We're very close. He's more than my patient," she said, looking down. "We met at a conference called Fit Minds, a mental awareness and hypnosis conference that's focused on the works of some ostracized scientists, some who deserve to see the light of day, but for whatever reason, they haven't been allowed to."

"When was this? Exactly."

"I told you, five years ago. In San Francisco. We were both living there at the time."

I tried to hide my surprise, but she caught it right away.

"You didn't know your father moved to San Francisco for three months, did you?" she asked. "He lived in the Haight. We met at that conference, and something just clicked. When he told me he was moving home to Illinois, I came with him."

She looked at me, and when I didn't respond, she sighed and kept talking. "I don't know who came up with the idea, really. I guess it was him, but I was there, right from the beginning, and looking back on it, it all seems so ridiculous, but when you're in the moment… It was one of those things somebody said and nobody disagreed with, and I guess it was a joke at first, but then we were doing it, and nobody stopped it, and—"

"Planning an abduction isn't something you just 'fall into,'" I said, cutting her off. I waved my free hand around the room. "What exactly are you doing here?"

"You wouldn't understand."

"Christine."

She sighed again and turned from me, training her eyes on a painting on the wall. "We're testing some of the theories of the late D. B. James," she said. "He's—"

"D. B. James?"

She turned back to me. "Yes. You've heard of him?"

The books.

All over my father's cabin.

"Sort of. Go on."

"He has theories on repressed-memory therapy—theories that were quickly shot down by the major medical associations and said to be another quack theory. But it's not true. It really works."

"Repressed-memory theory?" I asked. "Sounds like a fancy name for 'follow the shiny pocket watch until you feel sleepy.'"

She frowned. "You've been watching too much television," she said. "Tell me, what do you know about hypnosis?"

I shrugged. "I know you make people stare at an object until they pretend to fall asleep. And then they get up and do crazy things."

She laughed, but there was no humor there. "It's surprising to me how much misinformation still exists about my profession," she said. "Hypnosis is not just fodder for bad Wisconsin Dells's stage shows. It's used around the world for a variety of clinical practice. Thousands of people have any number of ailments cured each year by it."

"Like what?"

"What isn't it used for? Hypnosis can help with weight loss, smoking, fear of public speaking, fear of flying, even gastrointestinal issues."

"How is that possible?" I asked. "You can hypnotize yourself to go to the gym?"

"Look, if you're going to make fun of it, I'm not going to—"

"No, continue," I said. "Really."

She took a deep breath. "Hypnotherapy is as clinical a science as any other. The goal of it is complete focus, and the elimination of distractions that keep patients from concentrating on their problems. When you're able to focus your attention like that, you can begin to uncover problems and find solutions. Hypnosis isn't something that's done to you. I think that's the biggest misconception. You do it to yourself, with the help of an experienced, licensed professional."

"Unless you're in Vegas."

"Francis..."

"I'm sorry," I said. "But if hypnosis is used to treat all of these conditions, then why are you guys being so secretive? What was all of the outrage over D. B. James?"

"Hypnosis is generally approved for therapeutic purposes, like those I mentioned. But one of the more"—she paused to think about her word choice—"cutting-edge areas has always been, and remains, repressed-memory therapy."

"And that's...?"

"Using hypnosis not to treat a current condition, but to bring to the surface past memories that may be buried deep in the psyche, and that are otherwise unreachable."

"Shit," I said. "That's what you're trying to do to Sam Farr."

"Yes," she said softly. She cleared her throat. "The major psychological organizations say that the biggest threat is false memory retrieval. The idea that instead of bringing buried memories to the surface, repressed-memory therapy creates false ones, which can obviously have terrible effects on a vulnerable patient."

"Of course," I said. "Convincing little Carrie that she was abused as a child."

"That doesn't always happen."

"Always? So you admit it's possible?"

"Well, there are always risks with any medical procedure," she said.

"But, Christine, there's got to be a better way to do this. How come you're not going through the proper channels, and risking your career—not to mention the health of these men—if you're so sure you're on to something."

"Because that's what happens with cutting-edge research. Nobody wants to admit it, but do you think that they haven't been tested by the time these studies get full review-board approval and are signed off by some idiot in a suit in Washington? Do you think hardworking researchers would go through all of that effort without some proof, some evidence to know they're on the right track?"

"Yes, I think people wait and do things the right way all the time," I said.

"You'd be surprised, Francis," she said. "Were you doing things the right way by coming here tonight?"

I flinched but didn't respond to her question. "What about the rest of your team? Do they know exactly what they've gotten into?"

"Only Eric and Giselle," she said, motioning to the office door, which had gone silent. I wondered if he could hear us. "You met

Giselle earlier tonight. Alex and I hired them both about a year ago to do basic research, but then I realized I could trust them, and I filled them in. Neither knew anything about Sam Farr before they got here, but they were willing to help, for Alex's sake. And you have to understand who comes here for our studies. These are people at points in their lives where they are willing to put up with the risks for the benefits, and the possible rewards for science and mankind."

"You mean, these people are so desperate for a buck they are willing to sign whatever consent form you put in front of them and promise never to talk about what you did to them? Don't try to romanticize what you're doing here."

"You act like we're cutting out a body part," she said. "Our work involves therapies to help retrieve buried memories that are lost in the recesses of the mind. We pay them for a psychiatric session that they couldn't afford anyway."

She shook her head and stared at me, her eyes pleading. "You have to believe me when I say I had no idea Alex was going to take the child instead of Sam," she said. "I can't believe he did this."

"What exactly was the plan?"

"About a year ago, Alex told me he wanted to try to use one of D. B.'s therapies on Sam Farr—to access his memories from the night your brother died."

"He's fucking crazy."

"I thought the same thing at first. There was no guarantee it would work, first of all, and there was no way we could get him to do it."

"So you decided to abduct him?" I said, staring at her in disbelief. "Of all the options, of course that's where Alex would land."

"Well, it wasn't that simple, Francis," she said, moving even closer to me. "Your father tried everything else. He even talked to Sam about it, told him he knew of a technique that might help."

"When was this?"

"A couple of months ago, Alex went to Sam's job. At the gas station. He told him he just wanted to get to the truth, and if Sam didn't have anything to hide, he should be open to it."

"And let me guess, Sam Farr blew him off."

"Of course—"

"I would have too," I said.

"Yes, of course," she said again. "I wasn't that surprised by it, but Alex was. He couldn't understand it. He thought if Sam was truly innocent, then why wouldn't he want to know exactly what happened? Why wouldn't Sam do that for him? He told Sam he could end it all right then, just by agreeing to give it a try."

"Could he, though?" I asked. "Let's say Sam Farr had agreed to undergo your…repressed hypnosis—"

"Repressed-memory retrieval."

"Whatever. And let's say it showed he didn't know any more than he's ever said he did. Would my father have let it go? Would he have been satisfied?"

"I don't know," she said softly.

We sat there silently for a few moments before she continued.

"So, Alex told me there was really only one other option. That was to make Sam do it. He said he would do all the work. He just needed a couple of us on the scene to help out."

"What was the plan?"

She closed her eyes, shook her head. "It was staged perfectly."

"Not perfectly enough."

"No," she said, opening them again, and a tear rolled down her face. "Giselle, Eric, and I were there. We'd been following Sam and Matthew every Wednesday for weeks. Giselle and Eric were supposed to make sure that the two were separated. I was supposed to take the kid and help him get home. That was my role. He was going to be scared, because his father was missing. I was just going to get him to the main path, where the police could find him and take him home. We talked about that. But when I came around the bend, there was only Sam Farr there—no child. And your father was nowhere to be found." She straightened her shoulders. "I swear to you, I had no idea he was going to do that. If I did, I would never have agreed to help."

The story seemed believable, and yet I still wasn't sure I could fully trust her.

She'd done a pretty impressive job of lying to my face the other day. Maybe she'd had more to do with what had happened to Matthew than she wanted to admit. "How would it have worked anyway, even if you were able to get Sam Farr?" I asked. "I mean, you'd need him to buy in, to agree to do it, right?"

"Well, the sedative you have to take is very strong. That would have gotten him settled and ready. And then we would have begun the procedure right away. And your father and I can access the results from secure systems, from anywhere. We would have been long gone by the time he woke up."

"But even if it worked, wouldn't Sam Farr remember it after the fact? He'd know what you did to him."

"Some patients remember the therapy; others don't," she said. "That's a chance we were willing to take."

"He would have definitely remembered the kidnapping though."

"Again, a chance we were willing to take."

"Why were you so eager to help my father do something so horrible?"

She paused and looked at her hands. "You probably think I'm some dumb woman in love, right? A lovesick puppy? I'll admit I am in love with your father, but that's not why I helped him. I helped him because I understand what it feels like to be a parent with questions. I lost a child once, a long time ago, and I have a lot of unanswered questions about it. If this therapy could help another parent, well... I was willing to do what it took. Especially since we had no plans to hurt Farr."

"Besides the kidnapping."

She looked away and shrugged. "We weren't going to hurt him."

"Can you think of a reason Alex would take Matthew instead?" I asked. "I mean, he wouldn't want to try the procedure on him, right?"

"No, of course not. It wouldn't make sense. He wasn't there that night, obviously. Besides, D. B.'s techniques have never been tried on children. Only adults." She sighed. "I should have known something was going on."

"What do you mean?"

"That morning...there was something wrong with Alex, and he wouldn't tell me what it was. I should have pushed him more," she said, shaking her head. "I should have said something sooner, but I was so scared, both for the boy and for Alex. I know he won't hurt Matthew, not intentionally. You must know that, Francis. Your father is not a bad man. But if something happens to that little boy...I'll never be able to forgive myself."

She looked up at me, and I could tell she was waiting for something from me, some kind of reassurance.

"You're right," I said. "If something happens to him...I doubt you ever will."

Chapter Twenty-Three

Tuesday, 6:00 a.m.

The light that slithered through the cracks of my blinds the next morning prodded the corners of my eyes. I cringed as I woke up, and the flood of memories from the previous day washed over me.

When I'd gotten home, Amy had been sound asleep in bed, and I'd hit my own only a few minutes later, too exhausted to do anything else.

And, maybe, hopeful that all of it would just go away.

But when I opened my eyes, it wasn't gone, and the pain in my head was so severe that I rocked from side to side for a few minutes before I could summon the energy to sit up.

The news I'd learned the previous day was enough to make me want to give up all together—to leave the investigation in the hands of Delroy and the other cops. To head to the *Lansing News* today and do my job and let Alex figure it out on his own.

But it wasn't just about Alex.

It was about a nine-year-old boy.

Everything I'd learned convinced me that my father was responsible for Matthew's disappearance.

I dropped my feet over the side of the bed and leaned forward, struggling to push past the pain that throbbed between my temples. I massaged my eyes.

What did my father want with Matthew Farr?

Did he have it in him to kidnap a child?

Or hell, an adult?

And maybe the biggest question of all: What went wrong that day in the park?

I checked my messages and groaned when I heard the first one.

"Hello, Mr. Scroll. This is Principal Erin Murray. I got your message about wanting to meet. I'll be at home for most of the morning, so feel free to come by. Though I'm not sure what this could be about."

She left her address and hung up.

The meeting seemed pointless now after what Christine had told me, and yet I couldn't just ignore what I'd learned from Matthew's teacher. Pulling myself out of bed, I headed to the bathroom to shower and change. I owed it to the Farrs to go check it out.

Amy walked out of her room as I stepped out of the bathroom.

"Hey," I said, squaring my shoulders. I'd missed her yesterday, and now here she was, right in front of me.

I could do it.

I had to do it.

"Hey."

"Ready for today?" I asked. "Sorry we didn't get to talk yesterday about how things went."

"It was cool," she said.

"I know a new school is never easy—"

"It's not a big deal," she said, eyes wide, raising both hands to stop me. "I don't need the lecture."

"Of course it's a big deal. New classes, new teachers, new friends..."

"I'm fine," she said. "Really."

"Okay…" I took a deep breath. "Well, look, there's something I wanted to talk to you about."

She seemed to think for a moment before nodding. "Actually, me too."

I paused. "Really? Okay, you first."

It wasn't stalling. It was polite.

"Well, I was wondering—and it's no big deal if not…"

"What?"

"Well, you know that hashtag campaign for Matthew Farr? The missing boy?"

My chest tightened, and I tried to keep my expression neutral.

"Oh, right. Of course."

"I was wondering if you thought about doing any articles on him. Something a little more in-depth than what's out there. See, I have some really cool ideas for how to mobilize people to get out and look for him. I just think we could do more, you know?"

I swallowed. "Oh," I said. "Well, you know, the paper already has someone who's covering it."

"You mean the piece they had yesterday? It was total crap. It was the same information they already had on Channel 3, repurposed. Who wrote that?"

"Her name is Cynthia Green. She's actually really good at her job—"

"Come on, Dad. You could do better than that. Matthew has been missing for almost a week now. We need someone to really dig into it and not be afraid to ask the hard questions of the Lansing police. What do you think?"

I recognized the ambush way too late, and I stood there with my jaw open, struggling to come up with a reasonable response.

And knowing it sure as hell wasn't time to dive into Scroll family history.

"Well, I'm not sure I can—"

"You could try."

"I mean, I could ask, but—"

"It's not that hard, Dad," she said. "He's missing. Can you imagine what that little boy is going through?"

I blinked, stunned by how passionate she was.

Amazed and impressed.

But also terrified.

"Look," she said, grabbing her bag off the couch and heading toward the door. "Are you going to write a story, yes or no?"

"Well, it's more complicated than that."

"No, it's not," she said as she opened the front door and spun around. "It's just a suggestion. I thought maybe you'd be able to pitch something better, something that will actually help us find him. But maybe I should try another paper."

"Amy—"

"Don't worry about it," she said. "I'm going to the library after school, so don't wait for me for dinner." With that, she left.

Shit.

In my mind, I ran after her and said something, anything, because anything would have been better than standing there and pretending like there was nothing else to say.

In reality, though, I stood there with my feet glued to the floor, my self-respect waning with every second that passed.

After a few moments, I pulled myself together and reached for my phone. I dialed Detective Jeffries again, pretty sure I was close to using up all my favors.

"Can you get me the info for a Detective Younger?" I asked.

"Younger," he said slowly. "He retired a long time ago, but I think I have his number." He gave it to me, but before I could hang up the phone, he asked, "Any news? You find Alex?"

"Not yet," I said. "But thanks a lot. I think I'm getting closer."

I dialed the phone number, and a man answered on the third ring.

"Hello?"

"Um, this is Francis Scroll. Am I speaking with Ken Younger?"

There was a long pause on the other end of the line, and I thought he'd hung up.

"Hello?"

"Yes," he said calmly. The way he said it reminded me of his measured demeanor in the hallway outside my parents' bedroom.

"Do you remember me?"

"I do," he said. "How can I help you?"

"I was wondering if you had time to meet with me later today. I know it's really short notice and out of the blue—but it's important."

"About your father, right?"

He wasn't beating around the bush, so why should I? "Yes."

"All right," he said after a moment. "Meet me at Lady Beth's on Carmen and Jeffery. You know where that is?"

"I can find it," I said. "Thank you."

I was finishing getting dressed when my front buzzer rang.

Walking quickly to the intercom, I pushed the button, swallowing the lump in my throat. "Hello?"

"Hey, it's Cam."

I relaxed and buzzed her in before walking over to my front door and cracking it open. Stepping back into the living room, I flung the couch pillows into place and grabbed a plate off the living room table. I was putting it in the sink when I heard Cam's voice call out.

"Francis?"

"Hey," I said, walking out of the kitchen.

"Hey." She stood in the entryway. She was covered from head to toe in winter gear, her hat pulled low over her eyes, her peacoat stopping midcalf. Her bright-purple scarf was still wrapped around her mouth. She would punch me if I said it out loud, but she looked adorable. She was holding a Dunkin' Donuts bag in her hand and a tray with two coffees. "I was heading to the office, and I stopped to get breakfast. I got your usual too and was back in the car before I realized you weren't coming in. I decided to drop it off."

I moved closer and took the food from her. "Thanks a lot. Really. Will you stay and eat?"

"Nah, I have to get going."

"You came all this way just to drop this off?" I asked with a smile.

She shrugged. "Don't make a big deal out of it," she said, shifting the scarf away from her mouth. "How are you holding up?"

The words "I'm fine" were on the tip of my tongue, but they wouldn't fall out. I was pulled back to the moment outside my father's cabin when I wanted to tell her everything and didn't.

With her standing in front of me, her eyes wide and filled with concern, I didn't stand a chance.

"I'm falling apart," I whispered.

She took a deep breath. "I know. That's why I came. I'd be worried if you weren't falling apart. It's allowed, you know. You're allowed to lose it over something like this."

I nodded.

Cam placed a hand on my arm. "I'm not going to tell you not to keep searching for him because I know that's what you have to do," she said. "But make sure you're eating and sleeping and spending some time with Amy. Okay? You're no good to Matthew or Alex or anyone else if you fall apart."

"Okay," I said. "Thanks."

After Cam left, I downed the sandwich she'd brought me and finished getting ready before grabbing my jacket and heading out the door. On the way out, I grabbed the stack of photos of Matthew and Sam that I'd taken from my father's cabin. I stared at their faces, father and son, and the love evident in their eyes was breathtaking. Shoving the pictures into my pocket, I bolted out the door.

Thirty minutes later, I turned onto Principal Murray's street. I pulled up in front of her condo and parked the car. It was a large, modern building, and it was clear to me that she wasn't doing too poorly on her principal's salary. I got out of my car and walked up to the front door to ring her buzzer.

"Yes?"

"Ms. Murray, it's Francis Scroll."

There was a pause, and then I heard the buzzer. I walked into the building and moved quickly past the elevators. I took the stairs up to the fourth floor.

She was standing at her front door when I came out of the stairwell. I struggled to breathe normally, but the four flights had winded me. She looked different than she had in the office the previous day. She wore a pair of jeans and a tank top, and her long hair was around her shoulders. She was in her midforties, but from a distance, she passed for a woman of twenty-eight or twenty-nine.

She smiled as I approached, but it wasn't a kind smile.

"That's what took you so long. There's nothing wrong with the elevator, you know."

"I know," I said, stopping that line of conversation before it went any further. "Thank you for meeting with me. I will only take a few minutes of your time."

"Of course." She stepped back to allow me to enter. I walked inside and marveled at how beautiful her apartment was. It was tastefully decorated, and everything seemed tailor-made for the space. No item was out of place, almost like no one lived in the apartment.

I was always impressed by people who were able to keep apartments like that, free of clutter, mail, or dishes. As if their homes came out of a home-and-garden magazine. I wondered if they actually kept their homes that way or if they pushed all of their junk in a closet whenever they were having a visitor.

"No problem," she said, looking at the delicate gold watch on her wrist. "I remembered your name when I got your message. I met you in the office on Sunday, though I think you used a different name."

It was a simple statement, not a request for a response, and I nodded. Before I could come up with an explanation, she continued speaking.

"I'm not sure what exactly I can help you with. You seemed so urgent in your messages that I made this time for you, but I really don't have long. So, I would offer you coffee, but I'm sure you understand..."

"No, thank you," I said.

"What can I help you with, Mr. Scroll?"

"I am looking into the Matthew Farr case."

She nodded. "Yes, I figured as much. It's all we can talk about or think about. It's so sad. Though, again, I'm not sure I can tell you much. And we've been urged not to talk to the press."

"I'm here unrelated to my work at the *News*," I said.

"I see. Still, you'd do better speaking with his teachers. They know him a lot better than I do."

"Well, if you don't mind me getting right to the point—"

"I'd appreciate it."

"—that's not what I've heard from some of the teachers."

It was as if I'd slapped her. Her eyes widened briefly, and she leaned back against the counter. "Wow. So I guess when you said get straight to the point, you decided there was no need at all for any type of pleasantries, huh?"

"I'm sorry—"

"No, don't apologize. Look, I don't know Matthew Farr very well at all," she said, "contrary to what you may have heard from someone else. I tend to know the troublemakers around school, and Matt was far from that."

"Matt?"

She frowned. "Yes, it's a common nickname for Matthew, Mr. Scroll. Just what are you here for? Since we're not beating around the bush anymore."

"I've been told by some of the teachers, and I won't name them—"

"I wouldn't expect you to."

"—that there have been some concerns in the past about your interactions with some of the students, and that Matthew Farr's name has come up."

She didn't say anything for a moment. "I can't believe you would come into my home and speak to me like that with a straight face. It's appalling, really."

There was something in her expression, something I couldn't quite read, but it was almost…

Amusement?

"I don't mean to offend," I said, watching her carefully. "I only intend to get some more information from you about these accusations so I can put this to rest and move on to the next lead. Is that fair?"

"Absolutely not. But I will answer any questions you want before asking you to kindly leave my apartment and never come back."

"Can you explain your relationship with Matthew Farr?"

"I told you. I'm the principal at his school, and he is a student there. Nothing more, nothing less."

"I'm told he worked with you on some of the school programs."

"A lot of students have. I'm sorry to say that I don't get to work closely with all of the students who sign up for projects, but I'm grateful to every single one of them, and I let them and their parents know that."

"Would it be fair to say that you spent more time with him than you have with some of the other students?"

"Sure. More than some, less than others," she said.

"How about Todd King?"

Her eyes narrowed, and her cool demeanor faltered for a minute. "That's an incident I don't wish to—nor do I have to—discuss with you. It's been put to rest, and everyone involved knows I did nothing wrong. I care about my students, Todd included, but I won't let you or anyone else make it out to be something vile."

She tapped her foot quickly, and I could tell that mentioning the boy's name had made her uncomfortable.

"Can you tell me where you were last Wednesday between three and four o'clock p.m.?"

She paused, and I could see that for the first time in the conversation, I'd said something to truly throw her off. She'd expected the questions about her relationship with Matthew, and maybe even Todd, even though she'd pretended to be appalled.

But this had surprised her.

"Wait a minute," she said. "You came here because you think I had something to do with Matthew's disappearance? I swear, those teachers can gossip, but this is beneath them. For your information, I was working on a fund-raiser. At my church."

"You were there the whole day?"

She bristled. "From nine o'clock a.m. until about seven o'clock p.m. It's our largest fund-raiser, so it takes a lot of my time. That day, and today, are the only two days I've taken off all year. It's actually where I'm going after this."

"And there is someone who can vouch that you were there?"

"I cannot believe you're asking me these questions. Like I'm some sort of punk and this is an episode of *Law & Order*. That child is nine years old, and what you're insinuating is not only inappropriate, it's disgusting. But yes, there are about thirty 'someones' who will tell you I was at the church."

"Okay," I said.

She gave me the name of the church, and I thanked her for her time.

As I turned to leave, she stopped me. "You don't think there was another way you could have gone about getting the information you wanted without coming here to accuse me of something so horrible and embarrassing me this way?"

It was a fair question, and I couldn't help but think back to my conversations with Kira Jones.

Twice in two days I had been accused of being a jerk.

"All that matters to me is finding the kid," I said.

"Yes, I see," she said. "Well, I can tell you this. I will find out what teachers are responsible for this little visit. And it won't be a great day for them when I do. So it's nice that you have a singular focus on finding Matthew Farr," she said, "but don't make the mistake of thinking you can do or say anything you want while you're playing detective, Mr. Scroll. Everything has consequences."

Chapter Twenty-Four

I drove away from Principal Murray's apartment, replaying our conversation over in my head. She was hiding something, that was for sure, but I didn't think she had anything to do with Matthew Farr's disappearance.

And where the hell did she get off judging me?

I was just trying to do the right thing.

Right?

I checked my watch and headed toward Lady Beth's to meet Detective Younger. I pulled up outside and parked the car, just a couple of minutes before eleven.

I walked into the restaurant, scanning the room for any sign of Younger. I had a picture in my mind of what he looked like, but of course, he could have changed a lot in the past twenty years.

"Sit anywhere you like," the host said with a huge smile on his face, and I nodded. I looked at the faces of the other diners, but no one stood out, and more importantly, no one looked up as I made my way through the tables. I chose a booth by the window and sat down.

"Can I get you something while you wait?" a woman said, approaching with a menu.

"Just a coffee."

She nodded and walked away.

I didn't have to wait long. About a minute or two later, the door to the restaurant opened, and a man walked in. Immediately, I knew it was him. It wasn't just because he looked the same—stern features, intense gaze, and lanky stride—but there was something in his expression that took me straight back to that night twenty-three years ago when he practically dragged me out of my parents' bathroom. We stared at each other, and he nodded slightly before making his way to my table.

"Francis," he said, shaking my hand before sliding into the booth. His handshake was assertive and firm. "Long time." He was wearing a long wool coat, much like the one I remembered him in, and a tan scarf.

"Yes, it has been," I said. "Thanks for coming to meet me."

"No problem," he said, looking up as the waitress approached with my coffee. "I'll have one of those too," he said, then he turned back to me. "So, where do we start?"

"I don't know," I said honestly. "I really just wanted to meet with you because I think you may be one of the few people who still keeps in touch with my father. I'm hoping that means you have some sort of clue about where he might be."

If he was surprised that I knew it, he didn't react.

"When's the last time you saw him?" I asked.

He smiled, just slightly. He didn't take his coat off, and I wondered if that was because he didn't plan to stay long. "About a week ago. We had lunch. It was a long time overdue."

"What did you talk about?"

He smiled again. "You mean, did he tell me he had plans to kidnap a child? No, he didn't."

"Detective Younger, I'm just trying to figure out what the hell is going on."

He maintained eye contact for a moment, and then took a long, slow breath. "Look, Francis," he said, and he paused as the waitress returned with his coffee.

"You guys need anything else?" she asked.

"No, we're good for now," I said, and she left. I leaned forward, waiting for him to finish.

"Obviously, I wouldn't have come today if I didn't have something to share," he said, "but before I do, I need your word you'll check it out before you go to Delroy."

"I—"

"Your father and I don't talk that much anymore, but we became good friends after the trial. I'm worried about him. I just need to know you're looking out for him."

I didn't know what he meant exactly, but it seemed like the right time to agree. "Of course," I said. "That's why I'm here."

He took another deep breath.

"You know when people say things like 'I could just die right now' or 'Just shoot me' and they don't really mean it? That's what I thought was happening."

"What do you mean?"

"When we met, your father told me he wanted to try some sort of memory retrieval on Sam Farr. That he was working with some psychologist he thought could help. I actually thought it was a good idea," he said.

"You did?"

"Yeah," he said. "I know I shouldn't say that, but I did. See, I've always understood your father's need to know what happened that night. As you know, I testified against Sam at the trial. And to this day, I still think he had something to do with your brother's death. I'll never backtrack from that. But at the end of the day, our legal system did what it was supposed to do. He had a fair trial. I said my piece—everyone did. And he was found not guilty. That's where I couldn't agree with Alex."

"But you just said you thought what my father wanted to do to Sam was okay."

"I did, if Sam agreed to it. I didn't really see the harm. Sam should have wanted to prove us wrong, once and for all."

"But he didn't agree."

"No, and when Alex said he could *make* him do it, I thought he was joking. And then a week later, I saw the news."

"You didn't tell anybody?"

"There's nothing more to tell than that," he said. "I have no idea where he is. When you called, I figured I owed it to you to tell you that. But that's all I know."

I left the diner disappointed that he hadn't been able to tell me anything I didn't already know. As I was driving home, I made a split-second decision and turned the car toward my mother's. She still hadn't called me back, and I knew my best bet was simply to show up. I pulled up in front of her house and got out of the car.

I was about halfway up the walkway when I first heard the yells.

"I don't know why I've put up with this for so long. You're nothing but a whore, and an old whore at that!"

My mother's boyfriend, Jimmy, came bursting out the front door, and a suitcase came flying out behind him. His face was red, and he was carrying a backpack and a tool bag. He barreled down the front steps in my direction.

"Hey," I said, bumping into him with my shoulder and catching him off guard. He had been so focused that he hadn't seen me approaching. Jimmy stopped and stared at me, his eyes wild and angry.

"What the fuck is going on?" I asked. "Is there a problem?"

He continued to stare for a moment, frowning.

"You're kidding me," he said, spinning back toward the house. "You called your son?" he yelled. He turned back to me. "Nothing, man. I'm out of here. She's a liar, and a cheater, but I didn't do anything to her."

My mother walked out onto the porch. She was crying and carrying something in her hands, but she seemed okay. I hesitated before letting Jimmy walk by and hurried up the steps toward her.

My mother's eyes were glassy as she stared off the porch at Jimmy. She turned and looked at me for a moment, and I could tell she didn't quite recognize me. When she did, she gasped and stepped back, grabbing the corners of her sweater.

"Francis," she said, and it was nothing more than a whisper. "What are you doing here?"

"Is everything okay?" I asked, stepping closer. "Did he hurt you?"

"No, no," she said, moving back and looking down the stairs as Jimmy got in his truck and drove away, his belongings still scattered over her front lawn.

"No, he didn't." She watched as his car disappeared. "I mean, he hurt my heart!" she yelled after him and then turned back to me. "What the hell are you doing here? You should leave. It's obviously not the best time." She looked at everything on her porch in disgust before turning and walking quickly back to the house.

I followed her, stepping over the discarded items, my mind racing as I tried to piece together what had just happened.

"You wouldn't answer, so I just came here on my own."

"Well, I told you, I'm fine, but I need a little privacy right now."

"Please, Mom, I need to talk to you."

"I don't want to talk about this."

"Okay, look, your life, it's none of my business. If you say he didn't hit you, I'll believe you—"

"He didn't," she said. "Goodness, am I not allowed to get into a fight? If he'd hit me, you know I would have hit him back, that asshole."

"That seemed like a pretty big fight."

"Francis..."

"Okay, but it's not why I'm here. I swear. I need to ask you something else. It's about Dad."

She stopped, her eyes narrowing. "You've never said those words to me in your life."

I bristled. "Well, I'm saying them now."

She finally sighed and led me into the house. It looked a lot different than the last time I'd been there—it was almost completely barren, with only a few scraps of furniture in each room.

"Are you moving out?"

"No," she said. "And I thought you were going to only ask questions about your father. If you ask me one thing about Jimmy, I swear, I'll have you out of here—"

"Okay," I said. I swallowed. She walked into the kitchen, and I counted—actually counted—the pieces of furniture we walked by.

Six.

She gestured to one of the chairs in the kitchen, and I hesitated before sitting down. She grabbed a coffee mug and leaned back against the sink. I was pretty sure there wasn't coffee in the cup.

"Did you hear about the Farr boy?"

She froze and then nodded. "Yeah, I did." She shook her head. "It's terrible. That's why you're here?"

"Yeah, they think Dad took him."

"What?"

"Yeah," I said. "That's all they can talk about."

"I try not to watch the news all that much. Why the hell would they think that? I mean, Alex's lost it, but he wouldn't go that far."

"He was following them around."

"He what—"

"He'd been following their family for about a month."

"No..."

"I found pictures of them too. In his cabin."

She blinked and looked down at the mug.

"You knew about the cabin, didn't you?"

Her eyes refocused on me, and I couldn't tell if she was angry, sad, or nothing at all.

"Of course I knew about the cabin. Nobody has that many golf trips."

I shifted uncomfortably.

"Well, the family is accusing him of taking the boy."

"Did you go by Alex's place?"

"Yeah, he's missing. It looks like he hasn't been there in a couple of days."

"Wow, I didn't know that. I haven't talked to your father in years, since before he moved to San Francisco."

"You knew about that?"

"Of course," she said. "And don't look at me like that. Like I was supposed to send you a card and let you know. This is the first time you've come here in years, and it had to be for something like this."

"I've tried to call you."

"Sure. Sorry I missed that one call, that one time, Francis. I need to sit down." She walked out of the kitchen. I got up and followed her to the living room, where she sat on the couch. I sat beside her in an armchair, the only other piece of furniture in the room. She grabbed the remote control and flipped on a small television, which was sitting on the floor beneath the windows.

"Great, more news," she mumbled, gesturing to the TV. For a few moments, we sat silently, watching as a news anchor droned on about the upcoming snowstorm.

"So what did you want to ask me?" my mother finally said, turning to me. "Do I think he did it? Not really, but I wouldn't be surprised by anything anymore."

"Mom, I know this is going to sound weird, but…was Dad ever into…hypnosis?"

She laughed and then frowned, tilting her head to the side. "You're right, that is a weird question."

"It's an important one. Was he?"

"Your father was into a lot of things once. I guess hypnosis was one of them..." She looked out the window, but her unfocused eyes landed on nothing in particular. "Yeah, I think he was into it for a while. He was into any- and everything. He was sure there was some way to find out what happened to Lucas. Positive. I think he would have tried magic if he could," she said with a laugh. "If he could summon Lucas back from the dead just to ask him what happened, I think he would have." She shook her head and continued to stare out at nothing.

"I need you to think long and hard. Did Dad keep any notes about the hypnosis? Did you ever hear him talk about someone named D. B. James?"

She frowned and seemed to give it some thought. "D. B.? No, that doesn't sound familiar. I do remember that he was reading about a lot of different therapies, but he didn't want us to know about them. I found some papers under the bed once, and he got so mad. He said something about how it was so dangerous, he never wanted me or you to get involved. I let it go."

"Do you know where those papers are?"

"No clue. It wasn't the kind of thing I packed up and took with me after the divorce. I'm assuming they went into the trash."

"What was so dangerous about them?"

"I don't know," she said. "I know he used to talk about someone, a name..."

"You sure it wasn't D. B.?"

"No, it was John something. The last name was a flower... I think it was Rose. Yeah, John Rose. From Tennessee. He always talked about the Rose incident. I don't know—it was something he really didn't feel comfortable talking to me about. But I once heard him talking to someone on the phone."

"But you don't know who that was?"

"No."

I sighed.

"What's this all about, Francis? You're freaking me out."

"They really think he had something to do with it, and I'm just looking into it."

"And Delroy is okay with that?"

"No, he doesn't know. And it needs to stay that way."

"Why are you doing this now, Francis?" She reached into her pocket and pulled out a pack of cigarettes. "I mean, don't you think it's a little too late to get involved? We could have used you fifteen years ago."

I shook my head and shrugged. "I'm sorry, but I'm here now. And everybody I talk to seems to want me to let this go."

"Maybe because it's too late to try to fix our family." She leaned back in her chair and tapped her hand against the armrest. "You know, Francis, sometimes, it's best to leave the past in the past. What good is opening this stuff up now going to do?"

"I'm trying to find that little boy, wherever he is."

"So this is all about Sam Farr," she asked, frowning.

"No, it's about Matthew Farr. You do realize there's a child involved, right, Mom? Even if you still hate Sam…you can't possibly want to see his son hurt?"

She didn't say anything and looked past me out the window.

"Of course I hope they find that boy," she said as she put the cigarette in her mouth and lit it. "But am I going to go out of my way to help? No, Francis, I'm not. If you think that makes me a bad person, that's too bad. I wish I had something left in me to care about Sam Farr's son, but I don't. I hope you find him, but that's the extent of my involvement in all of this. Now"—she cleared her throat—"I really wish you would just let all this go."

We both turned back to the television, because there was nothing left to say. After a few moments, I stood up to leave.

"I guess I should get going."

My mother nodded, standing, but she didn't say anything.

I was stepping into the entryway when the sound on the television changed.

The previous monotone sounds of the anchor reading off a teleprompter changed suddenly to a loud, up-tempo song. We turned back as a colorful breaking-news graphic flashed across the screen.

"We have an update for you now in the case of missing nine-year-old Matthew Farr," the on-screen reporter said, and my mother gasped. My stomach lurched as we both inched back toward the screen.

"We have a report that Matthew Farr has been spotted at a gas station off of I-57 in Midlothian!"

The reporter said this eagerly to the camera, one hand pressed against a microphone in her ear. "I repeat, missing nine-year-old Matthew Farr has reportedly been seen at a gas station on I-57 in Midlothian, and..." The anchor paused to look at someone off camera.

"Oh my God," my mother said, the cigarette falling out of her mouth and landing on the carpet.

There was an awkward lapse as the reporter continued to speak with someone behind the camera. Finally, she turned back to the screen. "Yes," she said, nodding, "and it's now confirmed he is said to have been seen in the presence of his accused kidnapper, Alex Scroll. Authorities are on their way to the scene at this very moment."

Chapter Twenty-Five

Tuesday, 2:00 p.m.

The gas station off exit 349 in Midlothian was a rundown relic, with a modest but steady stream of daily traffic. There was nothing special about it: eight pumps, an attached truck stop, and a convenience mart with row after row of dust-covered potato chip bags. As I exited the highway, I slowed behind a line of cars that were pulling up to the station, which was anything but ordinary today. Cars were tucked into nearly every empty space—news vans, police cars, and the rest of us inching closer to the action. People swarmed about, and I sucked in a breath, terrified I'd see Alex's face in one of them, and the nightmare would reach its inevitable conclusion.

The cars behind me were honking viciously, and I strained to see what was holding up the line. A lone police officer stood where the road turned into the station, and I could almost see the sweat on his brow, the panic on his face. He held up a hand to direct traffic, but there was nowhere for the cars to go. After a few more moments of waiting, I veered off onto the barely existent shoulder and hopped out of the car.

"Hey, you can't leave that there!" someone yelled, but I ignored the voice and began to jog toward the station.

I stepped onto the concrete and tried to fight through my rising anxiety as I moved through the crowd. I was sidestepping a man with a camera on his shoulder when I heard someone call my name.

"Francis?"

I spun around and was eye to eye with Cynthia Green, the reporter from the *Lansing News*, who was covering the Farr case.

"Did they find him?" I asked immediately, the words thick in my mouth, the sun and the swarms making me nauseous, but the need to finally know overwhelming.

"I don't know," she said, her eyes scanning the crowd behind me. "I just got here too. What are you doing here?" She seemed suspicious.

"I was just in the area and heard the report," I said. "Thought I'd stop by."

She narrowed her eyes. "Cam has been trying to box me out for a year now," she said. "Did she send you?"

"No," I said, surprised at her concern. Cam hadn't mentioned anything to me about that. "I'm just curious about what happened to that little boy."

"Yeah, sure," she said.

She turned to walk away, and I followed closely, craning my neck to see over the crowd. Most of the action seemed to be taking place near the small building, and I inched closer. I was about twenty feet away when I spotted a tall figure with salt-and-pepper dreadlocks.

Delroy.

My first instinct was to duck out of sight, but I froze when I saw who he was with.

A young boy with sandy-brown hair stood with his back to me, staring up at Delroy. As I watched Delroy lean down to say something to him, the blood drained from my face, and I dug my fingernails painfully into my palms to keep from passing out. Delroy put his hand on the boy's shoulder and said something else before straightening to face the reporters.

"That's enough!" he yelled. "Keep moving! There's nothing else to see!"

I opened my mouth to take in more air, and suddenly, everything was swimming in front of me, the people moving too fast, the sun blazing too hot on the back of my neck. As I moved into Delroy's line of sight, he looked up, and the expressions that crossed his face ranged from confusion, to anger, to exhaustion.

"Francis," he hissed as I moved closer. "What the hell are you doing here?"

I didn't respond but stepped forward, my eyes glued to the back of the boy's head.

"Francis?" Delroy said again, shifting uncomfortably. "You shouldn't be here."

I kept going because nothing short of a cannon was going stop me.

I had to see his face.

As I stepped around the boy, Delroy put out a hand to stop me. "Francis!" he hissed again, a hair away from my face, but I didn't stop. I turned to face the boy, my shoulder bumping against Delroy's.

Then I looked down.

Into the face of—

A boy I'd never seen before.

Small, red nosed, and teary-eyed.

Scared.

But not Matthew Farr.

"It was a false alarm!" Delroy whispered in my ear. "What are you doing here? Are you nuts?"

I couldn't move, my gaze still locked with the boy's, who stared up at me helplessly.

"I heard on the news—" I started.

"It wasn't him," Delroy said. "This kid got on the wrong Megabus in Chicago and got dropped off here. The mom's on her way here now."

"And Alex?"

"No sign of him at all," Delroy said, watching me carefully. "He's not here, Francis. Somebody saw the kid wandering and assumed it was Matthew Farr. Not sure why they called in the pair, but people do it all the time. It's not the first false alarm we've gotten in the last couple of days, but it's the first one that got leaked to the press."

I took a deep breath and nodded.

"Still doesn't explain what you're doing here," Delroy said. "I thought I told you to stay out of this."

"I had to come, Cap," I said. "You know that."

His expression softened, just slightly, and he nodded. "Go home, Francis."

I turned to leave. As I moved back through the crowds, I fought feelings of both disappointment and relief. They hadn't found Matthew Farr with my father—but they were both still missing.

Cynthia Green was standing near the outskirts of the crowd, scribbling into her notebook.

"Hey," I said approaching her, and she looked up in annoyance. "It wasn't him."

"I know that," she said. "This case is so frustrating."

"Yeah. I'll see you at the office."

"Okay," she said, her eyes still on her notepad. I turned to leave, but she kept talking. "Oh, by the way, some guy was looking for you."

I froze. "What?"

She looked up. "The gas station attendant. He was looking for you earlier. He saw me talking to you and asked who you were."

"What did you say?"

She frowned. "What do you think I said? I told him who you were." She shrugged. "Weird guy. He got really hung up when I told him your name was Francis Clarke."

"What do you mean?"

"He just kept asking if I was sure that was your name."

"Where is he?" I asked, searching the crowd.

"I don't know. He was here a minute ago."

"Okay," I said, stepping backward. "Thanks."

I turned away from her and walked quickly toward my car. I didn't know who Cynthia had spoken to, but it wasn't the time or place to find out. As I approached my car, I took care to keep my head down, my eyes focused on the ground in front of me.

I almost made it.

I was opening the driver's-side door when I heard the voice call out, hesitant, but loud enough to make the scattering of individuals nearby look up.

"Francis? Dude, Francis, is that you?"

My hand still on the door, I considered just getting in the car and driving away. But the voice was so close. I lifted my head only slightly in the man's direction.

As I did, my heart skipped a beat. Peering at me from across the roof of my car was a thin man with a receding hairline. He squinted, carefully examining my face.

The man was wearing a striped shirt with a Citgo name tag on it.

"It's me, Jerry Morton!" he said. "From junior high! I knew that was you. What's all this Clarke nonsense? Didja change your name?"

"Oh, wow," I said, ignoring the last question. "Hey, Jerry, long time." I started to lower myself into the car but stopped as he continued talking, walking around the front of the car.

"What are you doing here?" he asked, shuffling along. "Looking for your dad? This is crazy stuff, huh?"

"Yeah, pretty crazy," I said. "Hey, I've gotta r—"

"Francis? Francis Scroll? I thought he looked familiar." It was a woman's voice, and I turned to see a reporter rushing in my direction, followed by a tall woman carrying a camera.

I froze, stunned, as everyone around me seemed to spring into action.

"Francis Scroll?" the reporter croaked out again. "Is that you? Quick, Maxi, get a shot!"

I realized what was happening too late.

I lifted my arm too late.

I recognized the newsworthiness of my presence at the station that day too late.

"Francis Scroll!" the reporter said, rushing around the car and placing a hand on the driver's-side door. "Can you make a comment for the record? Have you heard from your father? Please tell us if you have any information at all about where we can find Matthew Farr!"

I stared at her, mouth open, unable to think of a single response.

And then the flashes went off.

Chapter Twenty-Six

I backed up against the car, watching as the crowd seemed to multiply around me, faces peering at me, expecting something of me, waiting for me to react. I dropped into the seat, pulling on the door, which was still gripped in the reporter's fingertips.

She latched on tightly and frowned, daring me to slam her fingers in the door. We eyed each other, and I shook the door angrily.

"You want to let go," I said quietly. "Trust me." Her eyes widened slightly before she finally removed her fingers and stepped back.

"Mr. Scroll!" I heard someone yell through my window, but I had already started the car to leave. I pulled a tight U-turn, narrowly missing a car in the oncoming lane, and stepped on the gas.

I glanced in the rearview mirror as I drove away. Delroy stood near the edge of the crowd, watching.

I picked up my phone and dialed Amy's number, cursing as it went to voice mail.

"Ames, call me back as soon as you get this."

Shit. Whereas some people have good luck, I have Jerry fucking Morton. I tried not to think about what would happen if Amy saw the news before I got to talk to her. As I sped back toward Lansing,

I remembered she'd said something about going to the library. I would check the apartment first and then head there. She was just getting out of school, so she had to be at one place or the other, or somewhere in between.

She wasn't at home. I tore through the apartment, calling out her name, but was met with only silence. I grabbed my keys and raced back out the door.

Ten minutes later, I screeched into the parking lot of the Lansing Public Library and jumped out of the car. As I climbed the steps, I took a deep breath and tried to force myself to calm down. The building was modern, clean, and almost completely empty. There were only two main rooms, and it took me a matter of seconds to realize she wasn't there. Standing in the building's atrium, I dialed her again.

"Don't do it..." her recording started.

I sighed and hung up and began walking toward the exit. My hand was on the door when a thought crossed my mind, and I paused, turning back to the massive room.

It would only take a few minutes...

I strode quickly through the aisles toward the computers. Sitting down at an empty station, I typed in "John Rose, Illinois."

I frowned at the list of more than two thousand references. Shit. That wasn't going to work. What else had my mother said?

He'd originally been from Tennessee.

I did the search, and that came up with more than four hundred sources. A quick scan of them told me I wasn't going to find much that way, either. I typed in his name with my father's name, just in case I would get lucky, but that came up empty.

Shit.

Who was John Rose, and why had my father been so obsessed with him? And more importantly—did that have anything to do with Matthew Farr? With shaky fingers, I typed in the names of both John Rose and D. B. James.

Three results.

Okay.

It was a start.

I clicked on the first one, and the headline made me gasp out loud.

"Possible Suicide Linked to Hypnosis Quack."

It was an article in a small newspaper from 1974. The database only gave me access to the titles and publications, and I looked at the other results. One seemed to be completely unrelated, but the other...

...was an obituary for John Rose.

I took the titles of both articles and publications up to the librarian. "You have to use the reels," she said apologetically. "We haven't digitized those files yet." I followed her into a small, dusky room and waited. A few minutes later, she came back with a box of reels. Fitting them on the projector took another ten minutes, since she'd never done it before.

"I just started here last year," she said. "Nobody has had to look through these."

"Not even a student?" I asked, surprised.

"Nope," she said with a shrug. "You're the first."

I started by looking for articles about D. B. James. All of them listed him as a controversial researcher, except for one, published in a book about legendary scientists on the fringes. It heralded his work and called him forward thinking and innovative. The rest were local reports, and one was about some of his funding being taken away for "unsanctioned research practices."

I leaned forward and began scrolling through the newspaper until I came across the obituary.

In loving memory of John Rose, gone too soon, loving husband and father of four.

He'd died in 1974.

There was no cause of death listed.

I put in the other reel and began scanning it for more information about the article I'd seen in the database.

It was one of the last articles in the paper, and I slowed as I scrolled.

It showed a picture of John Rose—a nice-looking man with kind eyes and a soft smile. He had his hair combed to one side, and he looked uncomfortable in front of the camera. Was this him?

As I read the article, my pulse quickened.

John Rose had committed suicide—he'd jumped off a bridge. His death had been linked to…

D. B. James.

According to the article, D. B.—described as a "noted hypnosis quack"—had done some experimentation on John Rose. The writer noted that Rose had been a loving and happy father and husband, but after the treatments, he'd changed.

"He was a different person. We will be seeking justice for this," his wife had said in the article. I wrote down her name so I could look her up later.

What did it mean? How much did my father know about John Rose, and if he did know it, were he and Christine really using the same procedures?

I walked out of the room and thanked the librarian for her help.

I sat in front of the computer again and typed in *Marian Rose* and *1974*. Only one article came up.

She'd died six months after her husband.

I sat back in my chair and stared at the obituary. What the hell was going on here?

The connection between the three men was becoming clearer. My father had been looking into the work of D. B. James, but as he told my mother, he wanted us to stay far away from it.

And that had to be because of what had happened to John Rose.

Did my father think there was any truth to the accusations

about D. B. and his theories, and if so, had he been willing to expose Sam Farr to them anyway?

And maybe even Matthew Farr?

Alex couldn't be that crazy.

Could he?

Chapter Twenty-Seven

The Sam Farr Story

By: K. L. Jones

DRAFT v.9—Not to be shared without express permission of author, K. L. Jones

Sam Farr was ready.

He stood in the middle of Lucas's bedroom, his briefcase open on the bed in front of him.

The puppets were arranged neatly inside.

Sam stared at them as he paced back and forth, rubbing his hands together. Everyone was waiting for him downstairs.

It had been an incredibly long dinner party, and things hadn't been going so well with Lucas, but none of that mattered. It was time for his show. He had to forget about what had happened outside.

Don't think about it!

It would only make him mess up, and that was the last thing he wanted to do. He'd been practicing too long to mess up. This was his first big audience, and he needed to show them what he could do.

He heard the music and laughter flowing from downstairs, and he knew he needed to hurry up. He didn't want them to move on and forget about him. He tapped his thumbs quickly against each of his knuckles, loosening up his fingers.

Pointer, middle, ring, pinkie. Pointer, middle, ring, pinkie.

Sam stared at the display of puppets in front of him.

Nine of them, arranged neatly in the case, each one wrapped in a variety of plastic and bubble wrap he'd gotten from his mother. The wooden puppets delicately held on to the strings, and he smiled as he picked up two of his favorites.

Sam laced his fingers through the strings. He loved all of the puppets, but it didn't make sense to try to show off all of them, not tonight. No, he had to choose, and choose well.

Holding the two puppets, he squared his shoulders and walked out of the room.

Sam walked to the stairwell and placed one foot on each step, descending slowly, watching as the puppets swayed back and forth in his hands. Even in the dim light of the hallway, he could see the glimmer of the paint on them, and it made him smile. His parents had given him the puppets as a gift, and every Sunday afternoon, he took his time polishing and protecting them.

Now it was finally time to show them off.

Sam reached the bottom stair, turned, and walked slowly into the living room. Quickly, the conversation stopped. Everyone looked up at him—his mother with a wide smile, his father with something that looked a little bit like concern. The Scrolls were also watching him. Kate Scroll stood and walked over to the CD player and shut it off before turning to give him an encouraging smile. The complete and utter silence was suddenly deafening. Francis Scroll was in a corner reading a book, and he glanced up for only a second before putting his head back down.

The only person who wasn't there was Lucas. He didn't want to come down to see the puppet show, and that was fine with Sam.

He didn't need to be friends with him anyway.

"Why don't you come over here," Kate Scroll said, standing up.

Sam nodded, walking toward the front of the living room. It was so quiet all of a sudden, and he felt that he was breathing too loudly. Could everyone hear him? Could they tell how nervous he was?

"Thank you for sharing this with us," Kate said, putting her hand on his shoulder.

Sam smiled again, wishing he could hug her, and maybe cry for a minute, just to get all of his nerves out. She smiled back as Sam turned around at the front of the room to face his audience.

Sam cleared his throat and began to speak.

"Thank you all for coming this eve. What you are about to see, you will not believe!"

As he spoke, his hands shook viciously, and he swallowed, attempting to calm himself down.

There's no way you can perform if you're this nervous, Sam.

He lifted the first puppet and cleared his throat to continue, but when he spoke, all that came out was a nervous squeak. Sam stopped abruptly, feeling the words getting stuck in his throat.

The entire room was staring at him now, and he suddenly felt dizzy, his mind spinning out of control.

His father stood up and walked over to him. Crouching down in front of him, Brian Farr leaned forward. "Hey, are you all right?"

Sam looked up at his father and nodded.

"Hey, it's okay," his father said, staring at him meaningfully and putting a hand on the back of his head. "You're okay. Just take a deep breath and get started."

Sam nodded and opened his mouth, breathing in deeply as his father made his way back to his seat.

He lifted the puppets and tried again.

"This is the story of Annie McDerney," he started, his voice still shaky, but he locked eyes with his mother, and she smiled and nodded. Feeling a surge of energy, he tried to continue. "You will be very surprised by the magic inside, so please sit back and get ready for a ride!"

He made eye contact with his father, who was watching him carefully, and he swallowed again, trying not to cry. His father had always cared so much about him, he knew, even though he was hard on him sometimes. Brian Farr nodded once, and it was the encouragement Sam needed.

He turned and marched behind the couch and sat down on the floor.

Lifting both hands high above him, he let the puppets' feet dangle until they hit the top of the couch.

Now he was out of sight.

Now he was in his element.

Now he could begin.

"Once upon a time, there was a woman named Annie McDerney, and she walked through the streets, looking for her lost ring." As he spoke, he lifted Annie up and down, spinning her around to look near her feet.

Sam's nerves subsided even more.

"She looked under every trash can and behind every rock. She even looked inside Old Mr. Maggin's sock!"

The room erupted in laughter, and Sam froze. He couldn't believe it.

He cleared his throat and kept going. He was moving

through the story quickly now—too quickly, and he'd have to work on that—but besides that, it was flawless.

Perfect.

They loved it.

He moved left and right, along the length of the couch, making the puppets jump and turn and spin and dance, all to an animated, happy crowd. He didn't know it, but they were encouraged by the wine they'd been drinking, and the laughter flowed easily out of them. But for Sam Farr, it was a magical moment, and he was confident his performance was one of the best he'd ever done, even better than the countless times he'd practiced alone, no pressure at all, in front of his bedroom mirror.

He was close to the end of the skit now, and he continued to move with ease.

"Would Annie McDerney ever find her missing ring? Or would she have to say good-bye forever to her favorite thing?"

He spun Annie around again for one of her final moves—when he felt something snag.

Wait—

Annie had caught on something.

Maybe one of the pillows on the couch?

Sam frowned and poked his head up over the back of the couch to see what had happened. As he did, his mother rose out of her chair and approached him, her eyes on the place where Annie's leg had hooked on a tassel that flanked one of the couch's ornate pillows.

She didn't make it in time.

As Sam lifted himself up and reached forward to see what was wrong, there was a loud, cracking sound that seemed to reverberate around the entire room, filling it, stopping it, and bringing the laughter to a grinding halt.

Sam leaned forward and watched as Annie's leg remained entangled in the tassel, even as he pulled his arms back, lifting the rest of her body out of harm's way.

It took a moment for what had just happened to sink in.

Then Sam dropped his head back, closed his eyes, and began to wail.

Chapter Twenty-Eight

I was jogging up the front steps to my apartment building when a figure came barreling out of the door.

Amy.

The moment I saw her, I knew I needed to be the one to speak first, to say everything I'd been trying to tell her since she first arrived. But I could barely form a complete sentence.

"Amy," I said, my throat tightening and my heart rate speeding up, "I've been trying to call you. Where have you been?"

Good job. Start by blaming her.

She stared at me with those huge brown eyes, and instantly, I knew she'd heard. She stopped a few steps above me and just stared, and the pain and disappointment on her face was crippling.

"Amy," I said again, but she started to move, stepping around me without a word.

"Ames, wait." I reached for her arm, and when she spun around, there were tears in her eyes.

"For what?" she asked, and I knew they were the angry kind of tears, not the sad ones. "Wait for you to come up with some lame way of saying 'I was going to tell you'?"

"But I was going to—" I stopped myself, gritting my teeth and racking my brain for something else, anything that would get her to trust me.

"It's too late for that," she said. "Mom told me everything."

No.

Of course her mother hadn't told her everything. She didn't *know* everything, and even if she did, it wouldn't be in her nature to tell any of the parts that wouldn't make me look like a complete jackass.

"She did?" I asked. "What did she say?"

"She told me about how you changed your name and never bothered to mention that you were a *whole different person* when you were a kid. What the fuck?"

"I didn't lie to you, Ames," I said, and I knew I should say something about the cursing, but it seemed we were beyond that. "I just never found the right time to tell you about my family. You have to understand that."

"I *have* to understand that?" she asked. "Alex Scroll is my grandfather. Did he take Matthew Farr?"

"No," I said quickly, and I stopped myself, spreading my arms in front of me. "I mean, I don't know. I don't think so. I really wanted to tell you, Ames. I just couldn't find the time—"

"You know when would have been the right time to tell me? How about before I found out on the news during a freaking... missing person case? How about then?" She shook her head, and she stared at me with what seemed to be a mixture of disbelief and disgust. I don't know which one hurt more. "I gotta go," she said.

"Where are you going?"

"Out," she said.

"Where?" I said again to her retreating back, and I stood there helplessly as she darted down the block.

I dialed Reba, cursing as her voice mail picked up. In her singsongy recording, she told me she was sorry she missed my call and that it was very important to her. I hung up without leaving a message. As much as I wanted to be mad at her for talking to Amy before I got a chance to, I knew that wasn't completely fair. Amy had gone to her mother because she didn't trust me, simple as that.

She didn't trust her own father.

And I had no one to blame but myself.

Chapter Twenty-Nine

Tuesday, 5:00 p.m.

As I sat down at the kitchen table, the silence was interrupted by the trill of my cell phone. I glanced at the phone and sucked in a breath when I saw the screen.

It was a Skype call.

From Reba.

I answered it. "Hey," I said, and I glanced at the screen momentarily as her fuzzy picture formed.

"Hey," she said. "Where are you?"

"At home."

"Oh, okay." She paused for a moment. "Look, I know you're pissed—"

"I'm not, actually," I said. "I was at first, but then I realized Amy had every right to ask you. And you had every right to tell her."

"Why didn't you?" Reba asked. "Tell her, I mean. After all these years, and with her moving back to Lansing, she was bound to find out. What were you thinking?"

I gripped the phone tighter. It wasn't at all out of character for Reba to call out of the blue and ask me why I couldn't get my shit together. She'd asked me that same question in some shape or form every day we were married.

"I thought it would be more fun this way?" I asked and immediately regretted it. She didn't respond, and I cleared my throat. "I really don't know. How are things out there?"

"They're okay," she said. "Actually, you know what? They're really good. Sorry. I know it's not the best time for you to hear it, but...I don't know, I'm doing great. There's really no sense in lying about it."

"There are things that make less sense," I muttered.

"What?"

"I said that's good. I'm glad to hear it."

"Thank you, Francis, that's big of you." She said it emphatically, as if to drive home the importance of us being able to be happy for each other. "Things are going to work out. Amy will get past this. And hey, I guess you can thank me for taking some of the heat off of you, right?"

I frowned and glanced at the phone. "What do you mean?" I asked.

"I—" She stopped herself. "Wait, she didn't tell you what happened?"

"Amy?" I asked. "She barely spoke to me. Just said she'd talked to you, and that she knew everything about my parents."

"Oh, wow," she said. "Well, I guess I shouldn't be surprised she didn't say anything." She paused. "Amy asked if we could speed things up. She wanted to move here now, instead of waiting until she graduates. She said she's been practicing her Italian."

"She has," I said, my stomach dropping as a wave of emotion washed over me. "What did you say?"

"I told her the truth," Reba said. "With everything going on, I couldn't just say 'stay with your father; it's for the best.' She's a young woman now. A smart one. She deserved to know the truth."

My stomach flipped again, and the dread began to build. "What did you *say*?" I asked again.

Reba sighed. "I told her that in all honesty, it made sense for her to stay in Lansing. I'm on shoots every day, seven days a week. I can't remember the last time I got a full night of sleep. It's just...I don't think it's what she would expect. And who knows where I'll be two years from now."

"Damn it, Reba—"

"It was time to tell her," she said. "She's been keeping a little calendar in her purse, an actual *printed* calendar, Francis. Checking off the days until senior graduation. Counting the seconds until she can move out here to live with me! I saw it right before she left New York, and I almost said something right then, almost told her that—"

"You don't want her to come."

I realized we'd never said the words out loud, but we'd both known it, from the very beginning. We'd worked hard to make Amy feel like it was a tough decision, that we'd both struggled with it, but that simply wasn't the case. Not by a long shot.

"I told her I didn't think it's what she would expect."

"You said it yourself, she's a smart girl, Reba. She can read between the lines."

"And maybe that's okay," she said. "It's real life. Amy gets it. Why can't you?"

"It's not okay," I said angrily. "I don't care if she acts like a thirty-year-old. She's still a child. And you know what you're supposed to do? You're supposed to make your child feel like you want them. No matter what. Even if you're tired, or you're stressed, or you have a fucking photo shoot, or you move across the world, or you haven't gotten a full night's sleep. You do whatever you can to make them feel like the only thing you want in the world is to be by their side, even if you can't."

"That's nice," Reba said, and I felt pitied and ridiculed at the same time. "But not every parent is trying win parent of the year.

Some of us are just trying to make sure our kids turn out okay. Or that they don't turn out to be serial killers. Or *kidnappers*—"

I hung up the phone.

I've never once in my life hung up on anyone, but that was the last straw. I tried Amy, but it went to voice mail again. As I hung up, I was surprised to see the phone ring again, almost immediately. I frowned when I saw the unfamiliar number on the screen.

"Hello?"

"Hi, um…it's Patricia Smith-Bilks from Carmen Elementary School," a woman's voice said.

"Hi," I said. "Is everything all right?"

"Yes," she said. "I assume you went to see Principal Murray?"

"Yes," I said. "How did you know?"

"She sent out an email to a few of us, blind cc'd. Basically saying she was going to get to the bottom of who is spreading rumors about her. I figured you must have gone to see her. Anything helpful?"

"Not really, Ms. Smith-Bilks. She has a pretty tight alibi. She was at her church fund-raiser all day."

"Oh," the woman said with something that sounded like disappointment. "So they confirmed it? That she was there all day?"

"Well…" I started. "I haven't gotten a chance to ask, but I'm sure the story is easily corroborated—"

"You didn't go by the church?" she asked. "What have you been doing?"

I opened my mouth to respond and then shut it.

There was no good way to answer that.

"I've been following other leads," I finally said. "Quite frankly, much more promising than Principal Murray."

"Look," she said, "maybe I'm wrong about this. But you owe it to Matthew to make sure, right? At least go by the church. Please, for me. You can still make it out there today. They're working on the fund-raiser, and they're usually there until nine or ten o'clock."

I sighed. "All right," I said. "I'll go by and see if anyone is willing to talk to me. But I think you may be wrong about this."

We hung up, and I left for the New County Church, my mind still on Amy. No wonder she'd been so upset when I'd seen her outside of the apartment. She'd just found out she was trapped.

With me.

As I walked into the church, I was overwhelmed by the buzz of activity. People swarmed everywhere. A woman with a clipboard was yelling something across the room. She groaned and turned around and wrote something down. While she was still hunched over her board, I walked up to her and stood nearby, waiting for her to finish.

She looked up and frowned. "Yes?"

"Hi," I said. "I'm looking for Principal Murray. She told me she might be here today."

"Erin?" she asked with a frown. "No, I think she had something else to do today."

I nodded. "Do you know if she was here last Wednesday?"

"Last Wednesday?" she repeated, thinking about it. "Yeah, I'm pretty sure she was. That was our first big day of planning, and our Volunteers Opening Reception. Pretty much everyone was here."

She finally took a good look at me. "And you are?"

"I'm Francis Clarke," I said. "I am following up with some questions about a missing child at her school."

"Oh," the woman said, a look of surprise covering her face. "That's terrible. Well, yeah, I think you'll do better finding her at home, or at the school. She works pretty much 24-7. You could ask Diana, though," she said, pointing to a woman who was on the far side of the room, arranging a bunch of trays on a table. "They are both overseeing the food-and-drink committee."

The woman rushed off before I could thank her. I turned and walked across the room.

Diana looked up as I approached.

"Hi," I said. "I'm Francis Clarke. I was told I could look for Principal Erin Murray here."

"Erin's not here today," she said, rolling her eyes. "I mean, she's not the only one around here who has a full-time job, but this is the one week that almost everyone in the church takes off. It's such a huge deal."

"So this is your centennial celebration?"

"Yes," she said proudly. "We're raising the bar this year. Do you live in the neighborhood? I hope you'll be here."

"Yes, uh, sure," I said.

"Now why don't I believe that?" she asked. "You should definitely come. It's going to be a fun afternoon of food, music, and fellowship." She saw my expression and smiled. "But that's not why you're here today. Tell me, why are you looking for Erin?"

"She is helping me on a case, about one of the children at her school." I shrugged in a way I hoped would get her to stop asking questions. "I'm sorry to say it's confidential."

Her eyes widened, and I saw a glimmer of excitement there. "Oh, wow. Are you a cop?"

"No, a journalist," I said.

"Oh. Well, no, she's not here," she said. "She barely ever is."

"Sorry?"

"Oh, nothing," she said, and I could tell she wanted me to probe. Some people have an uncanny ability for that—making it seem like you're pulling something out of them when they're really dying to lay it all out there for you.

Diana was not one of those people. Her desire to talk about Principal Murray was completely obvious, but I played along.

"You guys work on the food-and-drink committee together, right?"

She scoffed. "Yeah, I guess you could say that. I mean, her name is on the program, but I mean…you know how these things can be."

I smiled and leaned forward a bit. "Let me guess, you're doing more than your fair share of the work?"

"Hey, you said that, and not me," she said with a laugh. "I mean, I'm no school principal, so I get that. She's really busy. I work part-time at the bowling alley, so it's not the hardest job in the world, but we all have lives outside of these things. And if you're too busy, that's fine. But then you don't sign up to help, you know? If you know you're not going to be able to put in the time."

"I know exactly what you're talking about. I've been there many times before. It's pretty frustrating… Well, I won't go down that road," I said, giving her a knowing look.

She chuckled and shook her head.

I cleared my throat. "But she was here last Wednesday, right?" Diana handed a bowl to a boy who walked up, and he carried it to a table on the other side of us.

"Um, last Wednesday?" She tilted her head to the side. "Yeah, she was. I mean, I guess you could say that. She was here long enough to sign in. But that doesn't mean she was actually here." She turned to the boy again. He stood behind her, waiting for some direction, and she frowned slightly. "Terry, could you count out ten packs of the spoons? The large packs." He nodded and walked away.

"What do you mean?" I asked.

"Well, like I said, she was definitely here in the morning for sign in, because that's how you officially get credit for being a part of the committee," she said. "But midday, I couldn't find her. I couldn't find anyone, to be honest. I really needed some help, and it was just me doing it all. Do you know that I had to lift a thirty-pound printer up two flights of stairs all by myself?"

"So you think she left?"

"Who? Erin? I have no idea. All I know is that right after lunch, I was looking for some help bringing in some of the utensil trays, and I ended up having to ask someone from another committee to help me. And then, when the printer showed up, Erin was nowhere to be found. But that's not surprising. It's been happening for years. I hate being on committees with her." Diana's eyes widened, and she covered her mouth with her hand. "Listen to me, just going on and on, and in a church nonetheless," she said with a smile.

I smiled back. "I won't tell anyone."

She nodded. "I don't mean to be rude. It's just a lot, and this fund-raiser is so important to us."

"I can see that," I said. My phone buzzed, and I looked down at it, hoping it was Amy. I sighed when I saw it was Reba. I silenced it and brought my attention back to Diana. "I'll get out of your hair. Just one more question. Did you see Principal Murray when she returned? Was there a time that you saw her back here that evening?"

"Of course," she said. "We had our opening reception that night. Around six o'clock. And she sure was back for that. Smiling and eating and laughing with everyone. She was in a great mood, actually. As if she hadn't been here all day working and was exhausted—because she wasn't. The rest of us looked horrible in the pictures because we'd been sweating and doing our jobs, but I guess she went home to change." She shook her head.

"Well, I know you will pull off a great event, and the food and drinks will be top-notch."

She smiled. "Thanks, Mr. Clarke. If she does show up this evening, I'll let her know you came by."

"That's okay," I said. "Don't worry about it. I'll catch her another time."

"All right," she said, and she turned to get back to work. "Oh, before you go. One last plug—it's going to be a great event."

"Thanks," I said with a smile, and I turned to leave. I had been hoping that visiting the church would simply clear up any questions

I had about Principal Murray and allow me to focus on Alex, Christine, and their botched plan.

But my visit had opened a lot more questions.

Principal Murray had disappeared from the church from about one to five p.m., during the exact time that Matthew had gone missing. The park was an easy fifteen-minute drive from the church.

It seemed so unlikely, so ridiculous.

So impossible.

I didn't need any more fake leads; I needed answers.

But the truth was she'd lied.

She'd wanted me to believe she'd been at the church all afternoon, and she hadn't.

So what was she trying to hide?

Chapter Thirty

Tuesday, 8:00 p.m.

I arrived home that night to an empty house.

I walked into the kitchen and found a handwritten note on the counter from Amy.

"Back tomorrow."

I crumpled the note in my hand. I picked up my cell phone and dialed her number. After four rings, it went to voice mail.

"Call me back," I said into the phone. "You can't just not come home, Ames. Come on."

I hung up and walked quickly from the kitchen toward Amy's room. I knew she'd kill me if she found me in there, but I needed to know where she'd gone and who she was staying with.

I'd messed up.

But I was still her father.

I went into her bedroom and looked around the neatly tucked blanket on her bed and the stack of books on her desk. She'd gotten her cleanliness from her mother, it seemed. Her laptop was on her desk, and I stared at it for only a moment before walking over and picking it up.

Just a quick glance…

I sat on the edge of her bed with her laptop. It was asleep, and when I opened the lid, the fan started up as the computer came back to life.

I blinked as the screen loaded in front of my face.

Madison Tribune.

What?

Amy had last been looking at a page from the paper, and I frowned at the screen as the familiar words danced in front of my face.

Sanders Takes Hot Dog Contest for the Fourth Time.

It was an article I'd written during my last year of college, a fluff piece about a hot dog eating contest at a summer festival. It was one of my first real assignments, and I'd been thrilled, milling through the crowds, notebook in hand, feeling incredibly self-important. At 350 words, and with just one quote from an onlooker who had been anything but sober, it hadn't been the best clip, but the article had stayed in my portfolio for years after Sanders's fourth and final win. It took a while for me to find something more newsworthy to replace it.

As I clicked through the other tabs Amy had opened, I found more of my articles. One about a new fitness chain in Madison, another about an improv group at a local business school. All stories I never thought I'd see again, let alone share with anyone.

There were also a few tabs open about the trial and Sam, but the majority of the tabs were about me.

Because Amy was trying to figure out who *I* was. It was *me* she was worried about.

I looked up in surprise as my cell phone made a noise from the kitchen.

A text message.

Amy?

I jumped back up, almost dropping the computer before setting it on the bed and racing out of the room.

I picked up the phone and stared at the small screen. A flood of relief rushed over me as I read the text from Cam.

Amy's here. She called and asked if she cld come here.

With shaky fingers, I wrote back. Thank God. Sry, should have told you I gave her your #. She okay?

A few minutes past with no response. Finally, her reply popped up on the screen: You said you told her everything.

I sucked in a breath. I could hear her disappointment, and I closed my eyes, unable to think of a single thing to say. Apologize for lying? Explain why I did it? As I leaned forward against the counter, my eyes still closed, my phone suddenly vibrated in my hand.

I lifted the phone up to my face, and my breath caught when I saw the phone number.

Unknown.

"Hello?"

There was a pause and a crackle on the other end.

"Hello?" I said again. "Amy?"

And then he spoke.

Barely audible, breathless, but undoubtedly *him.*

"Francis," my father whispered. "It's me. I need help."

Chapter Thirty-One

I gripped the phone so tightly, it should have broken in two. After days of wanting nothing else—praying and hoping he'd turn up—here he was, and I couldn't think of a single thing to say. I opened my mouth, but only a surprised croak came out, and I swallowed, closing my eyes in relief. Or maybe it was dread. With my free hand, I grabbed the edge of the counter as the room swayed around me. "Where the hell are you?" I finally managed to get out.

The phone crackled again, the static and wind scraping loudly at my ear, and I pulled the phone away from my face.

"Francis," I heard him say, "can you—"

More wind.

"Dad?" I said, the panic growing, along with the fear that he'd hang up and I'd never find him again.

"Francis, can you hear me?"

"Yeah, I can hear you. Just tell me where you are. Hello?"

The phone garbled, and my words were a lie. I could hear nothing but static, followed by dead air. "Hello?" I said again.

"...you...pick...can...Homewood."

"What? I can't hear you. What's in Homewood? Is that where you are?" Homewood was a small neighborhood west of Lansing, but it wasn't small enough to canvass. I needed something else. An address. A street. Anything.

The phone was cackling loudly now, the static so bad I could barely pick up a word he said.

And then, just as quickly as it all started, the call dropped.

Shit!

My phone lit up and buzzed again.

"Hello?" I said. "Dad, can you hear me?"

It was only slightly better than before, and I listened as my father's voice broke through the cackling. "Homewood…okay…say…light."

I tried to piece the broken words together. "Are you in Homewood? Dad, where? You have to give me an address."

But the phone was relentless. I cursed into the static. I would have to go down to the station to see if Delroy could help me trace the number. Could they even trace unknown numbers?

"I can't hear you," I said again, and I hoped he could hear me better than I could hear him.

I was ready to give up and head out to my car when something changed.

Maybe he moved to another location. Maybe he stepped indoors. Hell, maybe he stopped crumpling up paper next to the receiver. The howling, crackling sound that had separated us seconds ago suddenly stopped, and for just one moment, my father's voice broke through.

Crisp, haunting, and painfully clear.

"He's on the bench, Francis. In Deven Park. I'm sorry. I'm so, so sorry."

I was frozen in place, the dread washing over my entire body. It was suddenly impossible to breathe, let alone respond. The phone call dropped again only seconds later, but his last words rung over and over in my mind.

"I'm so, so sorry."

I grabbed my jacket and raced out the door, heading for the stairwell. As I bolted around each bend, I skipped stairs on the way down, holding on tightly to the railing to keep from falling. Later, I would chastise myself for not thinking to call the police right away. The sensible, logical thing that could make a difference in saving the boy's life. But in the moment, I could only think about getting there and seeing what state my father had left him in.

As I jumped in my car, I realized I didn't feel as surprised as I did resigned, like the person who finally gets laid off after months of cowering behind a cubicle wall. I'd known this was coming. Not *this*, in particular—I never could have guessed that my father would leave a nine-year-old boy on a park bench in the middle of the night—but something that would force me to deal with the tragedy that was my family.

I burst through a stop sign, and the driver whose turn I took laid on his horn. But I couldn't stop. I drummed my fingers against the steering wheel and pushed harder on the accelerator. *Please be alive. I just need you to be alive.* No matter what, my father was done for, and he deserved it. The only drop of hope I had left was that Matthew would be returned safely to his family. And that my father couldn't, in a matter of years, have become a murderer. It didn't seem like a lot to hope for, but the last couple of days had shown me otherwise.

Through the crackling phone, I hadn't been able to make out much, but Alex had sounded fully there. Scared, but sober. I didn't know if that made it better or worse.

As I approached Homewood, it hit me that I didn't know exactly where the park was. I'd been there before, years ago. I turned a couple of corners, searching for a landmark—anything that would remind me of which way to go. I could pull over and search on the GPS, but that would waste valuable minutes. *Think,*

Francis. As I made another turn, something up ahead caught my attention. I hit the brakes hard, and a screech of tires came from behind me, followed by a loud horn. I peered down the block at the bright-green awning of a Thai restaurant I'd been to a couple of times before, which was only a few blocks from Deven Park. I made a shallow U-turn and got back on the street I'd just turned off. This was it.

I came upon the entrance to the park, and my throat went dry. The gravel path caused the car to rock from side to side, but I pushed on, my chest pressed against the steering wheel as I peered out into the night. I put the car in park and jumped out. It took me a few moments to get my bearings, but then I was off, racing to the perimeter of the park, where there were benches spaced out every few feet. As my shoes hit the pavement, the loud tapping noise echoed in the silent night, matched only by the rasp of my breath. My teeth chattered as I ran, and the cold wind swirled around me. Somewhere along the way, my nose had started to run, and I sniffled, using the back of my hand to wipe at my face.

The first set of benches was empty, and it occurred to me that I should have driven straight through the park to save time. As I followed a bend in the path, my sights locked on another grouping of benches ahead.

Was I wrong? Maybe he'd made it all up.

Maybe *I'd* made it all up.

I kept running, my gaze darting through the shadows for any signs of life.

And then, on the farthest bench from the street, tucked between two barren trees, illuminated by the light of a single lamppost—

I saw him.

The dark outline of a figure, sprawled out on the large, wooden bench. I could barely breathe, but I pushed harder now, running faster, even as my stomach turned over and my throat tightened, and

I tried to prepare myself for what I was about to see. I slowed down as I focused on the hazy figure.

Something was wrong.

The figure on the bench was completely still, arms spread, head back.

And it was larger—much larger—than that of a nine-year-old boy.

As I drew closer, I could see it was not a boy, but a man, dressed in heavy sweats, nothing else. In the dim, yellow light, I could make out his closed eyes, his face bruised and bloody, his features almost unrecognizable.

Almost.

As the realization settled over me, my knees gave out, and I buckled to the ground.

It wasn't Matthew Farr on the bench.

My father had gone after the one person he'd hated for the past twenty-three years.

Sam.

Chapter Thirty-Two

I shuddered as I stepped closer to him, my eyes searching his broken, bloodied, and swollen face. I turned away, afraid I'd be sick, and took a few calming breaths before walking slowly toward the bench. Sam's left cheek had a raised, bloodred lump the size of a marble protruding from it, and his lower lip was split right in the center. I swallowed and forced myself to keep going, leaning forward to listen for his breath. As I did, his puffy eyes blinked, only slightly.

"Sam?" I said, and he peered at me from behind the folds of the bruised and inflated skin on his face. "Can you hear me?"

We stared at each other in the dimly lit park, and for a moment, I was ridiculously and unforgivably helpless. When he moved his battered lips but no words came out, it hit me that there was no more time to waste. I had to get him to a hospital.

Now.

I stepped back and reached into my pockets to find my cell phone and cursed when I realized it wasn't there.

"Shit, I left my phone in my car, okay?" I said. "I'm going to go get it. I'll be right back, I promise."

His eyelids fluttered, and I hoped he could hear me, hoped he knew that I meant what I'd said. After nodding in reassurance again, I turned and took off.

As I ran, I scanned the park for anyone who could help me, but it was empty at this time of night. I reached my car in less than a minute, but it felt like hours, and I quickly called 911. As I talked, I started the car, driving back through the park toward Sam's body. I pulled up beside the bench, hopped out of the car again, and raced around to him. He was lying in the same position, staring up at the night sky, raspy breaths pouring out of his chest.

"I called the police," I said. "They're coming."

He stared at me with one eye, and then he coughed, and it was a violent, racking sound. I paced back and forth in front of the bench, another plan forming in my mind. I'd driven past a hospital on the way to the park—it would take me five minutes to get there, tops. It was a risk to move him, but what if the ambulance couldn't get him to the hospital in time? What if they couldn't save him? And what if I could?

Without giving myself time to think about it, I stepped closer to Sam. "I can take you," I whispered. Sam was staring up at me, and I knew he wanted to speak, but his injuries wouldn't allow it. I could see the emotion in his eyes, and it stunned me.

He was scared.

Of me.

I opened the car door and turned back to face Sam. Looping an arm beneath his shoulders and one beneath his legs, I lifted him up in one motion and turned, placing him as delicately as I could on the backseat. He cried out; the noise was deep and guttural. I knew what I was doing was so, so wrong.

But I couldn't just stand there and wait for him to...

I couldn't.

I got back in the driver's seat and turned the car around, driving quickly but cautiously to the main street, careful to avoid any potholes or bumps.

As I sped toward the nearest emergency room with Sam Farr in my backseat, all of the events of the past hour flowing through my mind, the evening's lights seemed to take on a new and scary form. I squinted, struggling to see through them. The streetlights, the headlights, the brake lights all seemed to swarm in front of me, making my head spin. I blinked, hoping to moisten my contacts, but it didn't help, and I tried to concentrate on the road as best as I could.

I just had to get him there before it was too late.

For his sake and my father's.

For the sake of his family, and mine.

I may have been hurting him more, but that was better than the alternative. I drove up to the door of the emergency room and was out of the car and around to the back door in seconds. A few attendants ran out toward me, and I flung the car door open. Sam Farr moved, only slightly, and I knew he was awake, but I couldn't tell if he was actually looking at me. I turned back to face the ER doctors.

"Get a stretcher! We need a stretcher now!" I yelled at the medics.

They rushed by me, and I was pushed to the back of the car, the lights still burning my eyes, my body shutting down, and I knew the worst of it was just beginning.

Twenty minutes later, I paced in the hospital waiting room. Sam Farr had been in the OR for most of that time; he'd been beaten so badly that he didn't even look like himself. He'd also been kicked with incredible force in the chest. He'd lost consciousness as they took him into the building.

Sam Farr had, quite literally, been beaten within an inch of his life.

After all of the years my father and mother spent trying to get Sam Farr to see time behind bars, I wondered if secretly, Alex had been waiting for his chance to do this.

He was the one who would be behind bars now.

And still, the night's biggest question hadn't been answered: Where was Matthew Farr?

I'd just taken a seat next to the door of the waiting room when it opened, and a frazzled, terrified Miranda Farr walked in, her face wet with tears. When she caught sight of me, I had only a few seconds to brace myself before she flew at me, hands swinging, the anger flooding out of her. Her fist connected with my arm, and I pulled back, grabbing both of her wrists and trying my best to hold her at bay.

"How could you let this happen?" she asked, and she broke free, swinging at me again. "I trusted you to help me, to help my family, and this is what happened?"

"He's going to be okay," I said, even though I didn't know that. I didn't know what else to say.

"Your father is going to jail for this." Her entire body was shaking in rage, and I had no response but to nod. "Where is Matthew?"

"I don't know," I whispered. "I really don't know."

She stepped away from me, and I could see the hatred in her eyes. She turned and left me standing there, and I wished I'd had more to offer her. I slumped back down in the chair. I needed to talk to Sam to see if he could provide any insights as to where my father was—and how he'd ended up on a park bench in the middle of the night. As I sat there, I felt a vibration in my pocket, and then the low ring of my cell phone. I sat up quickly, almost falling onto the floor. I didn't recognize the number that was calling, and my heart skipped another beat.

"Hello? Dad?" I said into the phone, breathless, afraid.

"Um, Mr. Scroll?"

"Yes," I said curtly, disappointed that it wasn't my father. "Who is this?"

"Um, my name is Terry. I volunteer at New County Church."

I paused, trying to place the name.

"We met earlier when you came by and spoke with Ms. Diana."

"Terry," I said, frowning as I remembered the shy boy who had been helping Diana while I spoke with her. "Yes, hi. How can I help you?"

"I was hoping I could speak with you about something. It's really important. I hope you don't mind me calling you this late. I got your number from Ms. Diana."

"Of course," I said, trying to show patience but wanting to tell him to get to the point.

"It's about Principal Murray."

"Okay," I said. "What is it, Terry?"

"I wanted to tell you that you didn't need to keep looking into whether or not she was…I don't know. I think you believe she had something to do with the Farr kid, and that's not the case. That's completely wrong."

"Okay," I said. I leaned forward in the chair. After everything that had happened tonight, I knew he was right. But he was calling for a reason…

"How do you know that, Terry?"

"Well, that's the thing. I don't want her to get in trouble, but… we left that day."

"Who left?"

"Me and Principal Murray. We left. We went to…get something to eat." He stumbled over the last few words, and I could tell that he had planned them out.

And there was only one reason he would do that. My stomach turned over, and not for the first time that night. Murray had looked me in the eyes, and while she hadn't lied to me, she'd left out the most important part of the story.

"Did Principal Murray ask you to call me?"

"No," the boy said hoarsely, and I could hear the concern in his voice. "She doesn't know I called you. She'd be upset. She kept saying she didn't know how she would get you to believe she didn't have anything to do with the Farr kid without telling you she was with me. I told her it didn't matter, because we were just getting something to eat, and even so, I'm eighteen…"

"You're eighteen."

"I sure am."

"When did you turn eighteen?"

"Two months ago."

I took a long, deep breath. "Thank you for calling me," I said, and we hung up. Murray obviously didn't have anything to do with Matthew's disappearance, but she did have some explaining to do.

I made a call to Detective Jeffries and told him what I'd learned.

"Does Cap know what you've been up to?" he asked.

"No," I said. "And it needs to stay that way. For now. But you've got to look into this principal."

"I'm on it," he said.

I hung up the phone and went to see if there were any updates.

As I did, a tall figure approached me.

Just when I thought things couldn't possibly get any worse.

"What happened?" Kira asked.

"I really don't want to talk about it, if that's okay," I said, measuring my words, knowing the anger I was feeling had nothing to do with her.

"Well, yeah, but can you just tell me—"

"Look, this really isn't the time or place to conduct interviews for your book."

"I'm not here for the book," she said. "I'm here because I care about Miranda and Sam."

"Is that what you're telling yourself?"

"Yeah, it is," she snapped. "What the hell are you telling yourself these days, Francis?"

Chapter Thirty-Three

Three hours later, I stood at the edge of the door to Sam Farr's room, watching as Miranda embraced her husband and they whispered something to each other. At the foot of the bed stood a woman, her arms wrapped around herself, her eyes trained on Sam's battered face. Elizabeth Farr was shaking, and even from a distance, I could see the anguish pouring out of her body.

Brian Farr was also in the room, but he hung back, watching his family with a stern, troubled expression.

I watched Sam's face as he said something else to his wife, and she turned to pick up a cup of water. Placing a straw to his lips, she held it there as he took a painful sip.

He could barely drink water, but he was okay.

He was traumatized and hurt and battered and scared, but he was alive.

I stood around in the hallway, waiting for a chance to speak with him.

But I didn't deserve to be there.

I wasn't a cop or a family member. Not a doctor or a nurse. Not even Kira Jones. I wanted to run in the room and beg him for answers, promise I had his son's best interests in mind, do something to right some of my father's many, many wrongs.

But I didn't belong there.

Still, there was a part of me that knew Sam Farr held the key to it all. Whether he knew it or not. As I paced outside of Sam's room, it hit me that I was falling into the same trap my father had fallen into, and apparently stayed in, for all of his adult life. What kept him going all these years was this idea—this speculation—that there was someone else in the world who knew more about what really happened the night Lucas died than he did.

As I stood at the door, listening to their chatter and the sounds of the nurses and doctors rushing behind me, my breathing became shallow. I was in no position to talk to Sam Farr. I had no claim over the information he was holding. I needed to leave, to call Delroy and bring him up to speed on everything I'd learned in the past two days. I needed to go to Cam's to talk to Amy. She'd finally texted me back an hour ago with: I'm fine, don't want to talk. Home tomorrow.

Cam hadn't said anything after her last text either, and I was desperate to talk to both of them, even just for a moment.

I turned and walked down the hallway, heading toward the exit. I was about to enter the stairwell when I heard a voice call out.

"Francis?"

I turned around to see Brian Farr. I hadn't spoken to him since the night of the dinner party, and he eyed me carefully.

"Mr. Farr," I said, and I felt like an idiot, but I couldn't address him as anything else.

"Where's your father?" he whispered, the tears glowing in his eyes. "When is he going to stop?"

"I wish I knew," I said, stepping forward. "I really do. I'm so sorry."

"I don't understand why he can't let it go," he said. "I've felt for him every single day since that night. I've tossed and turned, knowing the entire city thinks my child could be responsible for your brother's death. But it's been *twenty years*," he said, and I could see the pain in his eyes. "Twenty years of this. When is he going to get that the past is sometimes best left in the past?"

It wasn't the first time I'd heard that sentiment in the past twenty-four hours. I watched as a tear rolled down Brian's cheek.

"I'm sorry," I said again. "I'll give you and your family some privacy."

"Well, no," he said. "He's asking for you."

"What?"

Brian used his palm to wipe at his face. "Sam wants to speak with you."

I cleared my throat. "About what?"

"I don't know," Brian said. "But please, make it quick." He turned and began walking back toward the room, never questioning if I would follow. I trailed him to the doorway, where Elizabeth and Miranda Farr were walking out. Neither of them looked at me.

Brian and I walked into the room.

"You all right?" he asked Sam, looking at me and back at his son.

"Yes," Sam said, barely looking at his father. Brian took a step closer to the bed, and Sam flinched, turning his head away. Brian sighed and stepped back.

"He's still upset with me about the book. I told him I think they should put it on hold, and he hasn't talked me to sin—"

"Dad, can we have a moment?" Sam asked, and though he said it softly, there was a degree of sternness in his voice.

Brian watched him for a moment, and then nodded. "Yeah, of course." He looked at me before turning and leaving the room.

It wasn't a small room, but it was oppressive and stuffy, and I curled my hands into fists as I approached the bed. Sam's face was bruised, swollen, and puffy, but he was looking at me through both eyes now. As I stared at him, I realized I hadn't talked to him face-to-face like this ever—we'd never said more than a passing hello at church when we were kids, or when he came to my house. I'd seen him at the end of his trial, but I hadn't had any direct contact with him.

Yet I felt like I knew him painfully well.

"Thanks for seeing me," I said, turning back to look at Miranda, who was still staring at us through the glass. "I really won't take up too much of your time. I just—"

"I get it," he said, nodding his head just slightly. "Miranda told me you've been looking into our son's kidnapping. She really appreciates everything you've done. We both do, Francis."

He said my name as if we'd been friends for years, and I tried not to show my confusion at his comment. Miranda had said that? She'd seemed ready to gouge my eyeballs out.

"And I know you didn't have anything to do with this, Francis. I know you want to find your father as much as I want to find my son."

I was shocked by his candor, but I tried to hide it. "Well, can you tell me what happened to you?" I asked. "I mean, to the best of your recollection."

His eyelids fluttered, and I could tell he was having a hard time keeping it open. "Yeah, I can try. He just snuck up on me. I guess he'd been watching us again, though I don't know how long. I was staying at my parents' house—Miranda and I both were. We thought it would be better if we were all there together, so we would be able to support one another, because this is such a difficult time for us all."

"I'm so sorry—"

He cut me off, the clichéd attempt at sympathy lost on him, or maybe just inappropriate by now. "I went for a walk," he said, staring into my eyes. "I went for a walk because I couldn't stand just being in that house anymore. I needed some fresh air. It was going to be a quick one—I didn't even put a coat on."

"Where did you go?"

"Not far," he said. "Only about a mile or so away from the house, toward Green Cove. I was turning around to head back when a car showed up. I didn't notice it at first, but then I realized it was trailing me."

"My father?"

He nodded. "He got out of the car and ran toward me before I had a second to think. He hit me over the head with something. I think it was an umbrella, because it wasn't that hard, but it hit me right here, and cut me."

He tried to raise his arm toward his face, but he winced and put it back down. "In my temple. I went down almost immediately, and he hit me again."

"What happened next?"

"He dragged me into the car, and we drove off."

"Where did he take you?" I asked.

"Nowhere. That's the thing. We just drove. I was out of it, but I remember my head bouncing up and down on the backseat. And he was going on and on about how he didn't have Matthew, and he was freaked out because everyone was saying he did. And he said he hated me. Over and over. There was so much hatred, but he was also apologizing for something, and I just didn't get any of it." The words rushed out of him, and then he paused. "I really didn't understand."

"So then what happened?"

"Well," he said, "we kept driving, and we talked."

"You talked."

"Yes," Sam said. "We talked for the first time in twenty years."

I watched his face, and there was something there that almost looked peaceful. He was staring off into the distance, and I wished desperately I could have been a fly on the window during that conversation in the car.

"What did you talk about?"

He tilted his head to the side and seemed to think about the question. Then he chuckled, a raw, odd sound that escaped him.

"We talked about our sons," he said, his voice breaking, tears running down his face. "Can you believe that, Francis? Your father and I spent about ten minutes circling the blocks, talking about our sons. He asked me about Matthew. About what his favorite ice cream flavor is, and what outfit he hates when we make him wear it, and his favorite bedtime story."

He sniffed, and I felt my heart racing. I looked back at the door where Miranda was standing perfectly still, her hand on the glass as she looked in.

Sam took a deep breath. "I told him chocolate. Matthew's favorite ice cream is chocolate. And he hates it when his mother makes him wear the brown sweater with the stars on it. He really hates that one." His voice cracked again, and he sat up straighter, squaring his shoulders. "And then he told me the same for your little brother. And I just…I could tell he was happy. He wanted me to feel the same thing he did, and I do. I feel it too. It's the worst feeling in the world to lose a child. I get it. I think he thought I was going to tell him something, something about what happened to Lucas, but I couldn't, because I don't have anything to tell."

"Then what happened?"

"I don't know," he said. "Somewhere during the drive, it all changed."

"What do you mean?"

"Well, at first, he seemed like he really did just want to talk. But then he kept asking me to tell him what happened that night."

"What did you say?" I asked gently.

"I told him I didn't know. That I couldn't remember. And that wasn't good enough for him. He pulled over, and he kept asking me. He came around to the back of the car and he opened the door and he—" Sam's voice broke, and he looked down at his hands.

"And what?"

"And he just started hitting me."

"Did you fight back?"

"I tried," he said hesitantly, looking up at me. "I'm not much of a fighter, and your father... It's like he snapped or something. I could tell he wanted to hurt me, or even kill me. That's all I remember. The next thing I knew, I was lying on the bench, and you were dragging me toward your car."

"You were scared of me."

"At first," he said.

I stepped back and stared at him. If my own father hadn't called me and told me where to find Sam, I might not have believed him, but I knew everything he was telling me was true. There was no way around it. My father had gotten what he wanted, and he would go to jail for it.

"It was one of the scariest moments of my life," Sam said. "It took me back to all of that stuff after the trial."

"What stuff?" I asked.

He blinked and looked down at his hands. "You know...the attacks and stuff." He whispered the last couple of words, almost as if he were embarrassed to say them.

"Oh, yeah," I said, thinking back to my conversation with Banks. "That must have been terrifying. How many were there?"

He looked up at me and shrugged lightly. "Everywhere I went, someone had something to say," he said. "At the grocery store, in the bank. Sometimes it was supportive, actually. Other times it wasn't. The worst one was the man with the bird on his chest..." He cringed.

"The what?"

He blinked. "It was a week or so after the trial, and I was taking a walk a block or so from home. It wasn't even that late. I remember because the sun was hurting my eyes. Then, out of nowhere, this guy came up to me—he was wearing a baseball cap and sunglasses, so I couldn't really see his face, but I remember he said, 'How does it feel to murder someone and get away with it?' and he just waited, like I had a response for that."

"What did you do?"

"I tried to get around him, but he pushed me, hard, against a tree, and he called me a murderer again. He said he knew I'd done it. I was scared, but I fought back and, in the process, ripped his shirt all the way open, and that's when I saw it—the most disgusting, largest tattoo I'd ever seen. It was a raven, I think, the eyes right on the man's collarbone, looking back at me, and that scared me more than the man himself. I think I froze, and I didn't know what he was going to do, but a car came around the corner at that moment, and I ran away."

I stared at Sam, and I thought about what Kira had said—even if we didn't know for sure what had happened when he was ten, he didn't deserve what had happened to him afterward.

I reached over and grabbed the tissue box, holding it in front of him.

It was probably the closest I'd ever get to a peace offering.

Chapter Thirty-Four

The Sam Farr Story

By: K. L. Jones

FINAL DRAFT—Not to be shared without express permission of author, K. L. Jones

Sam raced out of the living room, the puppets grasped in his hands, and he was glad nobody followed him.

"Let him go," he heard his father say to his mother as she stood up and tried to follow him. "He's going to need some time."

He'd broken his first puppet.

Sam had been as careful as anyone could be, and he'd broken one of them. He'd been worried about bringing them out around a group of people, and yet he was the one who'd broken it.

Sam ran up the stairs and sat down on the bench in the Scrolls' hallway. It was a long wooden bench with no back, anchored on each side by two small end tables. He leaned forward and looked at the place where his puppet had snapped.

Sure, it could be fixed. A little glue would do it.

But he would always know. Every time he picked up the puppet, he would think about how it was broken, damaged.

Sam sat perfectly still on the bench, the puppets in his hands. Five minutes passed, then ten. They were going to come looking for him soon, and they'd think he was a baby if they saw he was still crying. But he couldn't get himself to move.

He'd started rocking slowly back and forth when he heard the noise.

It was a loud thump, not too loud to make him think anything was wrong, but loud enough to make him curious.

He grasped both puppets tightly in his hands as he stood up. The noise had come from down the hall—from Kate and Alex Scroll's bedroom. Sam walked slowly down the hallway toward their closed door.

"Lucas?" he said.

He was still upset with Lucas for what he'd said to his friends earlier, but he wasn't going to worry about it anymore. Lucas was just like the other boys. Maybe he hid it a little when his parents were around. But he wasn't a friend, that was for sure.

Sam walked toward the Scrolls' bedroom and put his ear to the door.

"Lucas?" he said. "Are you okay?"

There was still silence, and he put his hand on the knob, wondering if he should go in. He would never go in the adults' room without their permission, but he had heard a noise, and Lucas wasn't saying anything.

What if he'd fallen?

The truth was, Sam really did want to see the inside of the Scrolls' bedroom. Even his broken puppet hadn't erased his curiosity about their home. He guessed it was just as pretty and nicely decorated as the rest of their house.

He pushed the door open gently and stepped inside. He took a deep breath, marveling at the large bedroom and the ornate decorations that filled it. The bed was covered with a shiny tan-and-gold bedspread. It was also covered with a million pillows, and Sam wondered how they slept with all of them.

Did they throw them on the floor every night? Sleep with them in the bed? Place them one by one on the chaise on the side of the bed? It seemed like a lot of work, but it sure was pretty.

"Lucas?" he called out again, stepping fully inside the room. Sam turned another corner and walked into the small dressing area. The door to the bathroom was partially open, and he hesitated before going closer. If it wasn't intrusive enough for him to have come inside in the first place, he surely shouldn't go into the bathroom.

If only Lucas would answer him back. And tell him what that noise had been.

Sam moved closer to the door and listened carefully.

"Lucas, are you in there?" He touched the handle and tried to peer inside.

"Lucas, what are you doing?"

He pushed the door open and went inside, and the sight in front of him almost bowled him over.

There in the tub...

The bright, colorful shirt.

Lucas Scroll...

Sam stumbled back and fell onto the floor, his eyes never leaving Lucas's body in the tub. He couldn't move; instead, he just sat there completely motionless for a few seconds, struggling to get a full breath. He sprang up and ran to the tub. Reaching in, he grabbed Lucas's body, the water pouring in waves over the side and covering his own clothes. He turned

Lucas over and saw the boy's face, bloated and pale, and he knew right then.

He was dead.

Letting him go, Sam tried to breathe through his mouth, but he felt like he was going to have an asthma attack. He turned and raced out of the bathroom, back into the Scrolls' bedroom, before running out into the hallway and toward the stairs.

As he did, he could hear laughter coming from downstairs, voices ringing through the house, and he ran toward them, wanting his mother, needing her. He raced down the stairs, holding the banister tightly.

As he turned the corner into the living room, everyone in the room looked up.

"What's wrong?" his mother said immediately, standing up, and all of the adults looked at him with expressions of confusion and concern.

"Lucas," he managed to choke out, feeling as if the world were coming down on him, suffocating him. The adults began to move, everyone except Kate Scroll, who stared at him in shock, and then, the wineglass in her hand dropped to the carpet.

"What's going on?" someone else said, and then they were pushing past him, running upstairs, and someone was bending down in front of his face, but he couldn't really see who it was.

Sam followed them back upstairs, unable to say anything else, because they would see soon enough.

In a matter of seconds, they would know.

As he reached the top of the stairs, he heard the first screams, loud peals, and he didn't know who they were coming from. And then Kate Scroll turned the corner into her bedroom, and Sam stood shaking out in the hallway, his mother still crouched in front of him.

He ran into her arms and hugged her tightly, and she

hugged him back, asking a million questions, but none of them really mattered. Sam continued to hold her, wishing it would all go away. He needed to get away. He turned and walked into Lucas's room where he'd left his things.

As he did, he heard a noise in the hallway, and then Kate Scroll was there, crying and screaming and demanding that Sam tell her what had happened.

"What happened to my baby?" she screamed. And then someone was holding her back, and Sam wished he could be anywhere else in the world besides standing there in front of Kate Scroll, who was so mad, mad at everyone, but mad at him the most.

He turned away from her while she was still screaming and grabbed his silver briefcase off the floor. Walking over to Lucas's bed, he began to put his puppets away, neatly, one by one, wrapping them carefully before placing them gently into the briefcase.

"What is he doing?" Kate screamed out, but Sam ignored her. There were too many people in the room now. Everyone thought he had something else to say, something to tell them about what had happened to Lucas, but he didn't.

He just needed to go.

It was too much.

The broken puppet.

Lucas and his tie-dye T-shirt.

The water—so much water.

Sam didn't know what he should be doing, but he knew he needed to finish putting his things away so his family could leave. He took a deep breath and tried to block out the rest of the room as he lifted another puppet and wound the protective wrapping around it—

Chapter Thirty-Five

Tuesday, 11:00 p.m.

I walked slowly down the hospital stairs, replaying my conversation with Sam.

I couldn't just go home—there had to be *something* else I could do. An idea started to form, and before I could stop myself, I got in my car and began to head toward Orland Park.

Twenty minutes later, I pulled up in front of Christine's office and turned off the engine. The streets were as quiet as the night before, and I thought about how naive I'd been, thinking I could walk inside Christine's clinic and steal my father's files. The lights were off in the front of the building, and I walked through the alley toward the back door, much more confident than I'd been the last time. I looked over my shoulder, but there didn't seem to be any mysterious figures lurking about in the shadows.

I walked up to the back door and banged on it loudly with my fist.

Nothing happened for a few seconds, and I banged again. Finally, I heard rustling on the other side of the door, and then a click before it creaked open. Christine stood there with a frown on her face.

"What are you doing here?" she asked, scanning the alley behind me. "What do you want?"

"I need to talk to you."

Her expression changed, and she seemed to consider it for a moment before stepping back and letting me inside. She shut the door behind me, securing the large dead bolts.

"What are you doing here?" I asked, looking around. It was a different space than the one I'd left last night; there were only a few lights on, and there was no one else in sight.

"Cleaning up some old files. I had Giselle and Eric take the night off," she said.

She stared at me with an expression that could only be described as defeated. The woman I'd met in her office at Cove Sparry Hospital had disappeared. That woman had been in control, even smug. Tonight, Christine seemed like a shell of herself, staring at me with exhausted, glassy eyes. "Talk to me about what?" she asked.

"Do you know who John Rose is?"

Her eyes clouded over, and she didn't really need to answer me. "Um, I've heard of him, yes," she said, looking even more uncomfortable than she had before.

"So you know what the potential effects of these procedures are? You know what happened to John Rose and why several organizations outlawed D. B.'s program?"

"Well, those 'effects,' as you call them, are nowhere near proven," she said. "You can't trust every critic who has something scathing to say, Francis." She spread both hands in front of her. "Look, I know where you're going with this. Everything we do in life carries risks. Absolutely everything. You know that, right? We looked into it. What they didn't want to report was that John Rose had a lot of problems of his own, problems that had nothing to do with false memories."

She looked away from me, and her face reflected anger. It

occurred to me that she'd probably had arguments like this many times in her career.

"Is that why you came here? To tell me how unethical all this is?"

"No, I came here because I realized that, even though my father was willing to try out these theories on people he didn't know, and of course, Sam Farr—he was scared of it. Did you know that?"

"What?" she asked. "That's not true. He always spoke about how harmless the process is."

"If it's so harmless, why was Alex so adamant that no one in his family should be even remotely exposed to it?"

"That's not true," she said again. "He said many times that he would trust the life of his own family with it."

"Well, he lied," I said. "Who best to have memories about what happened that night? If not the Farrs, then myself or my mother. But my father was completely against that. It wasn't just a coincidence that he never actually tried it on us. He was scared of the potential effects."

"I would never endorse a therapy I thought was harmful."

"Maybe you wouldn't. But my father did."

Christine seemed at a loss for words, and she wrung her hands together. "So that's why you're here, to tell me what a horrible person your father is?"

"No," I said. "I'm here because I need to know what you think. Given what I just told you about my father. Do you have any of the same concerns?"

"I told you, no," she said. "I wouldn't be doing this research if I did. Now why do you keep asking me that?"

"Because I want you to try it on me."

"What?" she asked. "No, I won't do that."

"Why not?"

"Because," she sputtered, "D. B.'s therapies aren't something you just toss around and try whenever you feel like it. It's a science, and that takes—"

"It's our only option," I said. "I was there that night. I need to know if there's anything left, anything at all that can help us. Isn't it worth it to find Alex?"

She hesitated, and I stepped forward.

"To find Matthew?"

She didn't say anything for a few moments, and then she looked away from me, focusing on a spot just past my head. But I could tell from her expression that I'd gotten to her.

"Yes," she said, drawing her eyes back to me. "I'll help you."

Chapter Thirty-Six

Follow me."

She led me down to the room I'd been in the day before with her turtleneck-wearing bodyguard.

"You can have a seat there," she said, pointing to the chair. I leaned forward and checked for the water bottle I'd stashed beneath it, but it was gone.

"I don't need to get undressed?" I asked, sitting down.

"Why would you need to do that?" she asked. "This is psychotherapy, not a prostate exam."

"But last time—"

"I told you, I saw you on the cameras the minute you walked in. We needed to make sure you didn't have any weapons," she said.

"Oh."

I was silent as she opened the cabinet above the sink and began looking for something.

"So what really happened to John Rose?"

Christine paused and turned back to me. She cleared her throat. "There were accusations that when John underwent D. B.'s therapy... that he came away with a few false memories."

"Such as?"

"That his mother beat him. Every day, for years."

"Hell," I breathed. "And then he jumped off a bridge."

She squared her shoulders. "It was a terrible event, but it didn't reflect on our industry the way his family tried to say it did."

"So what do you think? Were the memories John Rose had true?"

She raised both hands and shrugged slightly. "I don't know, Francis. How could I know? What I do know is that even if they weren't true, the therapy wasn't responsible for his tragic death. Right? All it does is provides information."

"But that's what his family said?"

"Yes," Christine said. She turned to face me. "We should probably get started."

My heart was pounding as she walked toward me with the small white cup and another water bottle.

"You have to take these." She held the cup in front of me, and I could tell she still wasn't quite convinced this was the right thing to do. "For real, this time."

"What are they for?" I asked. "Scarface wouldn't tell me."

She ignored me. "They are a part of the induction process," she said. "Just a mild sedative to help you relax as we begin the procedure."

I juggled the pills in my hand before tossing them back, following them with a swig of water.

The pills had been down for less than a minute, but the room began to sway, and her face began to get grainy.

"Are you all right?" she asked.

"Yes," I said. I knew then that my performance the first time around had been abysmal. I was having a hard time keeping focused. Christine had probably been laughing her head off the previous day at my pathetic attempt to appear as though the pills were taking effect.

"Okay," she said. "I'm going to need you to sit back and relax, and listen to the sound of my voice. Can you do that, Francis?"

"Yes," I said, and my voice sounded foreign.

"Good," she said. "Now take a look at the painting on the wall. Do you see it?"

I turned my head slowly and focused on where she pointed. I hadn't noticed the painting in all the time we'd been in the room, but now, I couldn't stop staring at it. It was a splash of colors, loosely forming the shape of what looked like a feather. The vivid teal, warm-brown, and bright-yellow brushstrokes danced across my vision, and I slipped further and further into slumber.

"Good," she said. "Now I want you to close your eyes, and I want you to stay with me. You're going to feel tired, but do not give in. That's the only thing I need you to do for me. Do not fall asleep. Can you do that for me?"

"Yes."

"Okay, Francis, keep your eyes closed and think back to the night of the dinner party. You know the night I'm talking about? It was a long time ago."

Of course I knew. It was why we were here. Right?

"Francis?"

"Yes."

"I asked you to tell me what you see. Can you do that for me?"

"I don't see anything," I said, my mind foggy, the painting still dancing in front of me even though my eyes were closed.

"That's okay," she said. "You'll see it soon."

I gripped the armrest and closed my eyes, fighting the urge to drift off fully.

"Picture your parents' home, the kitchen or the dining room. Any room you remember. Can you do that, Francis?"

Suddenly, I could see it. Fuzzy images of my parents' dining table. The bread rolls. The shiny silverware. The salad bowl.

"Okay," I said. "Yes, I can do it."

"Good, tell me where you are."

"I'm at the dinner table," I heard myself say, the words tumbling out of my loose lips. "I'm sitting down...at the dinner table."

"Good," I heard her say, her voice soft and rhythmic. "Now we can begin."

Grandpa Zach had brought me back downstairs to the living room, where there was a cluster of family members. My mother and father were still nowhere to be seen—I'd caught a glimpse of my father trailing behind another cop half an hour earlier, asking something about Sam, but then he was gone. I sat on the couch, where my grandfather had left me, and we stared at each other, him at a complete loss for what to stay to a thirteen-year-old who'd just lost his little brother.

About ten minutes had passed when a cop walked into the room and leaned over, whispering something into my grandfather's ear. He looked up sharply. "Kate?" he asked, and he looked back at me. "Francis, I'll be right back, okay? I need to check on your mother. Just stay right there."

I nodded, because there was nothing else I could do, and he hadn't invited me to come with him, so obviously, she didn't want me there.

I sat there for a few minutes, the oppressive heat suffocating me, and I yanked at my itchy sweater, which was now even more of a prison than it had been earlier in the night. After a few more minutes went by without any sign of Grandpa Zach, I stood and inched out of the living room and into the kitchen.

Nobody saw me. Nobody noticed. The patio door was cracked open from all of the traffic over the last hour. I pushed it farther open, just enough to wedge myself out, and I stepped out onto the back deck. It was freezing, and I sucked in a breath. Still, it was better than being inside in the dank, stifling heat.

Our house was aglow—I could see the lights of the police cars around the side of the house—and even though I was outside in the crisp air, I still found it hard to breathe. I moved away from the house and toward the steps. In the moonlight, I could see the first step, and it felt like if I just let my foot drop down onto it, I would be getting somewhere, and I'd have a chance.

"Going somewhere?"

I spun around and saw the detective who'd been upstairs in the bathroom—the one who'd tried to protect me from seeing Lucas's body—standing there, watching me. He was perched in the doorframe, one hand on the glass, and he waited for me to respond.

"No," I said, shrugging and spinning around.

"You should be inside."

"I was hot," I said as a shiver ran through me, and I folded my arms over my chest.

"Here," he said. He reached up and unwrapped the scarf from his neck and held it out to me. I hesitated and took it from him, wrapping it around my neck.

I watched him carefully in the moonlight. He'd been nice to me all night, watching me more closely than anyone else in the house, and I wanted to stay outside with him, where at least I could breathe, a little.

"You've probably seen a lot of those, huh?" I asked.

He peered down at me, and I folded the scarf tighter around my face.

"A lot of…you mean like your brother?"

I nodded.

"I have," he said. "It's my job."

"Isn't it scary?" I asked. "I wouldn't want that job if you paid me all the money in the world."

He looked back over his shoulder—the way I did when I didn't want to get in trouble for something—and then moved closer to me. "It's no walk in the park, that's for sure," he said. "But there's a reason I do it. It's because when bad things like this happen, the families deserve to know why. They deserve the truth. And someone has to be there to sort through it all, right? You can't do it; your mom can't do it; your dad can't. So they call people like me." He shrugged and straightened up. "Somebody's got to do it."

As he stood fully upright, the porch light struck his face, and my eyes focused on his collarbone. At first, I thought I was just looking at a shadow, but as I peered at the dark spot at the base of his neck, I realized it was something more.

The shape had been covered by his scarf all night, but as he leaned back in the light, I could see it clearly: the dark lines of the bird's head, its beady eyes.

A raven.

The detective followed my gaze and put his hand to his throat. "Let's go back inside," he said, and it took me a moment to respond.

"Okay."

As we stepped through the door, he reached out his hand for his scarf. "Thanks," I said as I handed it back.

"No problem," he said, winding the black-and-red-checkered scarf around his neck, burying the bird once again.

Chapter Thirty-Seven

I opened my eyes and found myself sprawled in the same chair, staring up at the fluorescent lights. I wasn't moving at all, but the room was spinning around me, and I held tightly to the armrests. I had the sudden urge to stand, to shake it off, and so I did, immediately stumbling back and knocking into the chair behind me.

"Whoa," a voice said, and a second later, Christine was by my side. She was standing over me, helping me back down into the chair, an expression of concern on her face. "Not too quickly." I tried to move again, and she placed a hand on my shoulder. "Really, Francis, you should stop moving."

It sounded like a good idea, and I stopped.

"How do you feel?" she asked.

I opened my mouth to speak, but nothing came out. I swallowed and tried again.

"Francis?"

"We have to go," I finally croaked out. "Now."

I was certain Christine did not fully understand my fragile state—otherwise, she would have taken the wheel. As we sped toward Detective Younger's house, the steering wheel slid beneath my fingertips, and I knew that at any moment, it could slip free, and we'd go crashing off the road.

I pressed the gas pedal as far as it would go, my heart lodged in my throat.

"You must think I'm an idiot," Christine said, and I turned to make eye contact. "How could I have let this happen?"

"Alex must have told Younger about the plan in the park," I said. "You couldn't have known that."

"Do you think he's still alive?"

"I don't know," I said. "It depends on what Younger's motivation was for taking him."

"What if we're wrong?" she asked. "Is that possible?"

She was asking the questions that were flowing through my mind, but I didn't want to admit it.

"We're not wrong."

I made a turn into a large subdivision, and we both leaned forward, looking for the address.

"There it is," she said. "6255."

I turned to Christine to ask that she wait in the car, but she cut me off. "If you think for one second I'm going to sit here and do nothing when Matthew could be inside..."

I opened my mouth and closed it. I shook my head. "No," I finally said. "Of course not. Let's go."

We got out of the car and quietly closed the doors. Walking quickly between a couple of houses, we moved toward the backyard of one of Younger's neighbors. We walked through the lawn, stepping carefully in the dark. When I reached the end of their backyard, I hit a short, white fence that was easy enough to pull myself over. I turned back and helped Christine.

We moved into the backyard of Younger's home and walked cautiously toward the patio. Climbing the steps, I was careful to stay in the shadows, and Christine followed suit. I needed to know who or what we'd face inside before we made any more moves. Most of the lights were off, except for a few on the first floor. We walked closer to the patio door, and suddenly, I saw movement inside. I stopped, and Christine crashed into my back.

"What?" she hissed, and I held up my hand for her to wait.

A moment later, a figure walked by, tall and muscular, and I knew it was him. He was home. I looked around to see if he was with anyone else, but he appeared to be alone.

"He's there," Christine said, and I nodded. I could hear the fear in her voice. I realized we'd both been hoping the same thing—that Younger wouldn't actually be home.

This made things a lot more difficult.

"Should we call the police?" Christine asked.

I hesitated.

"It's time to call them, Francis. Think of the best- and worst-case scenarios."

I thought about what Delroy would say when I called him and how upset he would be if I were wrong.

But what if Matthew really was inside?

I nodded and pulled out my cell phone, moving back from the patio door to dial Delroy's direct number.

"Francis," he said as he answered. "Is everything okay?"

I took a deep breath.

"I think I know where Matthew Farr is."

"You *what*?"

He was completely silent as I explained as much as I could. Delroy let out a string of expletives before saying he'd make some calls and get someone out there immediately.

"If you're wrong," he said before we hung up, "I hope you

know how much you've jeopardized this case. I told you to stay out of it and leave it to us."

He hung up on me, and I stood there shaking for a moment, unsure of what to do.

Christine cleared that up for me.

"Let's go," she said.

"Shouldn't we wait?"

"Matthew could be inside. You didn't drive out here to wait." She shook her head. "I sure as hell didn't."

I opened my mouth to stop her, but she was too quick. She turned around, and before I could stop her, she marched up to the patio door and banged on it loudly with her fist.

Chapter Thirty-Eight

"Christine!" I called out, but I was too late, and she stood there, shoulders back, ready to pounce.

A few moments passed, and I racked my brain for what we would say when he answered. We waited, shivering, and suddenly, Younger appeared at the door, squinting out into the darkness. He didn't see us at first—he seemed to look right through us, a scowl covering his face. He was wearing a T-shirt, and the top of the raven peeked out from beneath it. As his eyes adjusted, he frowned, his gaze settling on me. He reached down to unlock the patio door.

"Francis?" he said, stepping back for us to enter and looking up at me in surprise. "What the hell is going on?"

"Do you have him?" Christine asked.

He froze and frowned again in confusion. "What are you talking about?"

"The boy," I said. "Matthew Farr. You kidnapped him that day at the park. Where is he?"

"You've lost your mind," he said, and he turned to look at Dr. Christine. "Who are you?"

"Christine Sharpe," she said. "Where's Matthew?"

Younger looked back at me. "I don't know what you're talking about. You're making this up. Where's your proof?"

"What about the fact that you attacked Sam Farr twenty years ago," I asked. "You left that out when we met. How's that for proof?" I scanned the inside of his home for any signs of Matthew. I wanted to pounce, to jump at him, to claw, but I needed something else, one more clue that I wasn't wrong.

He looked shocked, and for a moment, I wondered if I really was losing it. Maybe I was so desperate to find another explanation, even after everything my father had done, that I'd latched on to the first person I could find to cover up my father's sins.

Maybe I was just as biased as the rest of the Lansing Police Department.

Then, Younger glanced briefly at the other side of the room, toward a corridor that led to the front of the house.

It was barely noticeable, and if I hadn't seen it, I may have backed down.

But I saw in that flicker the one thing that removed all doubt of his guilt: his calculated but desperate search for an escape. In that quick scan of his eyes, I saw—I felt—the intense need to flee. I did it every time I was in a room that was too small or too crowded: a quick assessment of my surroundings to determine what it would take for me to get out.

To get away.

Younger brought his eyes back to me and took a slow breath. "I really have no idea what you're talking about."

"Sam Farr told me a man attacked him a long time ago, a man with a huge tattoo on his collarbone," I said, stepping closer. "Before he described it, I never knew what I'd seen that night."

He frowned. "What?"

"When you gave me your scarf. I saw something on your neck. But I didn't know what it was until he told me about the man with the raven tattoo."

He put one hand up to his neck, and he clenched his jaw. He didn't move, but the surprised expression on his face softened, giving way to something else.

Something sinister.

He blinked but didn't respond as he dropped his hand to his side.

"Where's the boy?" Christine asked.

"I don't know what you're talking about," he said softly for the third time. But his voice had changed. He was no longer pretending to be shocked or outraged at what we were saying. He was almost…

Gloating.

He cleared his throat. "Now, I was making some dinner, so if you'd please leave…"

He turned to walk back into his kitchen.

"The cops are on their way," Christine said to his back, and he stopped in his tracks.

He turned back to face us, his composure broken.

"To do what?" he asked. "They have no evidence."

"They'll search this place from top to bottom," Christine said.

"They can't do that," Younger said, shaking his head. "You need due cause for that."

"Yeah, but it doesn't hurt to have the captain of the Lansing Police Department on my side," I said. "He knows a few people."

Something flitted across Younger's face, a rage he couldn't hide. "Fucking ungrateful cops," he muttered angrily, and he balled up his fists and then uncurled them.

"Hope you don't have anything to hide," Christine said.

His jaw moved quickly, and he blinked rapidly before closing his eyes for a few moments. When he opened them, he swung his arm and knocked everything from the top of his counter. A pot, his coffeemaker, and a few knives dropped to the floor. He paused, breathing heavily, and we all stared at the sharp knives.

He was stronger than both of us, but he was outnumbered.

I knew he was going to run a full second or two before he did. Before we could react, Younger turned and took off into the house, bolting at full speed out the other side of the kitchen and through the small corridor.

We ran after him, knocking into the kitchen chairs and each other as we raced into the hallway. We paused at the edge of a long, dark hallway leading toward the living room, and a staircase that led to the second floor. I heard a noise near the front of the house, and I moved toward it, Christine a step behind me.

I paused and turned around. "You should check upstairs," I said.

"What?" she hissed. "I—"

"Matthew may be up there. Please."

She nodded quickly and raced up the stairs. I took off down the hallway, listening for any sounds at all.

The hallway ended near the front of the house, and I emerged between the living room and a small dining area. It was dark, the only light being the moonlight that streamed in through the windows. I held my breath as I crept slowly through the main living area, my gaze darting to every corner for any sign of Younger. Before I knew it, I'd made a slow circle back toward the kitchen.

Shit.

Where did he go?

I drew in a breath at the sound of sirens in the distance; the police were almost here.

Should I head outside?

Flag them down?

I hesitated. We did need backup, but the cops would take their time when they got on the scene, time we didn't have, demanding an explanation about why Christine and I were here in the first place.

Younger would be far away by then. I walked farther into the kitchen, back toward the patio door.

Had he gone outside?

I hadn't heard the door open, but it was possible. My face was pressed against the glass when I heard a noise behind me.

It was the sound of a door being closed, softly. I spun around and moved back through the kitchen, toward the dark corridor where I'd just been.

I searched along the wall until I found the door.

The garage.

Someone had just gone inside.

I put my hand on the doorknob.

Steeling myself for what I'd find, I quickly pushed open the door.

Darkness.

My heart was pounding as I stood there, my eyes peering around the dark shapes in the large, open space.

Had I imagined it?

Was Younger out here?

I moved farther into the garage, pushing the door closed. If he wasn't already out here, I needed to be alert if he did come in.

I kept my eyes trained on the car—I couldn't see around the other side of it, but from where I stood, it seemed like the back passenger-side door was open. I was about to walk over to it when I stopped, remembering the last time I'd been trapped in the dark.

I needed light before I did anything else.

With one hand outstretched, I began to walk along the wall, reaching for the light switch. In the scant moonlight, I could see a bulb in the middle of the garage, but it was too high for there to be a cord—the switch had to be somewhere on the wall.

With my eyes still fixed on the back of the car, I dragged my fingers along the wall in search of the light switch. My fingers bumped into something cold and metal, and I turned briefly to orient myself. As I did, my foot hit something hard. It was a large trunk, a storage container nearly the size of a twin bed, and I wondered what Younger had stored in it. The noise echoed around the quiet garage. A second later, I heard a soft scuffling noise on the far side of his car, and I froze in place, peering into the darkness.

That confirmed it.

Younger was definitely out here.

"You hear that?" I asked. "The cops are on their way. You're not going to get away with this. Tell us where he is."

Silence.

I turned again and searched desperately for the switch, my eyes rapidly adjusting to the shapes that protruded from the wall.

Just a little bit of light...

I spotted it and flipped it on. As the room illuminated, I suddenly heard a loud noise, right behind me. I whipped around, and there he was, inches from my face, his arms raised, a large object high above his head.

We locked eyes for one second, and I could see the anger as he swung.

Chapter Thirty-Nine

I ducked as he brought the object down on top of my head—a shovel—and I cried out as it connected with the side of my face. The pain was so intense that my entire body buckled, and I crumpled to the floor, inhaling sharply as my wrist twisted beneath my body. Younger came crashing down on top of me, and we struggled, kicking, pushing, and using every ounce of strength we had to get the upper hand.

"What's wrong with you?" Younger yelled into my face, and his warm, foul breath suffocated me as his saliva sprayed on my cheeks. "They let that monster get away with it. How can you defend him? He killed your brother! I saw it in his eyes that night. I *knew* it. I couldn't just let that go."

"But why—" I tried to lift myself up, but he pushed his palm into my face. "Why take Matthew—"

He drew back and swung again, and I turned my head to the side. His blow landed on the point where my left cheekbone met my ear, and my eyes rolled back in my head as pain shot through my entire body.

"You're the worst kind, you know that?" he sneered, and as I peered up in his face, I could see his eyes were wild. "You should be *thankful* for what I've done. I finally figured out how to get to Sam Farr, how to get him back for what he did all those years ago. You should be grateful for what I did for you!"

I yanked my right arm free and pushed my hand into his face, using my fingernails to scratch at his skin, and he cried out as I rolled him off me. My head was spinning, but I pulled myself toward him, and then I was punching, in every direction, hoping to connect with *something*. But he was stronger—much stronger—and in one quick motion, he flung me backward. I fell again, my head hitting the leg of a workbench.

Something heavy fell from the bench and rolled onto the floor. I blinked as I breathed in and tried to pull myself up. Not a foot away from me, I caught sight of the hammer that had just fallen.

Younger raised himself and crawled toward me, grabbing a long garden spade that had fallen as he did. Reaching back, he aimed it straight for my face. I struggled to breathe, and to think.

Do something, Francis.

As he swung, I quickly rolled to my left and out of the way, and his body weight carried him down. The spade connected with the floor where I'd been only a second before. My fingers curled around the base of the hammer. Without giving myself time to think, I spun back, and with a guttural roar that contained all of the fear, anger, and self-loathing that had been trapped inside of me for the past two days, I swung. Hard.

And missed.

The sound of the hammer hitting the concrete echoed through my head and body, and I slumped forward. I knew the miss would cost me. Suddenly, I was moving, and not on my own. Younger was dragging me along the cold concrete. He knocked into something, and then he was pushing me, lifting me, and tugging me, propelling my body into a small space I couldn't quite identify—

The trunk.

When I realized what was about to happen, I lost every ounce of my ability to fight, and my instincts took over. I was kicking now, not smartly, but recklessly. The position was too awkward, my body too weak, my fear too strong. He kicked me one final time, and I fell backward, my body slumping farther into the trunk.

Before I could push myself up again, I heard a loud noise, and then the heavy steel lid came crashing down on my head. The lock was engaged.

Click.

If I'd thought it was dark before, I'd been mistaken. I blinked a few times as the horror of what was happening washed over me, and everything faded away.

When I opened my eyes again, I was in a box.

In those first few seconds, before I realized what was going on, I was relatively okay, and I lay there, my arm twisted miserably beneath my body, maybe broken, my knees scrunched up toward my chest. In those first few seconds, I was blissfully ignorant, unaware of the horror I was about to face.

I moved only slightly and felt the wall of the trunk on one side of me, and I gasped, pulling in a deep and shuddering breath and knocking my head against the bottom of the trunk.

The trunk.

I was in a fucking trunk.

The memories of the last few moments flooded back, and I yelled out loud, a vicious, terrified cry of shock and horror as the seemingly impossible manifested itself around me within seconds. The weight of it hit me all at once, and I felt as if my entire body would explode. My body began to shut down, and I could think of nothing besides the burning need to be free, and to take a full, exposed breath of fresh air.

I began to kick and flail, even though I knew it was wrong, knew it was futile, knew it wasn't going to help me. The box couldn't have been more than five feet long. The pain suddenly kicked in in my trapped arm, and I cried out, desperate to discover what was wrong with it.

"Let me out!" I finally screamed, finding a voice I knew was both wasted and useless.

Take a deep breath.

I needed to stop kicking. I was exerting too much energy and using up the little air I had in the trunk. And suddenly, I could visualize them, every single molecule of air, and I knew I was using them up with every breath.

Stop it.

I allowed myself one deep, calming breath and tried to think as rationally as I could. Kicking wasn't going to get me out of the box. Nothing would. This was it. I was going to die here in this lunatic's garage while Matthew could be—

Stop, Francis. Think.

I visualized my entire body, imagining every single button and zipper on my clothing—anything that might be helpful in my escape. My shirt was cotton; my shoelaces, useless; my—

The photos.

I gasped as it hit me, the small stack of wallet-size photos I'd taken from home that morning. The ones of Sam and Matthew Farr that my father had hidden in his cabin. It wasn't the pictures themselves that made me pause.

It was the paper clip holding them together.

The paper clip.

With my free arm, I twisted and reached toward the pants pocket where I'd stuck the photos. I cried out at the pain that surged through the arm tucked beneath me, and I feared I would have to stop because it was so intense. But stopping wasn't an option. I used the very tips of my fingers to slide the paper-clipped photos out of my pocket. Holding on to the clip only, I shook the stack of photos, letting them fall free, until only the thin piece of metal remained in my hand.

I used my fingers to unbend it and ran my thumb across the pointy tip of the paper clip. This was my only chance, and it wasn't a great one. The problem was, the hand that held the paper clip was nowhere near the front of the trunk. If I wanted to reach it, I was going to have to find a way to flip almost 180 degrees so my left arm was aligned with the front of it—where I thought the latch must be. Or, I could toss the paper clip to the front of the trunk and hope I'd find it with my other hand.

Too risky.

I decided to roll onto my face and let my arm swing over to reach it. As I did, searing pain roared through my body, and my arm began to shake violently. I pushed on, turning myself until my left arm was lined up with the opening to the trunk. Groaning loudly, I reached up with the open paper clip and felt around in the darkness. There had to be an opening somewhere.

I dragged the paper clip from one side of the box to the other, waiting for it to slip in an opening. It did, quickly, and I almost cried out, but it took only a second for me to realize it was simply a corner of the box. The paper clip hooked on to something I couldn't see, and I yanked, but it wouldn't budge.

Damn.

I pulled again, and this time, it clattered from my fingers into the bottom of the trunk.

My heart sank, and I clawed blindly for the paper clip, but my fingers connected with nothing but dust. I took a deep breath. I needed to find it; it was my only chance. I needed to calm down. More than that, I needed to count.

One.

Two.

Three.

But it wasn't working, and the painful absurdity of it brought tears to my eyes, which in turn shifted to something else. Something like—

Laughter. The first laugh escaped my body, and I knew instantly that I was losing it, going crazy, getting hysterical, but I couldn't hold it back. I really was going to die in the box. Alone, crazy, and laughing. Many times, in my nightmares, I'd imagined such a death, but now that it was here…

Another laugh escaped, and I didn't try to stop it as it rolled out of me. I let the giggles and the tears flow from my body and pushed on, using my hand to scrape the bottom of the trunk. I was piling the dust into the corners, and it only took about three swipes for my fingers to snag on something sharp.

The paper clip!

Fumbling to pick it up, I moved my hand toward the front of the trunk. I held the clip tightly in my fingers, feeling the small piece of sharp metal as it cut into my skin. But I couldn't afford to drop it again. I dragged it in a straight line across the front, waiting for an opening. Nothing.

My mind was racing as I moved the paper clip in all directions, searching for the lock. For many years, I'd thought if I could just force myself to be put in a confined space for ten minutes—maybe even five—I would get over it and be cured for the rest of my life. But the fear had been so terrifying that I could never go through with it. Now, here I was in that very situation, and I was almost positive it was making things worse, not better.

I ran the paper clip across the trunk again, and this time, it slid into a space that was different than the first one.

This wasn't a corner.

The lock!

I placed the thin metal into the hole and moved it around wildly at first, and then more carefully. I spun the paper clip in slow, deliberate circles to the left, using my finger to steady it. When it pressed against something firm, I knew it was the lock mechanism. I pushed with all my strength. The paper clip began to bend, and I groaned, trying to support it with my finger. I was pushing my finger through the lock as far as it would go, and the metal was cutting into my skin.

The paper clip continued to bend, and I knew if it bent any farther, it would be completely useless. I just needed a bit more strength and—

Click.

I paused, not daring to get too hopeful, then pulled the paper clip out of the hole.

Please.

Taking a deep breath, I pushed hard against the lid of the trunk, and it lifted about two inches before falling back down on top of me.

It was enough to give me hope.

The trunk was unlocked.

I pushed again and slipped my hand through the opening.

Reaching as far as I could, I used my fingers to finish opening the latch and then braced myself before pushing up again. The lid to the trunk flew backward, landing with a clang against the garage wall.

It took all of my strength, but I pulled myself over the side of the trunk, collapsing onto the filthy floor, drinking in gulps of the stale air as if it were fresh, pure mountain air. I lay there with my cheek on the cold floor, waiting for the nausea to subside and the room to stop spinning.

I heard a noise above me, and I looked up quickly, my heart pounding again.

In the dim garage light, I could see a figure sitting down about ten feet away from me.

I squinted as I pulled myself up.

Christine.

Her arms were bound behind her body, and her mouth was covered with tape. I walked over to her, pulling the tape off her mouth.

"Where is he?" I whispered.

"I don't know," she said, gasping for breath. "I heard the police cars. I heard them come in. But I think they left!"

"Damn it. He probably found a way to get rid of them," I said. "That son of a bitch. How long ago was that?"

"Just a few minutes," she said. "That means—"

"He'll be back in a minute."

"What are we going to do?"

I walked quickly over to the tools and picked up a pair of gardening scissors. I cut her free, but as she began to stand, I put my hand on her shoulder.

"What?" she said.

I wrapped the ropes loosely around her arms. "Stay here," I said. "When he comes back, I want you to run on my signal, okay?"

She blinked and then nodded. Placing the tape back over her mouth, I walked over to the trunk and closed it, locking it. I picked up the hammer from where I'd dropped it earlier and then stepped around the car and crouched, my heart pounding in my chest.

And then, we waited.

Five minutes passed, then ten. I heard scraping on the other side of the car as Christine got settled. She could get free if she needed to; I just hoped she could manage to stay still until he came back.

Moments later, I heard her gasp as the sound of footsteps approached. They were loud and confident, and I wrapped my fingers around the handle of the hammer.

Here we go.

The garage door opened, and the footsteps approached.

"They're gone," Younger said to Christine. "You stupid bitch. I don't know what you thought you were doing."

I took a deep breath as he walked across the room, closer to the trunk.

"Now what the hell am I going to do with you two?"

I leaned around the car and watched as he bent toward the trunk, unlocking it in one swift motion.

Now.

As he flung open the lid, he staggered back, an expression of shock on his face. As he spun toward Christine, I charged.

I knocked him back into the workbench, and we both went down. "Go!" I yelled at Christine, and she flung the ropes off her wrists and raced into the house, I hoped to find a phone.

The hammer was still in my hand, but I couldn't find the opportunity to swing. I kept my head low and pushed with my free hand, searching for my opportunity. I couldn't miss again. He scrambled back, reaching behind him presumably to find a weapon, but I had the upper hand. When he turned to reach toward a long metal pipe, I took my chance.

Swinging back, I let the hammer fly toward his head.

This time, I hit my mark.

The thud of the hammer hitting Younger was sickening. He let out a loud, anguished cry and then collapsed forward. I moved back, letting the hammer drop from my fingers.

Fuck.

He wasn't moving.

No, no, no.

I pulled myself closer to him as the door to the garage opened and Christine rushed back in. "The police are on their way back," she said. "Oh my God. Are you okay?" She stared at Younger's body. She reached along the wall for something. Suddenly, the garage was illuminated in light, and we squinted as Younger began to stir.

He peered up at me. I grabbed the collar of his shirt, locking eyes with him. Blood trickled down the side of his head, and his gaze was glassy, unfocused.

"Where is he?" I hissed. "You'd better tell me right now, or I will kill you, so help me God." I could barely get the words out. "Where's Matthew?"

He didn't say anything, his head wavering slightly back and forth.

"Please," I whispered, tightening my grip on his collar.

We stayed like that for a few moments, and then he began to laugh, a low, menacing sound that made me freeze.

"You'll never find him," he said, closing his eyes and leaning his head back against the concrete. "They don't deserve him, and you'll never find him." He opened his eyes again and then stared at me meaningfully. "Especially you. If there's one person who has no chance in hell of ever finding Matthew Farr, it's you, Francis Scroll."

Chapter Forty

I beat the shit out of him.

Only a few seconds passed between the moment when the words left his lips and when Christine dragged me off him, but it was enough. Almost too much. By the time she reached me, I'd hooked the thumb of my right hand under his two front teeth, dug my fingertips into the soft recesses beneath his eyes, and begun to whip his skull repeatedly against the cold concrete floor.

"Where is he?" I cried as Christine pulled at my waist. I dug in harder, unable to slow the tide of anger pouring out of me. "You better fucking tell me where he is right now, or I swear I'll kill you."

"Francis!" Christine yelled, and she pulled me even harder this time, violently, and finally, I lost my grip. I sprawled back on the floor, sobs exploding from my body.

The search for nine-year-old Matthew Farr began a little after twelve thirty a.m.

"We'll spread out and cover every inch of this place," Delroy said, locking eyes with me. He'd arrived in plain clothes alongside a team of police officers a few minutes earlier.

Cam was also there. An editor working overnight had heard the report on the police scanner and called to fill her in. She'd driven straight over. As she walked up to me, my breath caught in my throat.

"Hey," I said, "where's—"

I stopped when I saw a slight figure emerge from behind her.

"Amy," I said as she walked up. I turned to Cam and mouthed, "Thanks."

She nodded.

"I'm just here to help with the search," Amy said, not making eye contact with me and turning to scan the grounds. "Where should we get started?"

"Amy, wait," I said. She spun back around and stared at me, and I couldn't read her expression. She didn't seem angry, but she wasn't giving in, either. "I'm so sorry." She didn't say anything, and then, the words were falling out of me. "I didn't have any right to lie to you. And that's what I did. I lied. I told myself that by not telling you, it wasn't really lying, but it's all the same. I should have told you. I was ashamed of my parents, disappointed in them, but it's still no excuse. I shouldn't have tried to hide it."

She still didn't speak, but her expression had softened, just a little. I stepped closer and lowered my voice so only she could hear me. "I talked to your mother." Her eyes widened. "I understand why you don't want to be here right now, but I want you to know that having you here has changed my life. I've been waiting for it for a year and a half. If there's anything I can do to make it better, let me know. Okay?"

She blinked rapidly and bit her bottom lip before moving back. She stared at me, and for that one moment, she was that six-year-old girl, the one who needed me, and I wanted to reach for her, to pull her close. Finally, she nodded. "We should go look for him," she said.

"Yeah, of course."

She looked at me meaningfully before walking off to follow a group of volunteers. I watched her retreating back for a moment and then turned to Cam.

"Thank you so much," I said. "I'm glad she called you. Yours was the only number I could think to give her in case of an emergency. Didn't know *I* was going to be the emergency."

She nodded. "I'm glad she called me too."

"And I'm sorry I lied to you," I said. "I shouldn't have—"

"It's okay," she said. "I get why you did it, and she will too. Soon enough." She reached out and grabbed my hand. "Hey, we're gonna find him," she said, and she was so convincing that, for just a moment, I had hope.

The search team that had assembled in front of Younger's home was nothing short of amazing, and yet, it still didn't seem like enough. We needed more.

Matthew could be anywhere, in any condition.

Younger had woken up again, moments after I'd attacked him, a fact that I knew I should be thankful for, in the grand scheme of things. He was handcuffed in a police car out front. The last time I saw him, he was giggling softly to himself, calling out to anyone who walked by, "You won't find him!"

I'd taken just one step toward the car when Delroy appeared suddenly at my side and put a hand on my chest.

"What do you think you're going to do, Francis?" he asked, his eyes sad, tired but knowing. "Kill him? He's not going to give you what you need."

"I'll make him."

"Let the professionals handle that. What you need to do is keep looking."

I stared at Younger for a moment and finally stepped away.

I'd been wandering the surrounding lot alone for the past ten minutes, bundling my jacket around my face, feeling the weight of everything that had happened that night on my entire body.

Nothing.

No signs of Matthew.

Dead or alive.

The simple truth was we had no evidence he'd ever actually *been* at the house.

We'd searched the upstairs bedrooms—all four of them—plus the garage, the expansive lawn out back. We'd looked in every closet, around every corner. He could be anywhere. I could barely breathe, the weight of what happened crushing my chest. I wandered alone, my gaze coasting over the same places that had already been searched, with no plan and no direction. I passed a cellar door near the base of the patio and paused.

Again?

A team of cops had already searched it. I'd searched it. Like everything else. Still, if I gave up now, it would all be over. By the time the cops were able to get anything out of Younger, any small chance of hope would be gone.

I stepped onto the wooden stairwell, making my way into the musty cellar beneath Younger's home.

You'll never find him.

My eyes adjusted to the dim light, and my heart was pounding as I crept forward. I walked slowly into the room, which was illuminated by a single lightbulb.

"Matthew!" I screamed. I listened for any sounds. Kicking, screaming, calls for help, anything. But I was greeted with silence, nothing to let me know we were searching in the right place, or anywhere near it.

You'll never find him!

He had been so sure, so confident. He'd given up, but he would win in the end if we never found Matthew Farr, never returned him to his family.

I walked around the small cellar, looking in every corner for something else: an addition, another room, a hiding spot. Something they'd missed. But the cops had combed it already, and there didn't seem to be anywhere else to look. I replayed his words over and over in my mind.

You'll never find him. Especially not you.

I stopped in my tracks.

When he'd first said it, I'd thought he was just zeroing in on me because I was responsible for him getting caught. Because I was the one leaning over him at that moment.

But the way he'd said those words: *especially not you.*

Younger knew something about me, in particular, something my father must have told him. He was taunting me, preying on my weakness, which meant…

Matthew was being held somewhere he thought I'd never be able to get to. I spun back around, examining the cellar with fresh eyes. I needed to find the tightest, smallest space possible.

Come on…

I spotted a small air duct in the wall that was about three feet wide and four feet tall, and I gasped out loud, sucking in a sharp breath. I leaned forward and put my mouth against the grate, calling out into the darkness.

"Matthew!"

Nothing.

"Can you hear me? If you're in there, let us know so we can come find you!"

Still nothing.

I was turning to head back upstairs when I heard the smallest, tiniest noise.

"Help..."

It was a breath, a whisper, a hoarse cry for help from a distance, and I turned back to the vent. Leaning closer, my throat dry, I yelled again.

"Matthew?"

Silence.

"Can you hear me?"

"Yes," the quiet voice called out, and my heart broke. "Help me."

At that moment, my body wasn't my own. I launched toward the vent, testing the screws that held the cover. They moved easily. I unscrewed them with my fingers, wincing as the metal pinched my skin, and I removed the grate from the duct.

Especially not you.

Somehow, Younger knew about my fear, and he'd laughed in my face.

I leaned forward and was overwhelmed by the warm, suffocating air that entered my nostrils. Taking a deep breath, I lifted myself up and crawled into the vent headfirst.

Immediately, the breath got sucked out of me, and I paused, my feet still hanging outside in the cellar. My chest seemed to swell, and I opened my mouth, gasping for air.

I put my head down and pushed on, ignoring the fear that consumed my mind and body. Taking the deepest breath I could muster, I directed my hands and knees to move forward.

I had to keep going.

The duct was about fifteen feet long, and when I reached the other side, I dropped into a dark space. I landed on my side on what felt like a dusty, cold floor. I was thankful to be out of the duct, even though I was still struggling to breathe and felt horribly trapped, buried in the underbelly of Younger's house. I rolled over and stood, blinking in the darkness.

"Matthew?"

There was no light at all, and then suddenly, I heard a match being lit, and I saw a figure.

A small boy, quivering a few feet from me, holding a match in front of his face.

The room began to spin around me, and I knew something wasn't quite right.

The boy standing in front of me wasn't Matthew Farr.

His gaze was angry, accusatory, and I cowered back against the wall.

The expression on his face.

His colorful T-shirt.

Dripping wet.

"Lucas?" I said. My throat was dry, and I thought I would pass out from lack of air. I tried to take a breath through my mouth, but it wasn't working.

I needed to stay conscious.

He was right there.

I could save him.

I could save him, if only I could stand up.

A loud bang sounded, and then there were voices behind me. I moved toward my brother, who stood there shaking. The flame slithered toward his fingers, and he shook it out.

"It's okay, Lucas," I said as I walked toward him in the dark room.

He was so close, but I couldn't reach him.

"It's okay, I'll get you out of here."

As I stepped closer, a flashlight illuminated the space. An officer arrived, lowering himself carefully into the room. Another officer followed him.

One of the cops moved forward, reaching for the boy.

"Lucas!" I called out, and then the other officer was close to my face, speaking calmly, quietly.

"Shh," he said. "Sir, we need to get out of here."

"I found Lucas," I said. "He's okay."

He peered at me in the soft glow of the flashlight. "Yes, you did. Now come on. We have to go."

Chapter Forty-One

It didn't take long for me to come back to reality.

As we emerged into the fresh air, I watched the cops moving away with Matthew Farr. He walked by me, frail and terrified, and I knew my visions of Lucas hadn't helped the situation much.

But he was safe.

Delroy, Christine, Cam, and Amy walked up. "I can take Amy home," Cam said.

I nodded my thanks. "I'll see you back at the apartment," I said to Amy. "I have to finish up some stuff here."

We hugged, and she walked away with Cam, who gave me a knowing, reassuring nod as they left.

As Delroy and I went around to the front of the house, I was surprised to see that the car with Younger hadn't left yet.

Before anyone could react, I raced over to the car.

"Hey!" Delroy yelled, but I reached it before anyone else did and yanked on the handle, opening the door. I reached inside and grabbed Younger by his shirt, dragging him out of the car.

"Where's my father?" I asked.

"Is that all that matters to you?" he asked angrily, looking around him. "You really think Sam Farr deserves to live a picture-perfect life after what he did? You of all people should understand. Sam Farr killed that little boy. Your brother, Francis! And you just moved on!"

"Where's my father?" I asked again before the cops grabbed my shoulders and pulled me off Younger.

"I don't know," he said, not breaking eye contact with me, even as they dragged me away. "He told me about what they planned to do, how they planned to take Sam. And I thought it was a great idea. I went to the park that day and saw him there. Alex was just sitting there, watching his team as they got into place, and you know what he was doing? He was on his second bottle, Francis. Sitting in his car, drunk as a skunk, just watching it all happen. Letting his plan fall to pieces. I wasn't going to let that happen.

"But then I saw the way Sam Farr was looking at his son. And I knew right then that the boy was the only thing that's ever meant anything to him. Sam has always been untouchable—never seemed like he really cared what happened to him. But if you saw the way he looked at Matthew—I knew that was our only chance of getting him to admit what he did."

"So you took him instead," Christine said from behind me. "How could you?"

"How could I not? That's the real question, isn't it?" he yelled as the cops lowered him back into the car. "How could I not?"

As they took him away, Christine turned back to me.

"Are you all right?"

"Yes," I said, struggling to hold myself together. "I'm fine."

"You saved that boy's life."

"We did," I said.

She gave me her address, and then we drove in complete silence. I pulled up in front of her house, and she turned to me.

"Thank you," she said, "for everything. I know you're worried, but we'll find your father soon. There's no reason for him to continue hiding."

"Except for what he did to Sam Farr. What we all did."

She hesitated and then nodded.

"You really are in love with him, aren't you?" I asked.

She smiled softly and shrugged. "Your father is a very complicated man to try to love," she said with a slight smile. "We're very close, and I care about him a lot. But he has never been open to any sort of future, not when there's so much holding him back in the past. I just want him to be okay."

"You never told me how you met. Really."

She smiled outright this time. "I knew your father way before he knew me."

"Because of the trial."

"Yes, though I wasn't that concerned with him as a man, but instead, as a father."

"You were a supporter."

She rolled her eyes. "Everyone wanted to make it a supporter vs. nonsupporter story. But it wasn't so black and white. I was as invested in the case as anyone else in Lansing," she said. "But if you're asking me if I sympathized with your father, with your mother, with your family, then yes."

"You contacted him first?"

"I did," she said. "I was part of the original support team. And he told me one day that he needed a psychologist, and I told him I was trained. I was taking a hiatus at that time, but I'd always planned on going back. When I did, your father started coming to see me, first as a friend, but soon, I recognized his need to talk to someone, to unload the years of weight he'd been carrying. That he hadn't been able to talk about with..." She shrugged. "With anyone else."

"You mean with my mother," I said, and I didn't feel as angry as I should have.

She straightened her shoulders and looked away.

"What about you?" she asked, changing the subject. "Nobody special in your life?"

"Just my daughter, Amy."

"Her mother?"

"She's on the other side of the world."

"I see," Christine said. "And are you better or broken?"

"Sorry?"

"You're only two things after a divorce. You're better, or you're broken. And if you're broken, you just haven't gotten better yet."

"Oh," I said. "I don't know. I guess better, but that doesn't take much, given where we were."

She nodded. "Anyone else?"

I hesitated, and she leaned forward to let me know she wasn't going to drop it. "I guess there's someone," I said. "Sort of. She's… We work together."

"What do you mean 'sort of'?" she asked. "That usually means no more than it means yes. If it's a yes, it should be unequivocal."

"Should be," I said. "But in this case, it's not."

She frowned. "Why not?"

"I don't know," I said. "Cam's not really a romance person. And she's my boss. I don't think she's comfortable with us, you know, crossing that line."

"But you have already?"

My eyes widened.

She smiled. "I've been around the block a few times, you know," she said. "And aside from what I do professionally, I'm really good at reading people. If you feel the way you look, you shouldn't let her get away. Trust me. Life's way too short."

I couldn't think of anything else to say, so I just nodded.

"Are you going to call your captain friend?"

"Not tonight," I said.

"Okay. I'm not going anywhere." She got out and headed up her porch.

As I drove to my apartment, I could think of nothing else besides checking on Amy, taking a few painkillers, and falling straight into bed. When I walked into the apartment, Cam was coming out of Amy's room. She smiled softly. "Hey," she said. "She just dozed off."

I walked up to the door and stood beside her, watching Amy's sleeping figure. "Thanks," I whispered to Cam as we moved back into the living room. We stopped a few feet apart from each other. "Thanks for everything today."

"You're welcome," she said. "Any word from Alex? I mean, he can come out of hiding now, if that's what he's doing. Right?"

"Yeah," I said with a shrug. "That's what I thought too. But I haven't heard anything from him. I'm not sure I will."

"Well, the point is, Matthew's okay. And that's thanks to you."

"I don't know what I would've done if something—"

"And you don't have to know," she said. "Because he's okay. Don't let your mind go there, Francis. It's only going to drive you crazy."

"Crazier."

She smiled slightly and nodded. "Crazier." She took a step closer. "Amy's an amazing young woman. On the way here, she didn't say much, but she said something I think you should know."

"What?"

"She said she wished you'd stop being so hard on yourself because—and this is a direct quote—'even though it's been hard, maybe all three of us are better off now.' I'm not totally sure what she was referring to, but it seemed like—"

"She said that?" I asked.

"Yes."

"Better, not broken..."

"What?"

"Oh, nothing," I said. "Just something someone said to me recently."

Cam raised an eyebrow. "Well, I should get going."

I nodded, and she moved past me, toward the door.

Better, not broken.

"Wait, Cam."

"Yeah?" she said, turning back.

She stood in front of me, expectant, waiting, and my tongue felt like a pile of soggy paper towels in my mouth. I didn't know what I was feeling, so I had no chance of getting it out. I cleared my throat. "Um, I'll walk you out."

Something flashed in her eyes, but she didn't say anything. We moved into the hallway together, and she went straight for the stairs without saying a word. As we walked into the stairwell, I felt like the biggest idiot on earth.

Not only could I not bring myself to make a move, but I was forcing her to walk down the stairs. Still, I couldn't turn back now. We went down in silence, her a step ahead of me, and I tried to think of something else to say.

She beat me to the punch.

When she reached the bottom step, she whipped around. I had to stop myself from barreling into her, and I reached out a hand to grab the banister.

"Are you seriously going to make me do all of the heavy lifting?"

"What?"

"I swore to myself, after that night in Milwaukee, that I would never bring it up. Never. I'm always the one who brings it up. I always say something, put it out there. Has it worked out for me so far? No. So I talked to myself. I literally stood in front of the mirror and said, 'Cam, if he's interested, he'll say something. He'll do something.'"

I stumbled to find a response. "Cam—"

"Because for some reason, when you're a woman with a brain and a mouth, guys seem to forget you're still a woman, and you still want to be treated like a woman sometimes, and you still want the guy to make the first move, even though you know you can."

"I—"

"And I know this is not the best time to bring this up, but you keep looking at me like that, and I keep telling myself not to wait around, and I still am, and I'm tired of waiting for you to stop acting like there's not a thing, because it sure feels like there's a thing—"

"There's a thing," I said, cutting in, feeling like the biggest idiot in the world, but knowing this was my last shot. "That's for fucking sure; there is a thing."

It was the most eloquent thing I could come up with.

"Then what's the problem?"

"I don't know," I said. "I thought you weren't interested because you never said anything after Milwaukee—"

"*You* never said anything!" she said. "Do you know how that feels? You never said a word."

"I thought we both weren't saying a word!" I said. I shook my head. "And that was so incredibly…dumb." I took one more step down until we were inches apart. "I can't justify it. Of course I've thought about it, and every time I thought about saying something, it hit me that you're pretty much the only person I have, besides Amy, and if a relationship would ruin that, I don't know. I guess I just got scared."

"Oh, please. I am way too old for that bullshit, and so are you," she said. "Being scared of a relationship is for twenty-three-year-olds and pop stars. If you—"

I stepped forward and closed the small gap between us, dropping my lips on hers. She tasted like anger and sweetness and a bit of the Cam smirk, and after a couple of seconds, she gave in, reaching up to loop her arms around my neck and pulling me closer. It was a gentle, sweet kiss, and I let my hands settle on her waist. We stood like that for a long moment, drinking each other in.

We pulled away slowly, breathing heavily, and the expression on her face was intoxicating. I leaned in for more, but she put a hand on my chest.

"That's a good start," she said. "But I should probably go now. For real this time."

I smiled softly and dropped my hands from her waist. Together, we walked through the stairwell door and into the lobby. We went outside to her car, and she got inside.

"I'll call you tomorrow," I said, kissing her lightly again before she closed the door. She waved as she drove away.

I took a deep breath and turned to head back up the stairs. I was opening the door when I heard a woman's voice behind me.

"Francis?"

I spun around, looking for Cam, but instead, I came eye to eye with the last person on earth I expected to see at that moment.

Kira Jones.

I frowned. "This is not the right time," I said. "I'm not telling you anything, so you might as well—"

"Why haven't you been answering your phone?"

"I'm not telling you anything about Matthew Farr—"

"You found him?"

"Yes—"

"Is he okay?"

"Yes," I started, but she put her head in her hands and crumpled forward.

"Thank God," she said. "Where was he?"

"Not with my father, if that's your question, but I'm not going to talk to you about this. I can't believe you came here—"

"No, no," she said. "That's not why I'm here. I mean, I'm so thankful he's okay, but that's not why I came. Shit, so you didn't listen to my messages?"

"If you didn't hear me, I was very busy tonight," I said.

"I've been looking for you all day." She reached into her bag and pulled out a stack of crumpled papers.

"What's that?"

"It's my draft," she said breathlessly. "My draft of Sam Farr's memoir."

She held the bunched papers in her hands, and she stared at me as if she was waiting for me to understand, to grasp something. She was breathing heavily, and her eyes were wild, and she thrust the papers toward me again, some scattering and blowing off into the night.

"What the hell… Why are you giving me this?"

"It doesn't make sense," she said, her voice shaking. "It doesn't make sense."

"Kira, calm down and tell me what the hell is going on."

"I was writing it. I was in the middle of writing it, and I was looking at my notes from my last meeting with Sam Farr. And I realized it doesn't make sense!"

"What doesn't make sense?" I asked, raising my voice, too tired to stand out there talking about her ridiculous book.

"The story doesn't make sense, and I finally figured out why. Sam Farr has been lying about what happened that night, and I have proof," she said, lifting the stack of papers again. "He's been lying for twenty-three years, and the proof is all right here."

Chapter Forty-Two

Not for the first time that night, I felt as if I'd been lifted clean off the ground and tossed over the side of a cliff. The papers were swirling all around us now, dancing in the wind, taunting us and mocking us.

She was watching the papers and watching me, and I could tell she was having trouble concentrating, alternating between mumbled words and reaching out to catch the floating pages.

"What are you talking about?" I asked, grabbing one that had just smacked me in the face and peeling the paper away from my skin. I looked down at it, and the words seemed to crawl together, a failed attempt to make sense of something completely nonsensical, something unexplainably tragic.

"I was writing, and the notes didn't add up. I just..." She stopped and looked around her in dismay at the mess. She reached down and picked up a few more papers. "Can we go inside?"

I nodded, and we walked into the building, leaving Sam Farr's story to litter the street and sidewalk. As we went in, I held up a finger toward Amy's closed door and led Kira to the kitchen counter, where she sat down, shivering.

"What's going on?" I asked.

She took a deep breath, and then the words tumbled out of her. "I write off of my tapes. That's how I've been doing it. No structure, barely any fluff. Just the straight facts and details, based on what Sam tells me. He remembered so many details. I'm going to go back later and add more. Up until now, I was just trying to get the timeline down. But now that I know he's lying to me, who knows what I'll have to go back and fix."

"Kira," I said, resisting the urge to shake her, "you're not telling me what's going on. What happened?" I leaned against the counter. "What do you mean you know he was lying?"

"Because," she said, "Sam told me he went back upstairs after the puppet show. And he heard some sort of noise, and he went into the bathroom and found Lucas in the tub."

"Yeah," I said. "So?"

"And then he ran downstairs, and everyone followed him back upstairs, and then your mother, Kate, was screaming at him, demanding he tell her what happened."

"Right," I said slowly. "That's not a lie. I was there."

"I know," she said. "But what did Sam do after that?"

"He didn't answer her," I said. "That was one of the things the prosecutors harped on. He didn't say anything. He just put his toys away."

"His puppets."

"Yeah. She's yelling, and he's putting the puppets away like a little...robot."

"That was the problem," she said.

"What?"

"Don't you see? When everyone came back upstairs, they found him putting the puppets away. The other seven puppets. Sam Farr had a collection of nine, and he used only two for the show that night."

"So what?" I asked. "What's that got to do with anything? The significance of the puppets was analyzed over and over again. I know it's weird, but the kid liked puppets. What did that have to do with anything?"

"The puppets are *everything*," she said. "Because he only took two downstairs with him. Sam left the other seven puppets sprawled out across the bed of a boy he didn't know that well and that, it turns out, he didn't like all that much."

I paused as her words began to sink in. "You mean…"

"There's only one world where Sam Farr would have left his puppets upstairs, out of the case, sprawled out on the bed, as you, he, and everyone else that night described it. The puppets he guarded with his life. There's only one reason why he would have left them there, unprotected, while he was downstairs performing in front of you and your family, and that's because he knew there was nobody upstairs who could have harmed them."

"What?" I asked. "But…"

"When everyone rushed upstairs to find Lucas, Sam had only one thought: protect them. But he didn't need to protect them when he went downstairs to perform. Why? Because—"

"Lucas was already dead."

The words slipped from my lips, and even though I couldn't believe what I was saying, I knew they were true.

"The medical examiner was close, but not close enough. Or maybe he said what the town wanted him to say. Your brother didn't die after the puppet show. He was dead before Sam went downstairs, and Sam knew it."

"Why would he lie?" I asked. I stood and walked quickly toward the door.

"Where are you going?"

"Back to the hospital," I said. "I need to talk to him."

"I'm coming with you."

We were heading out the door when I stopped, and Kira crashed into my back.

"What?" she asked.

"But that means…" I shook my head as I tried to sort through what was bothering me the most about what Kira had told me. "That means he didn't die while we were all downstairs in the living room."

Her eyes widened. "You're right, Francis. There were a lot of other people who were in the house that night who may have known something about what happened to your brother. The timing changes everything. Who went upstairs after dinner?"

I closed my eyes and tried to revisit that night, picturing the rooms as people scattered. My father had been in the kitchen, talking to me about being in such a bad mood. Elizabeth Farr had been in the living room, setting up the "stage" for her son so he could start his performance.

That left…

"Brian Farr," I said. "I don't know where he was. He could have been upstairs and—"

I paused, my mind going back to the conversation I'd had in the kitchen with my father.

"And what?" Kira asked, peering at me.

My father had said she'd been upstairs getting a board game—Clue—to keep me from being so bored that evening.

She'd been delighted about her party but disappointed I was having such a bad time.

She was one of only two people who couldn't be accounted for at the moment Lucas had died.

"What is it, Francis?"

"My mother," I breathed, turning to face Kira and watching the blood drain from her face. "My mother was up there too."

Chapter Forty-Three

I didn't lift my foot from the accelerator for the entire drive.

I sped along toward the home of one of the two people who could help solve the mystery of what had happened to my brother.

And it was then that the tears started again.

Kira didn't say anything—she didn't reach over to comfort me, or search for a tissue, or anything of the sort. She didn't acknowledge my tears at all, and I was grateful for it.

I slowed only when I turned onto the street in front of my mother's house. I drove past the house and pulled over a few houses down. Using the palms of my hands, I wiped furiously at my face.

"Are you okay?" Kira asked, peering at me with concern.

"Yeah. I'm just not sure what I came here to ask her." She nodded as I put the car in reverse and backed down the street.

We opened the car doors and stepped out. As we walked up to the front door, I had to force myself to put one foot in front of the other and resist the urge to dart back to my car and drive away. Suddenly, I felt thirteen again, desperate to find a place to hide from it all.

I took a deep breath and rang the doorbell.

My mother opened it a full minute later and stared at me in shock.

"Francis. What are you doing here?"

"Can I come in?"

She moved back and allowed me to enter, a look of confusion on her face.

"Who is this?" she asked, looking at Kira, who followed me inside without saying anything. "Francis?"

"This is Kira Jones," I said. "She's a writer. She's working with me on the Matthew Farr case."

"Nice to meet you," Kira said, reaching out a hand toward my mother.

My mother shook it cautiously. We stood in the foyer, and then she seemed to think twice and ushered us farther into the house. "Well, since you're going to just stand there and look at me like I did something wrong, maybe we can get inside away from the door," she said.

We walked into the kitchen, and she stood with her hands behind her, braced on the edge of the sink. I stayed near the door. Kira walked inside and stood with her back against the fridge, and we all stared at one another.

No one spoke for a long time.

"What's up?" my mother asked.

"Where did you go after dinner?"

Her eyes widened, and she looked quickly at Kira before returning her gaze to me. "What are you talking about?"

"After dinner. On the night Lucas died. Where did you go right after dinner?"

She blinked and stared at me, and her expression changed from confusion, to shock, to complete and utter fear.

"What are you talking about, and why would you ask me that?"

She looked again at Kira for help, or an explanation, but Kira didn't say anything. My mother turned back to me, her eyes wider now, wild.

"Francis, if you have a problem, you should just say it," she said.

"You lied. You never told the whole truth."

"What?" she asked. "Why would I lie about that?"

"That's why I'm here. To find out."

She shifted, and her entire body was shaking. "Why are you bringing all of this up now? Is it because of your father? Because he took that boy?"

"No," I said. "He didn't take the boy. Matthew's been found."

"Well, that's great," she said. "Then why are you here?" She frowned, and I could see she was pleading with me to let it go. "If he's been found, then what's the point?"

"I told you, it doesn't make any sense," I said.

"Lucas didn't die after Sam's puppet show," Kira said, chiming in. "He was dead before that. He died at least half an hour before that."

My mother slumped back against the sink.

"What are you—"

"We can prove it. Now tell me where you went," I said, "because I know you were upstairs."

"What do you mean?" she hissed. "What are you talking about?" She stepped closer to me now, and everything changed. I saw what looked like a mixture of fear and rage in her eyes. "What the hell are you insinuating?"

"Just tell me the truth."

"It looks like you already know," she said, and my breath caught. "You don't think I've judged myself enough? I mean, I know you're here to find out what happened, but you must understand that I've kicked myself every day since that night, thinking about what I was doing, where I was, in the last few minutes before he died. Making out with another man right upstairs. You don't think I've hated myself?"

Her words started to sink in. "You mean…"

There had been only one other person upstairs.

"Brian Farr?" I asked. I struggled to get the words out. "Where were you? What...?"

"You want details?"

I didn't say anything, and she shrugged.

"We couldn't help ourselves, Francis. We were in love. Brian made me feel things your father never did. I couldn't stop him, and I couldn't stop myself. I'm so sorry."

I stood there, stunned, unable to move or respond.

"Oh, don't look at me like that," she said angrily. "Do you think that with all of the women your father took to that cabin, those young, silly girls... Brian and I didn't want it to happen; we fought it, we really did..." Her hands were shaking as she walked to the refrigerator and opened it, pulling out a half-empty bottle of wine. She pulled out the metal, rose-shaped wine stopper, paused, and turned it in her hand. "You know where he got this? On a trip with his *wife* to Las Vegas. He knew how much I'd love it."

I took a deep breath. "What happened next, Mom?"

"What do you mean? We came back downstairs. I came into the kitchen, remember?"

"You mean, you'd just—"

"I told you, I'm not proud of it."

"And Farr?"

She frowned. "He came down too."

"He was with you?"

"Yes," she said firmly. "He was right behind me, and..."

I leaned forward. "And what?"

The cloud that covered her face in that instant was one I wouldn't soon forget.

"I forgot my glasses." It was a soft whisper, and she looked up at me, her eyes wide, her whole body trembling.

"What?"

"I forgot my glasses. In your room. Brian went back up to get them."

I straightened, bumping into the table, and I turned to walk toward the front door.

"Where are you going?" she called out.

"To find him."

"Wait!"

Kira had followed me, and we both stopped and turned back.

"There's no need," she said.

"What?"

"There's no reason for you to go anywhere," she said.

"Why not? He's the only one left, Mom. Don't you get it? He had to have seen something, or heard something. And if he's lying, there has to be a reason. Don't you see that?"

"I do," she said, "but you still don't need to go to his house."

"Why not?" I demanded.

"Because he's on his way here."

Chapter Forty-Four

After all these years?" I croaked out.

"I wanted to tell you," she said.

"Impossible. If you wanted to do that, you would have. So that's who Jimmy was talking about?" My mind spun back to the day I'd come over and her boyfriend had stormed out. She *had* been having an affair.

With Brian Farr.

"But I didn't know," she said. "I had no idea he—"

At that moment, we heard a noise coming from the front of the house.

"He has a key," she whispered. "I called him earlier and asked him to come by. I don't know what to do. Should I tell him to go?"

"No," I said. "Talk to him. See if you can get him to tell you what happened."

She shook her head.

"Mom, it's the only way we'll ever know."

Kira and I moved into the pantry as footsteps strode into the house.

"Hey, what's wrong?" Brian asked as he joined my mother in the kitchen.

I put a hand on the wall and leaned forward to peer into the room, careful to stay out of view. I watched as they embraced, my mother's body tense, and I knew she was going to have a hard time pulling this off.

"Nothing?" she said, and Farr frowned at the seeming question. My mother turned and glanced in our direction, and I pulled back sharply.

Shit.

"Why don't I believe that?" Farr asked, but I could hear the smile in his voice. "What's wrong?"

My mother shifted and stepped back. "Francis called me today."

I leaned forward again, and I could see that Farr's body language had changed. He cleared his throat. "About what?"

My mother wrung her hands together. "He told me that you..."

Brian stepped closer.

I moved to the edge of the pantry, ready to pounce at any second.

"What?" Farr asked. "What did he tell you?"

My mother didn't respond.

"Kate, what kind of lies is he feeding you?"

"He told me you were upstairs," she said softly. "The night when Lucas... That Lucas died before the puppet show, and he has proof."

"What?" Farr asked, coming forward, but my mother stepped back. "What the hell are you talking about?"

"I don't know," she said, staring at him. "There's nothing you didn't tell me, is there? Please, Brian, I need to know. It sounds ridiculous to me too, so I'm asking to clear it up. You have to tell me the truth."

I could hear the pain in her voice.

And it was enough to make Farr stumble.

"I..."

"Brian?"

And in an instant, I knew.

"Brian?" she asked again, stepping back.

Farr swallowed, and the expression on his face changed suddenly. "It was an accident," he whispered. "I'm so sorry, Kate. I promise it was an accident."

"What—"

"It was an accident. He was there. Lucas saw us…when we went to Francis's room."

"What?"

"He saw us. When I went back upstairs to get your glasses, he told me." My mother stumbled back against the sink, and Farr moved closer, but he didn't touch her. "I asked him not to say anything, begged him not to. I tried to explain that there were some things he couldn't understand. But he was mean. And you know I would never say anything like that to you unless it was true. I'd never seen anything like it. He told me he knew exactly what was going on, that I was nothing like his father, that I would never be good enough for you."

I could hear the anger in his voice, and I knew he was in a rage, still, about the words of a nine-year-old boy.

"What happened?" my mother asked.

Farr shook his head, his hands clenched, his eyes trained on hers. "He was being so disrespectful, so callous, and I tried to get him to stop, and he tried to leave. I pushed him, and he fell," he said. As he spoke, tears gathered in his eyes. "I'm so sorry, Kate. I didn't know what to do. He was bleeding, and I wanted to clean him off, so I put him in the tub and turned it on—"

"Why?" my mother screamed. "Why did you do that? He might have—"

"No, he was already gone," he said. "I mean, I thought he was. I know he was, Kate. So I did what I had to, and luckily, you were playing those stupid songs you loved so loud that nobody knew. Nobody heard anything. It was all going to be okay, because it was an accident. I just needed more time to figure out what to tell you. And then Sam walked in."

My mother gasped. "He saw you?"

Brian nodded. "And then it hit me," he whispered. "What I needed to do for us. I made him promise not to say anything, and I told him to pretend that he heard something and found Lucas later on in the night so there was no way anyone would know." He wiped at his face. "I didn't know what else to do. I did it to protect both of us," he said.

"Wait. So you mean that all of that time…during the puppet show…Sam knew?" my mother asked. "How could you do that him? How could you ask him to do that?"

"For us! I knew he'd be okay. As long as he didn't say anything. Not one word. I did it for us. If anyone found out about us… I knew you weren't ready for that," Farr said.

"But what…?" Confusion covered my mother's face. "What about the fight you and Alex overheard?" she asked. "The one between Sam and Lucas. That happened later, after—" She stopped, and the realization seemed to hit her at the same time it hit me. "Oh my God, Brian," she whispered. "There *was* no fight. You had Sam—"

"He did it to help us," Brian said. "I told him to scream like he was really angry, just for a moment, and I'd come upstairs."

"Lucas was already—" my mother started, but she stopped herself. She swallowed. "Sam faked the fight, and nobody saw it but you."

"It wasn't perfect, but it worked," he said. "I had to do it. You weren't ready. You still aren't."

"What the hell are you talking about?" my mother asked, her entire body shaking. "You just told me you killed…" She leaned back against the sink, and I was worried she would pass out. Kira and I shared a glance, both of us prepared to run into the kitchen if Farr made a move.

"What did Francis find out?" Brian asked, stepping forward. "He just wants to keep us apart too, Kate. You know that, right?"

My mother didn't respond.

"He keeps poking into things—"

"He found your grandson," my mother hissed.

"I know," Farr said. "And I'm grateful for that. But he needs to keep his nose out of things. I should have taken care of him that day at the cabin—"

He cut himself off, and my mother looked up at him in confusion. My stomach flipped over as the significance of his words sank in. Farr had been at the cabin that day?

He'd attacked me?

I stepped forward to enter the kitchen, but Kira put her hand out, holding me back. She shook her head slightly and showed me her phone, which she was using to record the conversation.

My mother turned around to face the kitchen window.

"Please, Kate, you have to understand that this hasn't changed the way I feel about you," Farr said, moving closer to her. "I know it's hard, but...you have to understand it was an accident."

"It hasn't changed how you feel about me?" she asked, still staring out the window. "Killing my son has not affected how *you* feel about *me*?"

"No, that's not what I meant—" he started.

"Isn't it?" she asked.

He went closer to her, and finally, I'd had enough. I walked out of the pantry, and Farr looked up in shock.

"Step back," I said.

Farr looked from me to my mother and back again. "You tricked me?" he asked. He looked at Kira, who was still holding the phone in her hand, pointing it in his direction. He glanced at the back of my mother's head. She hadn't moved an inch, still staring out into the night, her hands on the edge of the kitchen sink. "Kate, how could you? You know none of this is going to stick, not twenty-three years later," he said.

"Mom, call the cops," I said, then turned to Brian. "So, it was you at the cabin that day?"

"You little—" He stopped himself and took a deep breath. "Miranda called me on her way there and told me she was following you. I told her to wait for me before going inside, but she never listens. When I got there, she was already driving away, and I just..." He shook his head. "I just needed you to stop poking around in the past. You didn't have to dig all of this up, Francis. What good has it done? It was the biggest mistake of my life."

He turned to look at the back of my mother's head. "I promise you, Kate, it was a mistake. I'm so sorry."

My mother still didn't move.

"Kate?"

I saw what she was about to do a second too late.

She reached in the sink, picked something up, and turned around.

"Mom!"

But I was too late.

I'd always been too late.

In just three quick steps, she was eye to eye with the love of her life, lifting her arm and driving the large steak knife deep into his chest.

Farr's eyes widened, and a bloodied gurgle escaped him before he took the first of his last breaths and crumpled to the floor.

Chapter Forty-Five

July, eighteen months later

At some point during the long drive out to Talcott Correctional Facility, the landscape changed; the trees became sparser, the air thinner, and there was a scent of sadness that seemed to rise from the dirt. On hot summer days, the unobstructed sun lent a muggy, rancid quality to the air that made it almost impossible to breathe. As I turned onto the two-lane road that led to the facility, I cranked the AC all the way up and prayed for the smallest bit of relief.

The massive building had four main entrances, each one advertised with an array of complicated signage, icons, and directions. Only two things were clear: I should avoid the last entrance, and I should leave absolutely everything that wasn't attached to my body in the car. As I veered toward the second entrance, I looked over at the young woman sitting beside me in the passenger seat.

"You ready?" I asked.

She looked back at me and nodded but didn't say anything. She was sixteen now, so to call her a woman was a stretch, but to call her a girl seemed laughable. Amy had spent the entire ninety-minute drive staring calmly out the window, her hands folded neatly in her lap.

As we opened our doors and stepped out onto the blazing-hot concrete, I wondered how many people were watching us and if they could see how nervous I was. I shut the door and froze, staring up at the large, imposing building in front of us.

Amy walked around the car and faced me. "*You* ready?" she asked, but there was a softness in her eyes.

I nodded.

The registration process was grueling. We waited, filled out forms, waited, showed our IDs, and waited some more. As we finished the final form, the registration attendant held up a card.

"How much would you like on your vending machine card?"

"Excuse me?" I asked.

She held the card higher. "In case you want to buy something. How much?"

"Uh, five bucks?" I said, and she nodded before punching something into her computer and swiping the card. She handed it to me, along with a key.

"This is all you can take inside. Store everything else in one of those lockers, and return with just the key and your vending machine card so you can be searched."

Amy's eyes grew wider, but she bit her bottom lip. We walked silently over to the lockers and stowed our wallets and phones. Amy's hands were shaking as she placed them inside.

"Hey," I said. "You sure you're ready?"

She swallowed and looked up at me before nodding slightly. The words "you don't have to do this" were on the tip of my tongue, but I held them back. We'd been down that path several times already, and I knew what her answer would be.

The search was quicker than I'd expected and included a quick pat down, a check in our shoes and beneath our tongues. Then, a guard led us down another hallway and into room the size of a high school cafeteria. There were rows of tables, and they were filled almost to capacity with visiting families. Most talked quietly with the inmates; a few people were sobbing, and a few were laughing. Amy and I shuffled behind the guard, who stopped at the sole empty table.

"You can wait here," he said, motioning to a seat. Amy and I sank down into two of the blue bucket seats. The guard turned to face us and spoke in a rehearsed, emotionless monotone. "We're bringing him down now. When he arrives, you are allowed to greet him briefly, and then he will be asked to sit down. From that point on, he will not be allowed to move until the visitation period is over. If you would like to get a snack from the vending machine for him or for yourselves, you are free to do that. Please use the card you purchased. If you need to go to the bathroom, let me know, and I will escort you. You will be subject to another search upon your return. Please keep your voice at a conversational level and be courteous to those around you. All visitation sessions are recorded. Do you have any questions?"

Amy and I stared at him with our mouths open, and he waited, completely motionless.

"Uh, no," I said, and I turned to look at Amy.

She shook her head.

The guard walked away, and we sat there, staring straight ahead. I found it hard to breathe, but I clenched my fists and took a slow, deep breath, unwilling to let Amy see me break.

"Want some water?" I asked her, and she swallowed before shaking her head.

The minutes went by, and I watched the inmates talking to their parents and friends, their wives and children. They devoured their treats from the vending machine like it was Thanksgiving. The sound of all of the voices in the room was just above comfortable, and I squirmed in my seat.

But as much as I wanted to flee, I knew I had to get used to it.

We'd be back. And when Amy asked to go visit her grandmother, we'd go there too. Because she wasn't going to run from it.

She needed this, and so, I needed it too.

Fifteen minutes had gone by when the metal bars at the end of the room opened and a guard walked in, followed by a tall, thin man who took my breath away. He'd received nine years for what he did to Sam Farr. I didn't know what I was going to say to him, but I hoped the words would come when we were finally face-to-face.

Amy must have seen my reaction, because she leaned across the foot or so that separated us and placed her hand on my arm. I turned to face her, and she stared at me with the bravest, sweetest, most courageous expression I'd ever seen. And I doubt I'd ever loved or admired anyone more.

"Hey," she said, and there wasn't an ounce of hesitation in her voice. "We're ready."

Reading Group Guide

1. *Boy, 9, Missing* follows an unconventional structure. How does Kira's memoir serve as a narrative device within the story?

2. What is the central motivation behind Francis's decision to search for Matthew? For Alex? Are these motivating factors the same?

3. Do you agree with Kira's statement that, regardless of what happened in 1992, ten-year-old Sam Farr should not have been held responsible? Did your feelings change after you found out what really happened that night?

4. How is Francis's relationship with his daughter similar to his relationship with his parents? How does it differ?

5. Why does Francis resent his parents? Do you feel that his resentment is justified? Likewise, why might his parents resent him?

6. How does Francis handle his claustrophobia and panic attacks? How does this parallel the way he handles the rest of his life?

7. How does Francis handle guilt at different stages of his life?

8. Why did Sam Farr lie in his story to Kira Jones? Why hasn't he told the truth about what his father did all those years ago?

9. Francis tries several times to tell Amy about his past but fails to do so. What excuses does he use to justify his avoidant behavior?

10. Why do you think some people were so quick to believe that Sam Farr was a murderer? Why were others so quick to defend him?

11. Francis and Amy go to visit Alex at the end of the novel. How do you think this meeting is going to turn out?

A Conversation with the Author

What was your inspiration for *Boy, 9, Missing*?

I have always been fascinated by the changing relationship between parents and children—what kids expect from their parents, and what parents expect as their children become adults. The inspiration for *Boy, 9, Missing* started there, around the question of what kinds of support and understanding parents and their adult children expect from one another, particularly during a time of crisis.

To which character do you feel closest?

Francis, for sure! He is, for lack of a more eloquent description, a hot mess. He's trying to do the right thing, but he doesn't really know why. Deep down, he hopes that showing up now will make up for the fact that he wasn't there in the past. What he knows for sure is that he doesn't want to be the guy who doesn't care anymore.

How did you decide on the narrative structure for *Boy, 9, Missing*?

I enjoy stories that showcase a variety of viewpoints around a single topic or event. The night of the accident was experienced by two families but felt by an entire town. Kira's story allowed me to delve into one particular experience of the night—albeit through a rather shaky and unreliable account of it.

How long have you been writing?

I've written stories and poems since childhood. My father is a writer and artist and a mystery buff, and he instilled in me a deep love of suspense. Even now, when I go home to visit, we gobble up all of the old mysteries we can find. My very first story was titled "The Case of the Missing Ring." I illustrated it myself too. Let's be honest: it may have been cute, but it was not very good.

Are you an outliner?

To say I'm an outliner is an understatement. I handwrite a detailed outline for almost every scene of my novels. Then, I rewrite the outline adding in more details. Then, I do it again and again. I've filled notebooks with outlines, and my purse is filled with crumpled pieces of paper containing plot sketches, character profiles, etc. I don't start actually writing the book until most of the plot has been inked out several times. For some people, this stunts their creativity. But I like to think that the outlining stage is where I let my "soul glo." The writing part is where I put it all together into something coherent.

What do you love most about writing?

The control (should I not admit that?). There is very, very little in life that we have complete control over. In the initial stages, when I'm drafting a story on a blank page, every twist, every dot over every *i* is up to me. That's incredibly cool and incredibly scary.

Who is your favorite author, and why?

I own almost all of Ken Follett's books. He is such a masterful storyteller. I am always in awe of authors who are able to transport you, quickly and completely, into their worlds. He has definitely inspired me as a writer.

What draws you to the mystery/suspense genre?

Mysteries provide the reader with a question that just *has* to be answered. They're fun, they're exciting, and you often can't look away. They draw you in and hopefully keep you there long enough for you to get to know and care about the character. Because at the end of the day, that's really what matters—the character. The mystery just opens the door for you to step into his or her world.

Do you ever get writer's block?

Sometimes! It usually happens when I try to force myself to write on an off day. On those days, it's best if I just step away and come back later. Forcing myself to reach a certain word count or complete a scene that doesn't want to be completed almost always ends in some quality time with the Delete key.

Do you have any writing rituals?

No real rituals, but I do have some pretty ingrained habits. I do most of my writing in my living room, curled up on my couch. I can write with the television on in the background, but not if there's music playing. I plot in my car; I have an hour-long commute to work, and I often spend that time talking through (yes, out loud) difficult plot points.

What do you do when you're not writing?

I like gardening, cooking huge meals for friends and family, and watching classic mysteries.

Acknowledgments

Thanks to Shana Drehs and the entire Sourcebooks team for their expertise and incredible passion for books.

To my wonderful and talented agent, Barbara Poelle, for her guidance and support.

To the SCH Marketing crew for being amazing, and to Tom Carr and Dawn Carlson for their constant encouragement (yes, Dawn, I did write today!).

To Sade Adekunle, Jackie Azpeitia, Mesmin Destin, Yolanda Hare, Marissa Jackson, and Chenée Lewis for all the laughs, love, and friendship.

To my entire family; to my grandmothers, Antoinette and Lanell; and to Sylvia and Roosevelt for treating me like one of their own.

To my mother, Constance, and my father, Guy-Claude, for never missing a single beat and setting the parenting bar incredibly high, and to my big sister, Guiandre, for still, to this day, protecting me from all of the bad, scary things in life.

And finally, to Damian, for being there every day to listen to me talk about this dream of writing and the characters that live only in my head. Thank you for caring about them as much as you care about me and for always encouraging me to follow my heart.

About the Author

Photo by Damian Chaplin

Nic Joseph is fascinated by the very good reasons that make people do very bad things. She writes thrillers and suspense novels from her home in Chicago. As a trained journalist, Nic has written about everything from health care and business to aerospace and IT—but she feels most at home when there's a murder to be solved on the next page. Nic holds a bachelor's degree in journalism and a master's in communications, both from Northwestern University. For more information, visit NicJoseph.com or follow her on Twitter @nickeljoseph.